Better Together

Nicola May

Copyright ©**Nicola May** 2014

Published by Nicola May 2014

The right of **Nicola May** to be identified as the author of this work has been asserted by the author in accordance with the Copyright, Designs and Patents Act 1988.

The story contained within this book is a work of fiction. Names and characters are the product of the author's imagination and any resemblance to actual persons, living or dead, is entirely coincidental.

All rights reserved. No part of this book may be reproduced, stored in a retrieval system, or transmitted in any form or by any means, electronic, electrostatic, magnetic tape, mechanical, photocopying, recording or otherwise, without the written permission of the publishers.

*When you are joyous, look deep into your heart
and you shall find it is only that which
has given you sorrow that is giving you joy.*

*When you are sorrowful look again in your heart,
and you shall see that in truth you are weeping
for that which has been your delight.*

Kahlil Gibran

PART 1

On the Rebound

Chapter One

Jess checked herself in the mirror. Not bad for a thirty-nine year old, she thought to herself. Shoulder-length dark hair with a straight cut fringe, the barest of wrinkles due to her decade-long vigil at the Clarins counter, and a toned, size 12 body due to her twice-weekly hour with James the personal trainer. She could easily pass for thirty-three and revelled in the exclamations of 'Surely you're not nearly forty!'

She pulled on her ankle-length black velvet coat, placed her hat at a jaunty angle, and headed out into the crisp December air to drive to the Lemon Events Christmas party, being held at their premises in a little village in Oxford.

The party was in full swing when she arrived. A jazz band blasted out in the corner of the impressive converted barn, groups of people were drinking a pink-coloured punch and whoops were coming from the ice rink that had been set up in the courtyard in the middle of the quadrant. She was greeted by Sam, the handsome MD of Lemon Events with a kiss on both cheeks.

'Jess! Good to see you. You look great.'

'Cheers, Sam. Thanks for the invite.'

'Well, we have to keep our best clients happy,' he flirted.

Jess had been an event manager for ten years and had she had fed work to Lemon Events throughout this time, which the company had found invaluable.

'Punch?' he enquired.

'OK, but just the one as I'm driving tonight. I've got a

big day tomorrow: – the launch of Haven Wines' new sparkly offering at The Brewery in London.'

Jess flitted around chatting to various acquaintances, sipped her punch, dunked marshmallows in the chocolate fountain and was amazed by the tricks of a close-hand magician. As she was putting back on her watch, which had been expertly removed by the magician, she heard a voice behind her.

'Impressive, isn't he?' She turned around and opened her mouth in surprise.

'Dan Harris, what on earth are you doing here?' Her wide smile gave away her delight at seeing him.

'Well, Jessica Morley, I happen to have started working here two weeks ago.' He grinned openly and without any warning, Jess's heart skipped a beat.

'It's really good to see you,' he went on. 'I did want to get in touch after the Battersea event, but changed my phone and didn't transfer your number.'

Jess and Dan had worked together on an event two years previously. Both had been attached but had spent an amusing evening after the event in the Holiday Inn, Wandsworth, smuggling in a McDonald's, drinking warm lager and arguing the case of whether horoscopes were a load of rubbish, until the bland hotel bar had closed and they went their separate ways. There had been a connection then but, both being attached, they knew it was just a passing flirtation.

'So are you freelance here again then?' Jess enquired.

'No. I bit the bullet and decided to go permanent and get responsible in my old age.'

Jess laughed. 'Old age! You must be at least twenty-seven now?'

'Twenty-four on January the fifteenth, to be exact.'

Dan looked and acted way older than his twenty-three years, with his six-foot-two frame, knowing hazel eyes and responsible demeanour he called easily have passed for thirty.

'Surely you're not commuting from Bath every day?' She said.

'No way. We moved down to Windsor a couple of months ago.'

'Wow, quite a life change, eh? And how's that little girl of yours?'

'Not so little. She's nearly three now, and so beautiful, just like her father.' His eyes twinkled and Jess couldn't stop herself from looking right into them. 'And you and Phil?' he asked.

'Didn't work out. Bad case of commitment phobia on his part, but life goes on and I'm in a really good place at the moment.'

'Good, good. It really is lovely to see you. Did I say you were looking great?'

'Mr Harris, I do believe you are flirting with me!'

'Ms Morley, I guess you also probably think my rising sign is in Capricorn,' he joked.

'You must come to my fortieth party; it's in a couple of months.' Jess carried on. 'It will give you a chance to meet some new people in the area.'

'Forty? Surely not!' He laughed out loud as they had had this conversation about her age back when they had first met. 'I must ring Alex. With only one friend in the locality, she's finding adjusting to a new area difficult. Your party will give her something to look forward to.'

'Great. I'll catch you before I leave. I must go and speak to Sam re any new projects coming up.'

Jess finished up with Sam and walked to the bar to get herself another drink.

'Let me.' Dan pushed to the front of the bar. 'I've been told to look after all of our best clients. What's your poison?'

'Just fizzy water with a twist of lime please, got a big event tomorrow.'

Dan smirked. 'I am sorry, but I don't allow mixers at a Christmas party. I insist you have a glass of wine with me for old time's sake.' Jess could tell he was a little bit drunk. He really was good-looking, she thought. His dark hair was cropped short and his features were large and friendly.

'Oh, OK then, but just the one as I have got to drive.' Jess was usually strong-willed enough to say no to a drink when she was driving, however, this young man seemed to be able to persuade her with ease.

She took a sip of her wine. 'Ooh I needed that.'

'Nectar, pure nectar,' Dan sighed gulping his lager. 'So where we going after here then?' he enquired. 'Any good clubs your way?'

'Dan Harris! You have a home to go to as do I. It's getting late.'

'I have a pass tonight. I'm staying with a mate down the road, so if the gorgeous Jessy Morley wants to hang out with a cool dude, I'm all yours.'

Jessy was more than tempted. The wine had already begun to make her feel a little light-headed. 'No clubs, but two bottles of red wine and a Bose sound system at mine.' Shit, had she really said that? She carried on. 'Deal or no deal?'

'Sounds like a deal to me. Shall I get your coat?'

When they got outside, he exclaimed, 'Cool wheels! Get that roof down and get that music turned up.'

'It's minus four out here!' Jess objected.

'Come on, Jessy Morley. Life is all about fun.'

Jessy turned the key of her new Audi convertible. She already knew life was all about fun: she had had some wild times, none of which she regretted, and the exuberance of this young man and the thought of the exhilarating drive in the cold, starry night excited her.

'Will bloody Young, he can come off for a start,' Dan said rudely. 'What else have you got?'

'U2, Stereophonics or Kate Bush.'

'Jessy, perlease.' Dan started fiddling with the radio stations until Daft Punk blared out across the country lanes. 'Does your lighter work?' he asked.

Dan held the joint to Jessy's lips just as she was rounding a sharp bend.

'Shit, Dan, careful. I don't smoke. . .' Before she could finish her sentence she had taken a large drag of some sweet-tasting weed. She shrieked with delight and then proceeded to cough really hard.

'Good, eh?' Dan enquired.

Jess felt heady but oh so good. She was relieved to pull up outside her house in one piece. She giggled as the electronic roof banged to a halt over their heads.

'You're naughty.' She pushed her finger into Dan's chest.

'You love it!' he replied, leaping out of the car. 'Morley Mansions, what a charming residence.' He assumed a posh accent.

'Morley Mansions, what are you like? But it certainly does the trick,' Jessy said modestly. She had worked hard at making her Victorian mid-terrace a haven of comfort. She wasn't particularly tidy. Her bookshelves were messy and various ornaments and artefacts could be found on every surface. An empty tea cup was still on the coffee table from that morning. She switched on her twinkling twigs, and a lamp in the corner of her cosy living room, and went through to the kitchen.

'Red wine for you, sir?'

'Well, if there is no beer then I s'pose I'll have to.' Dan smiled. 'I do actually love red wine; I'm not that much of a philistine.' He was taking in his surroundings and started looking through Jess's book collection.

'Chick lit, I knew it. Don't suppose you've got any Stephen Hawking?' he smirked.

'Dear boy, at my age I know what the Universe is in a

nutshell anyway.' She laughed smugly as she knew he'd be impressed with this. Never before had she met a young man so knowledgeable . After jeering at her love for Will Young on their journey, he had confessed to his liking of Radio 4's Reith Lectures.

'And what's this: *Open Poetry*?' he asked.

'Oh, I got a poem published a few years ago.' She had won something like £15 for being a runner up and then had to buy the book for £25 to see it in print.

'Cool, what page is it on?'

With the red wine and weed now taking effect, Dan dramatically struck a pose on a leather cube in the corner of the dining room and began reciting. Jess took a large gulp of wine in anticipation of his reaction. She wanted his approval.

'GONE'.

He continued dramatically.

I thought I saw her today
Her warm smile, her wavy brown hair
I blinked back a tear and she was gone again

Gone, that word of finality
Go on in the middle, with a lonely e on the end

The bottom of my world fell out when she left me

Dan nearly lost his balance and fell off the cube. 'I knew it would be lost love shit.' He continued his sarcastic recital.

Empty, incomplete
Tears on New Year's Eve
Pain at my sister's wedding
Flowers for all anniversaries

She was here today
Her cuddly frame, her comfortable smell
I opened my eyes and she was gone again

Hurting, lonely
Tears on my birthday
Pain at my niece's first steps
Flowers for all anniversaries

At my mother's graveside

'Oh Jess, I'm so sorry. If I'd have known...' He tailed off and Jess was sure she could see tears in his eyes.

'It's fine, don't be silly. It was a tribute to her, she was so beautiful. She died a long time ago now. Guess that's why I take life as it comes and try to fit in as many adventures as I can. Now, get off that pouffe and come and sit down.'

Dan joined Jess on the sofa. She liked the softer side of him she had just seen.

'Body language is another one of my interests,' Dan said knowingly.

Jess was sat with her hand resting way up her thigh. She moved it immediately and he laughed out loud. 'I don't even want to know what that means,' she smirked and looked directly at the young man next to her, suddenly feeling something that she had never ever experienced before. Dan too must have felt the same as he all of a sudden just jumped up from the sofa.

'I have to go,' he said.

'Yes, you do.'

It was as if there was an electric current running between the two of them. A force so great, it made her feel euphoric. If she had run her hand between them, Jess honestly thought she would have received first-degree burns. With her job, she'd been all over the world. She'd met and dated a lot of men but never before had she experienced this actual force between two people.

'Did you feel that?' she said, astonished, and then suddenly embarrassed by the intensity of her feelings, she jumped up too.

'I have to go,' Dan repeated.

'OK, a taxi back to yours will take about twenty minutes from here.'

'Shit! I've left my house keys at the barn.'

'What about where you were supposed to be staying?'

'Carrie will be long in bed by now, plus it will take an hour to get there.'

There was a pause. Dan bit his lip. Jess took control.

'OK, you sleep in my spare room. I have to leave at seven to go and set up for my event, so I can drop you en route to work at the barn or you can get a cab. Sorted.'

'Spare room,' Dan repeated and took another gulp of wine.

Chapter Two

Over in Windsor, ten miles away, Alex Meadows – mother of Evie and partner of Daniel Harris – woke up and looked at her watch. 2.30 a.m.. Ever since their four-year relationship had begun, Dan had always called her to say goodnight. He must have run out of battery, she thought, and drifted back to sleep.

Chapter Three

'OK, I'm in,' Jess shouted downstairs. She had pulled on some baggy black pyjama bottoms and a lacy grey and white camisole, and leapt under the covers of 'the comfiest bed in the whole world'. It was a king-size sleigh bed. Once you'd sunk into the expensive mattress and under the Egyptian cotton duvet, you just didn't want to get out.

'You have to walk through my bedroom to the bathroom, so no looking!' she warned him. The intensity of the situation downstairs had died down and they had set about getting ready for bed.

Dan walked through pretending to ignore Jess. In her drunkenness she had the urge to start singing 'Don't cha' but she managed to stop herself.

He poked his head around the bathroom door and said, 'You got a spare toothbrush by any chance?'

Jess got out of bed and Dan looked her up and down.

'Ms Morley, how do you expect me to keep away from you when you put on something like that?'

Jess had actually put on her least sexy bed-wear purely for this reason. As much as she desperately wanted this man, she knew morally it wasn't the right thing to do. She was on a mission to find a suitable suitor and an attached twenty-three-year-old didn't quite fit the category. Hopping back into bed, she pulled the covers up high so that just her pretty, oval-shaped face was showing. Her bluey-green eyes shone with desire.

Dan walked past her but, instead of carrying on through the door to the spare room, he paused and looked down at her.

'Damn, you're gorgeous,' he said and leaned down to brush her now trembling lips softly with his. Jess took a deep breath and felt as if she was floating. He knelt down by the side of the bed and pushed a strand of her hair off her face. She could smell him, a sweet smell that just made her want to taste him.

'Lie next to me,' Jess whispered.

Dan climbed into bed fully clothed. As he pulled back the covers he could see Jess's now erect nipples through her flimsy camisole. Jess herself could feel the sense of danger, the untamed pleasure that she would get from this man with whom she felt such chemistry.

'Hold me, just hold me,' she said. The warmth of his soft mouth on hers made her feel like she was sinking to the bottom of the soft mattress.

'Jesus, Jess,' Dan murmured. 'You're beautiful.'

They searched each other's mouths with a loving intensity. Dan's fingers gently began to stroke her body. Jess gasped with pleasure.

'We can't,' she panted.

'I know.'

'I want to.'

'So do I.'

He kissed her passionately again and nothing else in the world seemed to matter.

What seemed like hours later, drenched in sweat, Jess suddenly laughed out loud in after-sex hysteria.

'I thought I told you to go to the spare room,' she said.

Dan lay next to her, looked into her eyes and smiled.

'My, my, Mrs Robinson. I shall have to get drunk with you more often.'

Chapter Four

Alex woke up with a start.

'Mummy! Mummy, I want some milk.'

It was 6 a.m. Alex groaned. Why couldn't her daughter just sleep in for a little bit longer?

'Go back to sleep,' she shouted.

'Mummy, but I want milk!'

Alex stumbled out of bed. She caught a glimpse of herself in the mirror and knew that, although her cropped dark hair and elfin features normally made her look younger than her thirty-three years, she felt old and tired this morning. Her mouth was claggy and her eyes, small and squinty. She knew she shouldn't have smoked all those cigarettes last night, but when her mate Sal came over they always managed to drink at least two bottles of wine and get through at least a pack of Marlboro Lights. Her arm was smarting from the recent tattoo she had had, an early Christmas present from Dan.

She lifted the little one from her cot and gave her a kiss. Scruffy white-blonde hair was stuck to a pretty little, bright pink face.

'Morning, little miss.' She carried her through into her untidy bedroom and laid her on the bed.

'Milk, please, Mummy, milk now.'

Alex threw on her kaftan, grabbed her mobile, put CBeebies on the TV and went downstairs to warm some milk. No text from Dan. She dialled his number but it went straight through to answerphone.

'Morning,' Alex said in to the handset sleepily. 'Guessing you had a good night? Two very important ladies want to talk to you so give us a call when you get this.'

By 8.30 a.m. Alex was beginning to get a little worried as she had still not heard from Dan. She called Carrie's home number

'Hiya, it's only me, just checking that my delinquent boyfriend is not demanding you make him a full English breakfast?'

'Hey, Alex. He didn't stay here in the end. I thought he'd be home with you?'

'Oh, well he's not.'

'No need to worry though, Al. He met up with an old client of the company and carried on drinking with her.'

'Her?'

'Yeah, Jessy Morley. I've known her years. She's a really nice lady. He probably ended up crashing at hers, as his car was still at the barn when I left.'

Alex had always trusted Dan implicitly; he was the most honest person she had ever been with. They had met when he was twenty and she was twenty-nine. The nine year age gap had never seemed a problem, and not long into their relationship she had fallen pregnant. Instead of him running away at the prospect of parenthood at such a young age, he was really excited. They'd been happy until recently.

Alex desperately wanted another baby and had been feeling insecure when Dan said he wasn't ready just yet. Instead of discussing and getting through this hurdle, Alex had found herself reading books every night while Dan played his computer games.

She felt a pang of jealousy that he was maybe staying at another woman's house. She took the warmed milk upstairs and got back into bed.

'Where's Daddy?' Evie asked.

'At work, darling. We'll see him later.'

Alex lay back on the bed and began to question her

relationship with Dan. Were they really happy? Had they been playing at parenthood because neither of them was brave enough to let the other go? She realised that they hadn't made love for over a month now. Suddenly, warning bells went off in her head.

'Mummy, why are you crying?'

Chapter Five

Jess woke up before her alarm. Dan was still holding her close. She turned over gently, looked at her beautiful sleeping partner and smiled. She had never felt like she did last night. Yes, of course throughout her life she'd had amazing sex on numerous occasions, but last night was different. Even if they had just kissed and he had not touched her, she knew it would have been the most erotic and sensual sexual experience she had ever had with a man. What she had with Dan Harris was chemistry with a capital C.

'Hey, Mrs Robinson, how you doing?' Dan said sleepily.

'It's all good, Mr Harris, but I have to get up now. I can drop you to work at seven if you want me to.'

Dan grabbed hold of her and gave her a long and loving kiss.

'No time to start me off again young man, sorry,' she smiled. 'I really enjoyed last night by the way.' She jumped out of bed and went to get showered.

Dan pulled the covers up over him as he realised the enormity of what had happened last night. Never before had he cheated on Alex. In fact, never before had he cheated on anyone. He could blame the drink, but no. He realised that he hadn't even thought about home for one minute; he had been so overtaken with emotion for this marvellous woman. It was at this precise moment he realised that his relationship with Alex was over, in fact, it had been over for months.

'Don't get up,' Jess said softly. 'There's an iron there

to sort out your crumpled clothes, help yourself to a shower and there's a taxi number on the coffee table downstairs. You don't want to be two hours early with a hangover like yours.'

Dan sat up again. 'Wow! You look amazing.'

Jess had put on a fitted black trouser suit and shocking blue shirt, her hair was straightened and make-up perfect. She felt content, walking on air, almost as if she had honey running through her veins.

'Bye then,' she said brightly but for some strange reason wanted to cry. 'I'm far too big to be a bit on the side, you know. Thanks for a lovely evening – and I really mean that.'

He waved as she disappeared down the stairs. Then, 'Shit, shit,' he said out loud as the front door banged shut and hurriedly looked for his phone.

Chapter Six

'Oh, Sal, it feels so wrong. I've never ever distrusted Dan in my life.' Alex announced to her best friend, whilst dragging hard on a recently lit cigarette.

'Mummy, want *Ballamory*. Want *Ballamory*!'

'Shit, I forgot about Evie upstairs. Hang on, darling, I'll come up and put it on for you.'

Back in the kitchen, Alex planted a kiss on her mate's cheek. 'Thanks for coming over, by the way, Sal.'

'Always here for you, you know that. I've called in to work and said I had car problems.' She brushed Alex's cheek lightly with her fingers. 'However, I really don't think you've got anything to worry about. You know Dan, he's so honest. He'll call you in a minute, I bet you.'

'No, Sal, I know him too well. There's something wrong.'

Beep, beep – the reassuring sound of an awaited text message ran out across the kitchen.

'See,' Sal said smugly. Alex grabbed her mobile from the table. Just seeing Dan's name on the screen made her smile, but this was short-lived.

'Mrs Robinson, thanks for last night x'

Alex repeated the message out loud and went white. Sal put the kettle on, lit another cigarette and handed it to her friend.

'I knew it, just knew it, I had the most dreadful feeling in my stomach when I spoke to Carrie this morning. Shit, Sal, he's fucking cheated on me with. And he wasn't even clever enough to send the text to the right bloody person.

'Maybe it was meant for you, Al. After all, he is your

toy boy.'

Alex put her hand to her head. 'Sal, of course it wasn't meant for me, I'm not stupid.'

Sal placed a reassuring arm around her friend's shoulder, as Alex continued her betrayal-induced rant. 'Well, that's it, Sal, no more bloody lies. It's about time I told Daniel Harris the truth about his precious little girl.'

'No, Alex! No way! Think clearly here. If you tell him, it will be Evie who suffers the most, not Dan. You know how much she loves him. Sometimes, there are things that just have to remain a secret, and I think this should be one of them.'

'OK, OK, but I just want to hurt him like he's hurt me.' Alex was visibly shaking. She picked up the phone.

'Don't tell him, Al,' Sal pleaded. 'You don't even know he's done anything wrong yet. He might have just been thanking her for a drink, a lift even. Find out first before you go mad at him.'

Alex didn't need to think. She felt a white-hot anger.

'Good morning and how are my beautiful girls today?' Dan tried to sound as calm as possible but inside he felt like he was dying. 'Sorry I haven't called you yet,' he went on, his voice trembling. He wasn't used to lying. 'My mobile is out of juice and I'm really busy this morning.'

'Busy? Lucky you. So how was last night?' Alex seethed.

'Good, good. Ended up staying with Matt as had late drinks with a client in Warfield. Anyway, gotta go, loads to do, call you later, be home around six. Kisses for Evie.'

Alex's voice suddenly turned into a deep, slow growl. 'Who the flying fuck is Mrs Robinson?'

Chapter Seven

Jess arrived at The Brewery, just in time for her meeting with the Operations Manager. She was glad that she was at a familiar venue. She was also relieved that she hadn't had to set up last night, as she would have missed our on her fateful meeting with the luscious Daniel Harris.

Despite having been arranging events for the past fifteen years, she still loved her job. The sense of satisfaction from arranging staging, lighting, show content, music, and then seeing it all come together, gave her a complete buzz.

She smiled all day long and didn't feel one ounce of tiredness. She questioned herself on how she could be so affected after such a brief interlude. The boy was practically married and had a child, he was in fact young enough to be *her* child! Despite this, however much she tried, she couldn't get him out of her head.

She got in after eight, poured herself a large glass of wine and put her feet up on the coffee table. She noticed a Lemon Events business card. Keeping up *The Graduate* theme, on the back, he'd written *Benjamin Braddock wants you to mail him on his personal mail! Add me to messenger too! X*

Jess smiled broadly and turned on her laptop. She would send a mail that he would get in the morning. She would keep it short and sweet.

To: dharris@hotmail.com
From: jmorley@yahoo.co.uk

Dear Benjamin

It was good to see nearly all of you last night!
You can reach me on this mail.
Mrs Robinson xx

Dan called Jess immediately. 'Oh, Jess, you'll never guess what has happened. I stupidly sent Alex a text that was meant for you. I'm so used to texting her.'

'Oh, Dan.' Jess wasn't sure what to say. She could feel Dan's anguish down the phone.

Dan had thought of nothing but Jess since the moment he left her. He loved her vitality, her smile, her warmth, her body! She was fun, she was happening. Her age wasn't an issue at all. But he wasn't a philanderer. He loved Alex, but if he was honest with himself he wasn't *in love* with her any more.

He continued, 'Jess, please listen to me. I really did have a great time last night. I was actually phoning to tell you that and also to explain that I need to sort stuff out with Alex. We've got Evie to think about. I have to try and make a go of it, for her sake. I've hurt her so badly. I'm still at work, because I just can't face her.' He paused. 'I'm really scared, Jess.'

'It's OK, Dan,' Jess replied softly, shocked by the tears that she was holding back.

'It will be fine. Alex doesn't have to know everything.'

'Thanks, Jess, I really must go. Be cool.'

'Bye, Dan, I will – and good luck tonight.'

Tears began to slowly fall down Jess's cheeks. She had never believed in love at first sight before but, on that crisp December night, what she felt for Dan was the way she imagined true love must feel. Dan was a decent bloke; he would sort it out with Alex. She would be a fool to leave him, and it would break his heart to have to abandon his little girl.

She poured herself a glass of wine, opened up her laptop and began to type a proposal for a new event.

Chapter Eight

'Em, I can't believe I feel like this after just one night with someone.'

'Do They Know It's Christmas' blared out from the local wine bar.

'My head is telling me he's completely wrong for me but I just cannot stop thinking about him.'

Emma and Jess had been friends for thirty-four years; they had met at primary school and had been close ever since. Emma, with her curly, dark brown hair and green eyes, was tall and willowy. She had kept her figure and looks despite giving birth to three beautiful children. It had always amazed them both that Emma had succumbed to being the earth mother and Jess was now the single career woman. Throughout the years it had been Jess who dreamt of the rose-covered cottage in the country, adoring husband, and brood of kids, whereas glamorous Emma had wanted to be dresser to the stars and marry one of them. She had been married to Mark for the past fifteen years and despite the fact that they bickered like children most of the time, their relationship was solid. Emma was a great artist and painted large mural-type paintings in her garage to supplement their income and 'keep her sane' amongst the madness of family life. Despite being extremely close to her siblings, Jess actually confided in Emma, more than in anyone else in her whole life. Nothing seemed to shock her.

Em took a slurp of her Sauvignon. 'Come on, Jess, you know what you're like. You always wear your heart on your sleeve. I think you've actually got to see sense on this one.'

"Do they know it's Christmas time at all?" The chorus boomed out, drowning the Christmas revellers.

'He wouldn't even have been born when this song came out first time,' Emma realised.

They both laughed.

'And I was having my first sexual experience as he was in the maternity ward,' Jess added.

'You probably were even driving past the hospital in your blue Mini with the ladybirds on the side. This is some age difference, Jess, even for you.'

Jess had always liked younger men. Even Philip, with whom she had been with for two years, was five years younger. Yes, she was young at heart but deep down she knew the reason she picked these younger men was that she was actually quite frightened of commitment herself. Any man who had crossed her path and had offered her the world had frightened her off. She became bored of their intentions. On the other hand, if any man posed as a challenge, she would jump in with both feet, give them the world and then frighten *them* off. Heartbreak would ensue and the whole pattern would start again.

Emma thought it had stemmed back to the death of her mother. She thought if Jess got close and loved anyone completely, they would leave her and she would feel the same terrible loss she felt then.

'But Emma, I think this is different. Age has no barriers in the game of love and all that.'

'You'll get hurt and I'll be buying shares in Kleenex again,' Emma replied knowingly.

Jess looked at her friend with her big honest eyes. 'I do get what you're saying, Em, but I'm desperate to see him again.'

Emma softened. 'OK, so you know what you have to do on this one, don't you?'

Jess looked at her quizzically. She always relied on

Emma's sensible advice, as her own track record with men had been appalling to date.

'You *have* to leave him alone, well alone, not even a text, or a sneaky email. He's young, he won't like being hounded. He's told you that he needs some time to try and sort things out with Alex and that is what you have to let him do.'

'I know, I know,' Jess replied like an insolent child.

'It's the only way, Jess. Hunter-gatherer instinct and all that. Men love to be the chaser. If he feels the same for you he'll come back to you.'

'Wasn't it Sting who sang 'If you Love Somebody Set Them Free'?' Jess piped up.

'He's probably never heard that either.'

They both laughed out loud.

Chapter Nine

The lead up to Christmas was a mad time for Jess; she had an event on nearly every night, dinner-parties for rich City businessmen, and her biggest money-maker, the annual Christmas party for AG Technology at the Grosvenor House Hotel. This involved entertaining a thousand employees with a comedian, live band, and four-course dinner. She loved the buzz of an event of this size; the stress of it almost ran her ragged but the rewards allowed her to take the majority of January off.

A day hadn't gone by when she hadn't thought about Dan but she had managed to take Emma's advice on board. Even though she'd sometimes had to almost sit on her hands, she hadn't contacted him in any shape or form. She carried on her routine of going to the gym, seeing friends and planning events for next year.

She was going to spend Christmas with her sister Phoebe and husband, and her two beautiful nieces this year. Her dad and his partner Maria were going to France to stay with friends, and her brother was travelling around Australia.

Christmas Eve arrived and Jess started to pack up her car for the drive to her sister's. She wondered what Dan was up to. It wouldn't be a very happy Christmas for him, she thought. Even if they had managed to sort it out, it would be hard for Alex to trust him now. She threw the last bag into the boot and went back into the house to make sure everything was locked. Noting that she had forgotten to switch off her laptop, she quickly checked for any new messages. She looked at the screen and did a double-take. Her heart began to beat faster as there, sitting in the inbox, was what she had been waiting for, for the past three weeks.

Chapter Ten

Alex turned over and snuggled up against the warm, soft body next to her.

'Morning,' she whispered.

She luxuriated in the fact that Evie wasn't in the next room so there would be no crying out for milk today. She was soothed by the gentle love-making of the night before and for the first time in weeks felt content.

Finding out about Dan had been a complete shock, but in some ways a relief. They had been playing happy families for so long. She was frustrated that she hadn't been getting the respect she deserved as a partner or mother, and was glad it had all come to a head. She could now concentrate on making Evie's life as happy as possible and fulfilling her potential as a stand-up comedienne, something she had always wanted to do.

'Morning, gorgeous girl. How much time have we got before Evie is back?'

'Hours and hours yet,' Alex replied dreamily.

Alex melted into the slow and loving kiss from her partner's soft mouth. She pulled away and put her finger against those lips as if to shush them, and moved slowly and deliberately down her partner's body. Her tongue caressed every inch of perfect, sweet-smelling flesh. As she licked and teased an inner thigh, she became completely turned on by the groans of pleasure that ensued.

'Good, so good,' Sal murmured.

Chapter Eleven

To: jmorley@yahoo.co.uk
From: dharris@hotmail.com

Jess
Hope you're doing OK. Just wanted to send you a little note to say that Alex and I have split up. We did our best to work it out but we realised that we've been living a lie for quite a while now. I would love to see you again. If you fancy a drink sometime next week, text me!
   Happy Christmas!
   Dan x

Jess began to dance around her small living room.
   'Happy Christmas, Jessica Morley!'
   She sang 'Onward Christian Soldiers' with such gusto at the Christmas Eve carol service that Phoebe laughed out loud and got glared at by the rest of the congregation. Georgina, Jess's eight-year-old niece, looked on in horror, thinking that finally Auntie Jessica had gone completely mad.
   She decided to hold out on texting Dan until that evening as she had kept Emma's hunter-gatherer comment in the back of her mind. He could now wait for the wonderful Jessica Morley to contact _him_!
   She poured herself a large sherry and drafted a text.

Happy Christmas, Mr Harris.
Drinks next week
sounds good x

Short and sweet, perfect. Not giving anything away but saying that yes, she wanted to meet him. She was happy with that. Send!

Although she was bursting to, Jess had managed not to tell her sister about Dan just yet. Phoebe was five years Jess's junior. She was shorter than Jess, at just five feet two and had inherited their father's blond locks, which she always wore tied up in a ponytail.

'It's easier this way.' Was her standard reply when Jess insisted she showed off her long, fair tresses every now and then.

Phoebe lived a charmed and happy life. She had never been very ambitious; in fact she had wanted to start a family from the minute her periods had started. She had married Glen when they were just eighteen and they were still as much in love with each other now as on the day they met. Glen had inherited his father's successful catering business and, from the day that Georgina was conceived, Glen insisted that Phoebe should not have to do another day's work in her life, which of course delighted her.

Jess knew her wise and far more sensible younger sister would think she was completely mad even entertaining the idea of dating a twenty-three-year-old boy. Especially when all she ever harped on about was meeting the man of her dreams, settling down and having children before she was forty! Hmm, three months to go. She'd have to get a move on!

Christmas Day came and went without incident. Georgina and Annabel shrieked the whole way through it and Jess was actually quite glad to get into the comfort zone of her Audi to drive the 50 miles back home. She had decided to travel back on Boxing Day to miss all the traffic, and was excited at the prospect of eating all the cold leftovers that Phoebe had packed up for her. She would scoff and watch crap telly for the rest of the day –

bliss.

She turned on the radio and sang along with Wham's 'Last Christmas'. Just as she was pulling up outside her house she received a text.

You free tonight by any chance? Yours at 7? Dan x

Bored with playing the hunter-gatherer game, Jess turned cavewoman and replied straight away.

Cool. See you then. Jess x

So much for slobbing around the house eating cold stuffing. She had to find an outfit, get bathed, get perfumed, and get ready to entertain!

Chapter Twelve

'Mate, are you sure you know what you're doing?' Matt enquired. He was seven years older than Dan and sometimes he felt like a big brother to him, rather than a friend.

'You've just come out of a four-year relationship and you're thinking of meeting up with someone else already, sixteen years your senior. It'll end in tears, you mark my words!'

'Matt, she's hot. I just know from the other night the sex will be amazing. She's fun too. I could do with a laugh.'

'Rebound and all that though, mate. Just don't get into something you can't get out of.'

'Look, I'm only going to meet her for a quick drink and then I'm going to Henley to see Dave later. It's his sofa's turn tonight. I just want to chat through what happened the other night. I did sort of leave her out in the cold a bit. It'll be fine.'

'Go and have fun then. Happy Christmas and all that. See you New Year's Eve as planned, yeah?'

'Sure. Bye, mate.' Dan turned off his mobile and headed towards Warfield. He didn't want Alex to know where he was. If she phoned, he wasn't sure he would be able to lie convincingly. Although they had split fairly amicably he didn't want to cause her upset by realising he was meeting Jess, in her eyes the catalyst to the end of their relationship. He would call and check Evie was OK later.

Chapter Thirteen

When the doorbell rang, Jess double-checked herself in the mirror, blew on her palm to check her breath was minty fresh, and ran downstairs to answer the door. Dan was better-looking than she remembered. He had obviously made an effort too, wearing dark Levis and a freshly ironed black shirt.

'Well, hello, Ms Morley. Fancy seeing you here.'

'Evening, Mr Harris. Do come into Morley Mansions.' She swept her arm past him in welcome.

They smiled at each other.

'Good to see you,' Jess said, feeling like she had reverted to a nervous teenager.

'You too. I'm officially on the rebound so I thought just a quick drink maybe?' Dan smirked. 'I'm staying at a mate's in Henley tonight so you have me for precisely two hours.'

Jess felt like she was going to cry with disappointment but hid it gamely.

'Sounds good to me. Why don't we go out for a drink then? It will be really quiet as it's Boxing Day and I don't ever buy Stella in.'

Dan laughed. 'Cool by me, I'm happy to drive as I'm going on after.'

Jess moved an old McDonald's wrapper and Coke can on to the back seat and placed a tired-looking dolly at her feet. Her chariot roared into life.

'The Horse and Hounds in Ringfield would be cosy at Christmas-time, I reckon. OK with you?' she said.

'Cool, cool, I know where that is. Hold on, Mrs

Robinson.'

And hold on she did. Jess clung onto the door handle for fear of her life. She looked briefly to her side, checking to see if Jenson Button had got into the driver's seat. The vibration of the souped-up exhaust on Dan's old Golf GTI made her legs wobble and she thought she might be sick with fear as they approached a roundabout at 70 miles per hour. She struggled to hear what he was saying over Eminem's rant booming out of the eight well-positioned speakers, and then realised Dan wasn't talking to her at all, but was reciting the rant of his American idol.

She felt like she needed a bottle of wine and a straw when they eventually parked up.

'Stella?' Dan offered.

'Large glass of red for me please,' she replied shakily.

They took a seat in the corner next to a beautifully lit Christmas tree.

'I still love Christmas, you know,' she said dreamily.

'And you've certainly been around for a few,' Dan joked.

'Hey, less of the cheek, you.'

Their legs touched and Jess felt that same spark of electricity she had felt on her sofa that first night. Dan didn't move away.

'Being honest with you, Jess, I actually arranged to see Dave later as I knew that we'd be at it like rabbits if not. And as I am officially on the rebound, that wouldn't be acceptable, now would it?' He looked right into Jess's eyes to gauge her reaction.

She held his gaze. 'No not acceptable at all.' She squirmed in her seat, imagining already what it would be like to be at it like rabbits.

'How are you anyway?' she went on.

'I'm doing OK actually. I would only admit this to you, but I feel like I've got my life back again. I'm actually genuinely really, really happy. Alex and I were not going anywhere. I was beginning to despise being with her. Eventually Evie would have picked up on the bad vibe, but as it happens, she's young enough to accept what's going on without hopefully disrupting her life too much.'

'Well, I'm really glad you've come out of it OK.' She took a large gulp of wine, and then went on. 'So, are you going to get your own place? I guess there are only so many sofas you can sleep on.'

'The plan for now is that we all stay in the house we are in until the lease runs out at the end of Feb – separate rooms obviously. It seems the best compromise at the moment, as I'm not sure if I can afford a place on my own since we'll have to pay for Evie to go to nursery now. When the time comes I'll have to sort out what I'm gonna do house-wise.'

Jess liked the maturity of Dan where Evie was concerned. He always wanted the best for her and, for someone so young, she thought that was a lovely quality.

'Another Stella?' Jess enquired.

'Jeez, Jessy, you knocked that back.'

She had indeed downed her wine very quickly. She intended to have at least two more before she set foot in that car with Jenson again.

'Better have a half as I'm driving and its Christmas and all that.'

They chatted and flirted until Dan suddenly remembered Dave. 'Shit, I'd better drop you back.'

Dan took a large toke of a joint when he got back in his car. Jess also took a big slug of it and proceeded to cough for five minutes, to Dan's amusement. Jess was thankful that it mellowed him out as, instead of a booming rapper, Ian Brown's F.E.A.R came out of the multiple speakers and normal driving was resumed.

'Do you want to come in for a coffee before you go?' Jess enquired, not wanting to lose the exhilarating company of this young sexy man.

'Mrs Robinson, surely you should be offering me alcohol.'

Dan actually did not want to go anywhere. Just the thought of getting Jess naked and touching her full, pert breasts was all he could think about. He watched her walk through to the kitchen, her firm little bottom looked amazing in her tight jeans and he felt an immediate stirring in his loins. He shouted through to the kitchen.

'I'm gonna call Dave. OK if I stay with you for a bit?'

'A bit of what?' Jessy flirted. 'Sugar?' she enquired.

'I was thinking more spice,' Dan replied cheekily.

Jess walked into the lounge and put the coffee cups down. Before she'd even had a chance to sit, Dan grabbed her towards him. He went straight for the buttons on her crisp white shirt and, instead of unbuttoning it, he ripped it open and some buttons fell to the floor. He kissed her passionately and longingly. Jess responded with as much force. It was as if they'd just been told they were the last two people on the planet and the world was going to end.

'I want to taste you,' Dan murmured. He moved down her body, kissing her ample breasts. His tongue deftly teased her erect nipples and Jess groaned with pleasure as their lovemaking commenced.

They came together. Dan closed and opened his eyes as if he couldn't believe what had just happened.

'Fucking hell, Jess. Happy bloody Christmas!'

Chapter Fourteen

'Matt, mate, it's me, you got a minute?'

'Hang on a sec, let me put you on hands free. Well?' Matt enquired.

'Mate.' Dan hesitated.

'Come on, Danny boy, spit it out.'

'She's bloody amazing; I have never had sex like it in my whole life. All night – we were at it all night and it just got better every time. She's gorgeous Matt. Her body is surprisingly really fit too.'

'So what's the vibe, Dan? You seeing her again?'

'I can't not. I really like her. It's not like she seems old or anything. We actually get on really well, we're at a level. She makes me laugh.' Dan tailed off. By describing Jess, he realised that he really *did* like her.

'And does she realise it's a bit of fun?'

'Jeez, Matt, I've only stayed with her once, it's not marriage. She knows I'm on the rebound. I told her that. It'll be fine.'

'Just be careful, hey, for both your sakes. You've got a lot going on in that head of yours at the moment and, from what you've told me, she sounds like a decent lady.'

'She's a big girl, Matt, she can handle herself. She's certainly not stupid. In fact I can thoroughly recommend the older woman.'

They both laughed.

'See you New Year's Eve.'

'Yeah, see you, mate.'

Chapter Fifteen

'Coffee, Jess?' Emma shouted through to the lounge where she was playing Peppa Pig Houses with Laura, Em's youngest.

'Tea please, ta. I'll be through in a minute. Just giving Baby Pig George his dinner and putting him to bed.' Laura shrieked with delight.

Jess and Emma sat down in the kitchen.

'Pray tell, dear friend, what the duces is happening? You look like the cat that got the cream.'

'He's bloody gorgeous!' Jess exclaimed. 'I've never experienced love making like it. I just can't explain the feeling, it's like suddenly I've found a creature who presses all the buttons mentally and physically.'

'And how does he feel, do you reckon?'

'Well, I think he feels the same. I don't think you can do it with someone like we did the other night and it just be pure sex. It was just too real and too special. And I just know he felt it too,' Jess reassured herself. 'He did say that he was on the rebound though and that maybe it would be better if we only saw each other as mates in future, until he sorts himself out a bit.'

'OK, so Jess that is a warning sign if ever I heard one.'

'But Em, I know he doesn't mean it. He wants me as much as I want him, I just know it. He's just being sensible.'

Emma had her knowing look ready. 'Jess, please be careful. I love you and I know it all seems wonderful at the moment, but you need to be realistic here. He's told you how it is.'

'Em, I've spent two nights with the bloke.'

'Yes, Jess, but I know you so well and from the way you're talking you are so going to fall in love with him.'

'What are you doing tonight anyway?' Jess enquired changing the subject.

'We can't get a babysitter so we're going to see it in at home, just the five of us. And you?'

'I've actually got all the new magazines that are out, a bottle of Chilean Red, and I'm going to stay in. I can't be arsed to go through the rigmarole of the whole forced New Year's Eve enjoyment thing. I go to enough parties with work.'

'You know you're always welcome round here. What's Lover Boy up to anyway?'

'He's going round his mate's house with Alex and Evie, 'cos they can't get a babysitter and neither of them will compromise. Matt's girlfriend will be there too, so it'll be just the five of them, how cosy.'

'You bothered by that?' Em asked.

'Weirdly no. I know there is no way anything would happen between him and Alex now. There's too much water under the bridge and anyway, even if it does, what can I do about it? Right, I'm going to head home to my magazines and copious amounts of alcohol.'

'Lucky you, I shall go and bath these bairns of mine.'

Jess got home and ran herself a deep bath. She wanted to call Dan but thought she should let him come to her. She pushed his comments about being mates to the back of her mind. That was not what she wanted at all.

Midnight arrived and so did the text she prayed may come through.

I don't mean to be blunt,
but you're beautiful. Happy New Year
Mrs. Robinson X

Chapter Sixteen

'Come on, come on. Answer the bloody phone' Alex said impatiently into the handset of her mobile phone. After ten rings, she eventually got an answer.

'Hey, what's up? I told you to try not to call me during work hours,' the man at the other end of the phone said rudely. Alex grimaced and took a deep breath.

'Happy New Year to you too.' She knew she couldn't let him wind her up, especially not before she had said her piece. 'I need more money. My dear other half has decided to have it off with someone else, so we are splitting up.' She sighed and added, 'I must have *Philanderers Apply Here* tattooed on my forehead or something!'

The man ignored her smug comment and continued, 'But, Alex, I give you £500 a month already. Surely that's enough?'

'Enough when Dan was bringing home the bacon to support us all, yes. But I'll have to find my own place now. I will of course have to go back to work but, with nursery fees for Evie, I still don't think I will earn enough to manage on my own.'

'But Dan will obviously give you money for her, won't he? Unless you've told him about me, that is?'

Alex went silent. She wanted to taunt this man, who had so readily dismissed her the minute she had told him she was pregnant with his child. She was so lucky to have met Dan when she did, and was so easily able to pass Evie off as his.

'Of course I haven't told him. I'm not that stupid. I don't want anything at all to upset Evie. It's hard enough for her that we are splitting up, as it is.'

The man at the end of the phone softened. 'Look, I'll pay a grand into your bank account today. That should tide you over until you find a job. Then, why don't you work out some figures and we'll talk again?'

'OK. Thank you,' Alex replied curtly and hung up.

Chapter Seventeen

BEEP: *Dead excited about tonight are you?*
BEEP: *Maybe ☺ See you on the train at 6 x*

'Birthday boy!' Jess hung out of the train window as she saw Dan rushing through the ticket barrier.

'Phew, just made it,' he gasped. 'Hey, nice hat, Mrs Robinson.'

'Well, thank you, sir.' Jess kissed him on the cheek. 'Your birthday surprise awaits, young man.'

The Soho Hotel was even plusher than Dan had expected. They were greeted in reception by a large stone sphinx and a stunning-looking girl, dressed in a smart black uniform.

'Good to see you again, Ms Morley.'

Jess loved it here; she had run various events at this hotel and they always treated her like royalty.

'We've upgraded you to a junior suite as it's a special occasion.' The receptionist nodded towards Dan and smiled. 'Happy Birthday, sir.'

'Fuck, what an amazing room!' he exclaimed as he threw himself on to the massive bed. 'Champagne too!'

'Of course, only the best for the birthday boy. Look in the fridge.' Neatly lined up were four cans of Stella.

'You're a bit special, aren't you, Mrs Robinson?'

'I do try.' Jess smiled.

Since Boxing Day they had lunched and messaged and talked for hours. This was Jess and Dan's first whole night together since and the anticipation bristled around the room.

'And now I actually have a surprise for you, Mrs Robinson.'

Jess looked at him quizzically.

'Go and sit over on the sofa, shut your eyes and hold your hand out.'

She did as she was told. Opening her hand to find a bit of folded-up paper, she looked at Dan quizzically.

'Go on – unwrap it then.'

She unwrapped the small packet to find four orange-coloured pills.

'Dan?'

He laughed, loving the fact that he had done something to surprise Jess for once.

'These, my darling lady friend, are our entertainment for the evening.'

'Oh my God! Look, Dan, I'm not so sure. I've never taken drugs, apart from the odd puff of weed, ever before in my life.'

'You're going to love it!'

Jess hoped there weren't any gas ovens around to stick her head into, as she was sure if he asked her to do that she would obey without question! What was it with this boy?

'I'm scared,' she confessed.

'I'll look after you. You will be absolutely fine, we're going to have a ball.'

He kissed her full on the lips and brushed her fringe off her face. He noticed that she smelt gorgeous. Dan proceeded to stand on the bed and put his arms in the air and began to speak like a ring-master.

'Jessica Morley. What you have here tonight, for one night only, is a fuck-off huge bedroom, with a sumptuous lounge area.' He pointed to the end of the suite. 'Plus,' dramatic pause for effect, 'over in that corner, a marble tiled bathroom, with a Jacuzzi for two and a walk in shower and – drum roll, please….'

Jess tapped her hands on the glass coffee table as her

sexy young partner continued. 'Finally, Ms Morley, for your delectation and delight, you have champagne, a love drug and, of course, me and my huge cock!' Dan did a star jump off the bed and Jess laughed out loud.

Dan was happy. He loved hanging out with Jess. He was also really excited at the thought of taking some pills with her, as he knew how horny she would get. Jess, too began to feel excited. As she had never mixed in circles that had taken drugs, she had always wondered how Ecstasy would make her feel.

'Right,' said Jess. 'Let's go for dinner and then we can come back here and party on.'

Dan put his hand on hers, 'Jessy Morley, we don't need food tonight, just supplements. Now let's get this party started.' He poured the champagne and they clinked glasses.

'Cheers.' Jess cocked her head to the side and smiled.

'You ready?'

She nodded.

'Just take a big swig, wash them down and relax,' Dan urged.

'Both of them?' Jess enquired.

'Yeah, I reckon.'

Chapter Eighteen

Alex lifted Evie out of her car seat and carried her to Sally's door.

'Auntie Sally's.'

'That's right, Wevie, clever girl.'

'Is Daddy here?'

'No darling, Daddy's gone to London to see some friends tonight.'

'Hey, how you doing?' Sal greeted Alex at the door with a kiss on the cheek.

Her bobbed blonde hair was wet and she was wearing just a white towel over her size 14 frame. 'Let me whizz upstairs and get dressed and I'll be right with you.'

Alex sat Evie on the lounge floor, gave her a packet of raisins and put on CBeebies. She went to the fridge and poured two large glasses of wine. Then she lit a cigarette. Sal came back into the kitchen. 'Right, I'm all yours. How's it going?'

'He wants me back.'

'You *are* joking!'

'Exactly what I said. He walked in last night, blubbed like a baby, said sorry for what he'd done about a million times and thought it was the right thing to do, to try and make a go of it for Evie's sake.'

'Not your sake then?'

'Well, he did say that we hadn't ever really discussed what the problems were with us, and maybe if we did that then we could work it out.'

'And what did you say?'

'I told him to fuck right off!'

'Good girl.'

'So, more crying ensued and then I think he realised that I meant it and that was that. He just skulked off to bed with his tail between his legs.'

'Has he seen the old hag again?' Sal asked.

'Not as far as I know,' Alex shrugged. 'He said that it was just a one-off, a silly drunken mistake, and she was far too old to even consider having a relationship with anyway.'

'So where is he tonight then?'

'It's his birthday tomorrow and he's gone to meet up with an old friend of his in London. They are going to a few bars and he's crashing there.'

'And you believe him?'

'Well yeah, why wouldn't I? And to be honest, if he is lying I actually don't care any more. I've lost total respect for him now.' Alex took a large gulp of wine.

'How's Evie doing?' Sal added.

'She's not picked up on anything yet, so that's a good thing anyway. I'm finding it tough coping with her on my own, though. I didn't realise how much Dan actually did, to be honest.'

'So are you going to tell him that Evie is not his?' Sal enquired.

'No definitely not. Dickhead can pay for the rest of his life, and now that Dan's gone too *he* will have to pay up as well. I'll be quids in.'

'I don't blame you, Al. They've both wronged you. In fact, it's divine retribution.'

Alex sat back in the wooden kitchen chair and suddenly felt sad. As much as she and Dan had not been getting on over the past few months, she did really miss having him around the house. It was tough and lonely sometimes, being a single parent. Dan would always be more of a father to Evie, than Dickhead ever would have been, and she was relieved that she hadn't blurted it out in anger, when she had first found out about his indiscretion. Dan wasn't a bad man and at least he had the decency not to continue having an affair behind her back.

The girls sat in silence for a while until Sal piped up. 'Look Al, about us the other night.'

Alex had almost forgotten about it already. 'Sal, it's cool. I was so in need of some love and attention, and the fact that I got it from my best mate was perfect. I actually feel like I've been unfaithful to Dan now, and that makes me feel a hell of a lot better too.' Sal looked a little perturbed by this comment. Alex softened.

'Look I'm sorry, what I said came out wrong. I wouldn't have changed a thing about the other night. But let's face it, it was a one-off.

Alex smiled 'Can't really imagine explaining to Evie that her pretend father ran off with a geriatric, and her mother turned lesbian due to the shock of it!'

It was Sal's turn to giggle. 'Nice pussy and all that, honey child, but I like cocks too much girlfriend,' she added in a funny voice.

'Sally Walters, you are pure filth! Now let's get that little girl of mine fed and in bed, and we can get pissed.'

Chapter Nineteen

Dan had loaded the CD player and his music blared out over the Soho Hotel suite.

'How's it going, Mrs Robinson?' He knelt down in front of her, stroked her face gently and held her hands as she sat on the sofa.

Feel a bit wonky actually, Mr Harris, bit hot.' She could hear her voice, but thought it didn't sound like her. Dan proceeded to fan her with the breakfast menu.

'It's all good, Jess, I promise you, it's all good. Here, have some water.'

'Whoa.' Jess felt really strange. 'I need to take some clothes off.'

'That's cool, Jess, no worries.'

She stripped off her jumper to reveal a lacy black bra which showed just the right amount of cleavage. 'Dan, am I OK?' she questioned.

'You're more than OK, honey; in a minute you are going to feel amazing.' Dan was completely attentive: he fanned Jess, stroked her face, and touched her lips with his just so she knew he was right there.

'Need to lie down,' Jess said.

Dan helped her up. She lay down back to front on the huge bed and put her legs high up on the 6ft satin headboard, stretching out her arms wide.

'Here, have some more water.' He lay down next to her and put his legs up too.

Jess's face had completely relaxed; she had a wry smile on her face as the Gorrillaz blared out 'Dare.' Dan stroked her face. 'Has anyone ever told you how beautiful you are?' he said tenderly.

'I've lost count.' Jess laughed. 'God, I feel amazing,' she murmured.

She reached over to stroke Dan's face, turned to her side and kissed him. It was the most sensual, tender kiss she had ever experienced. She was lost in the moment. If she had died there and then she wouldn't have cared.

Finally, she pulled away from him. 'And now, Mr Harris, for your eyes only, I am going to do the world famous Jessica Morley Soho Hotel pillow dance.' She grabbed a pillow with both her feet and began circling it above their heads.'

Dan leapt up, ripped his shirt off and proceeded to dance around the room. Jess dropped her pillow and stretched her body right out into a star shape.

'You dancing with me, Jessy Morley?'

'No, I'm stretching.' She yawned. 'But in a minute, I am going to be your private dancer,' she said woozily.

Suddenly she felt a rush of energy go right through her, from her toes to the top of her head. She jumped off the bed, ripped off her jeans to reveal black, lacy, shorts and threw her head back in delight. 'Baby boy, I'm a dancing.'

She lifted her arms in the air and began to dance and dance and dance.

'I feel like a twenty-four-year-old.' She shouted grabbing Dan's erection through his boxer shorts.

'You're lucky it's after midnight then, aren't you?' He smiled at her exuberance. She pulled away, grabbed a bottle of water from the mini bar and downed it in one. Dan laughed out loud at Jess who was now bouncing up and down on the sofa. She looked oh so sexy.

'Get here, you,' he said huskily.

Jess hopped down from the sofa and he grabbed her from behind. He could feel the curves of her body gyrating against him, droplets of sweat from her forehead fell on to his hands. Never before had he felt such a wanting for another human being. He walked her slowly towards the bed so that she gently fell forward, pushed her panties aside and slowly entered her, caressing her breasts as he did so. Jess squirmed with pleasure.

'Whoa, I need a rest,' Jess panted.

They fell on to the bed.

'You like?' Dan enquired

'I fucking love it!' she replied.

A chill-out track came on. Jess lay on the bed stroking Dan's arms and planting butterfly kisses all over him.

'Do you know what? The minute I saw you at the party I wanted you, Jessy Morley. In fact, the minute we shared a warm beer in the Holiday Inn in Wandsworth I thought you were pretty special.'

'I feel exactly the same. I've never felt such a connection with anyone like this before. Just mates though, eh, like you said?' Jess smiled at him wryly.

'Jess, I love hanging out with you, I think you're really cool.'

'We can be mates that stay overnight then, is that a deal?'

'Deal.'

Jess shut her eyes momentarily and clenched her knees into her chest.

'Jess?'

'Hmm?' she responded dreamily.

'I always want to be honest with you.'

'That's good.'

'And, well.' He hesitated for a second. 'Just so you know, I did see if Alex would get back with me again. The thought of Evie coming from a broken home just hurts so me so much, especially as it would be my doing.'

'And?' Jess enquired, not allowing herself to get upset.

'She told me to fuck off actually. Can't say I blame her really. I thought long and hard afterwards and realised that it would have been foolish to even try. Alex and I would never have worked out. I was just twenty when I met her and I've already grown into a different person.'

Jess leaned over and kissed him on the cheek. 'Thanks for telling me,' she said sincerely.

'I love Evie so much,' Dan sighed.

'I know you do, darling. Everything will be fine, don't worry.'

'You'll never guess what else?' Dan carried on. 'She only had a lesbian fling with her best mate.'

'No way!' Jess laughed out loud.

'It's not funny,' Dan said indignantly. 'She was bloody unfaithful with another woman. It's still a betrayal.' Jess said nothing more and snuggled into him.

'Jess?'

'Yeah?'

'Great tits too, by the way,' Dan smirked.

'Well, thank you,' she laughed

'Pussy's pretty delicious too.'

'Daniel Harris!'

'I mean it, Jess. I think you are gorgeous with a capital G and thanks so much for arranging this for me. I really do appreciate it.'

And then the love making commenced: in the Jacuzzi, in the shower, on the sofa, against the desk. They eventually fell asleep on top of the bed, in each other's arms.

Jess awoke with a jump as the maid knocked on the door. 'Dan, wake up. It's eleven-thirty and we've got to be out of the room in thirty.' She groaned. 'Give us an hour please,' she called out.

She snuggled into Dan. 'Happy Birthday, baby boy! That was the most amazing night I've ever had in my life. I'm glad I shared it with you.'

'It was pretty special, wasn't it?'

Dan turned over to kiss her sensually. As he did so, Jess

became aware of wetness between her legs. She knew it wasn't just from her.

'Shit, shit!'

'Jess, chill out, baby. What on earth's the matter?'

.'Dan, for one, I can't remember if we used condoms every time last night and if we did, which I doubt, one of them has most definitely burst.'

'Don't panic its fine, we're in central London. I'm sure a Boots will be open, you can take a morning after pill.'

'OK, OK. I won't panic. Damn, I was waiting for the first day of my period to go back on the pill. But you're right:, the morning after pill must be foolproof. Let's get up now so we can zap those sperms of yours.'

Chapter Twenty

'Em, it's me, pick up if you're there.' Jess was in the fruit and veg section of Tesco.

'Hey there, how you doing? I've literally got 5 minutes, as I've got to drive Aaron to football practice.'

'I'm panicking slightly, I just felt really strange, got like flashes in front of my eyes and felt really faint, like I've never felt before, I'm worried I might be pregnant.'

'Oh Jess, I'm sure you can't be. But look, whilst you're there, why don't you get a test. You can put your mind at rest. I'll be back at 7.30, come round then and do it here, with me. I'm sure you can't be though.'

Chapter Twenty one

Matt says:
'Yo, Happy Belated Birthday mate, how was it?'

Dan says:
'I was up nearly all night.'

Matt says:
'No way, how come?'

Dan says:
'It begins with E.'

Matt says:
'Ha ha – and she was cool with that?'

Dan says:
'More than cool, she loved it – we had a great night.'

Matt says:
'Ha – I bet you did!'

Dan says:
'I really like her mate. She's lovely.'

Matt says:
'Glad it's going well. All OK at home?'

Dan says:
'Bit sticky but Evie's OK – and that's all that matters.'

Matt says:
'Sounds like you want to be more than mates with Mrs Robinson.'

Dan says:
'I do like her a lot. I can talk to her about anything, she's very cool.'

Matt says:
'Better get on. Let's go for a cuzza and a few beers soon. If you get brave, maybe I can meet your new lady friend…'

Dan says:
'Ha… defo up for curry, laters mate.'

Chapter Twenty two

Jess put her head in her hands. 'If I'd have been with him for a year, even ten months, I'd be the happiest woman in the world, but I've been seeing him for less than three weeks. Shit Em, what am I going to do?'

Mascara created thin black streams down her cheeks as she began to sob.' I know he won't want me to have it. He virtually frog-marched me to Boots!'

Emma put her arm round her distressed friend. 'It'll be fine, whatever the outcome. Call him. He might surprise you.'

'I can't.' Jess wailed. 'He's with Alex tonight sorting out finances and said we'd talk tomorrow.' Jess slept fitfully. Since the wonderful birthday night Dan had called Jess every day on his way into work. 'Morning Mrs Robinson, what's the vibe?'

'The vibe is shaky I'm afraid.'

He could tell from her voice something major was up. 'Oh Jess, please tell me you're not.'

'I am.' She said quietly and started to cry.

'Call you right back.' Dan said and promptly pulled over to be sick.

Jess made herself a cup of tea and sat upright on the sofa. She had always dreamed that the day she found out she was pregnant would be the happiest day of her life. She'd imagined that she'd be with her partner, waiting for the positive result and then they'd fall into each other's arms crying with joy at the amazing news. Instead, here she was now, not knowing what on earth her partner was going to say to her. Half an hour passed and Dan still hadn't called back. She was startled by the doorbell. 'Hey, you. I turned straight round and came to you.' Dan gave her a big hug.

'Can't believe our luck, can you?' Jess half smiled.

'I need a drink.' Dan sighed.

'Dan, it's only 10 a.m.'

'I don't care.' Dan went to the fridge and got himself a Stella from the stock that Jess now kept for him on the bottom shelf. He joined her on the sofa and held both her hands. 'I'm not going to beat around the bush here, Jess. I am so sorry but there is no way I want this baby. I won't be able to cope. It's going to be hard enough being a part-time Dad to Evie. This is just too much for me to deal with at the moment.' Jess gulped, she didn't expect this to be so cut and dried. Dan continued. 'Ultimately I realise it's your final decision and I respect that but I don't want to have any more children, not for a long while yet.' He had tears in his eyes. 'I'm really sorry but that's how I feel.'

Jess suddenly felt anger rising up inside of her. 'I, I, I, what about me and how I feel?' Jess raised her voice and dragged her fringe back roughly off her face. 'This is a big decision for me, Dan. I'm nearly forty years old; it might be my only chance to have a baby.'

'Jess, the ease with which you fell pregnant this time round, I severely doubt it.'

He continued calmly. 'Be realistic, Jess – it's just not the right time. We've known each other five minutes. To be honest with you, I care for you more now than I actually cared for Alex when she told me she was pregnant, so it's got nothing to do with how I feel about you it's just I'm not ready for another child.' Tears slowly began to fall down Jess's cheeks. 'Bringing up a kid is hard, Jess, it's not all cooing and gurgles you know. The first six months are a living hell. We're having such fun, it would all just stop.'

Jess contained herself. 'I can see where you're coming

from but…' She hesitated. 'But, I'm older, wiser. I've got my own place and I'm financially secure. We *could* do this. *I* could do this. You wouldn't even have to be that involved, if you didn't want to! I've *always* wanted a baby.' Jess's voice faltered.

'Well if that's the case then go get yourself pregnant by someone else and have a baby.' Dan even shocked himself at his bluntness. Jess pushed past him and ran up the stairs. He ran after her. 'Shit Jess, I'm sorry.' Jess was angry now.

'Maybe I want *our* baby.' She shouted. She went into the en-suite bathroom and washed her face with cold water. Dan was sitting on the bed when she came out.

'What a fucking mess, Dan.' She took a deep breath and regained control.

'OK, we can sort this, Jess, I care for you so much that the last thing I want to do is make you unhappy.' Dan put his hand on her leg. He could feel her pain but he had made his decision and there was no going back on it.

'Give me a couple of days, Dan, I need to get my head around this.'

They hugged tightly.

'I'd better get to work.' Dan said.

'Yeah, yeah you go, I'll be fine.'

'Call me anytime, Jess, if you want to talk before Friday. I'll make sure Alex has Evie.'

Chapter Twenty three

'Phoebe, it's me'

'Hey, Jess, long time no hear.' Caught up in the moment Jess actually hadn't spoken to her sister for a couple of weeks. 'I've been busy, you know...' Jess's voice began to falter.

'What's wrong, Big Sis?' Phoebe knew her sister so well.

'Pregnant, I'm bloody pregnant, Phoebes.'

'Okay,' Phoebe said slowly, 'anyone I know?' She continued almost jokingly.

'It's a long story – well a short one really.' Jess began to cry. 'Can I come over and stay tonight please?'

'You don't need to ask, get in the car now. Glen's away, so perfect timing.'

It was 7 p.m. by the time Jess got herself sorted and began the hour-long drive to Phoebe's house. Georgina and Annabel were waiting at the door, excited at her arrival.

'Auntie Jessica, Auntie Jessica. Look at the picture I did at nursery today.'

'No, no, look at *my* new reading book.' The two girls started to fight. Phoebe sighed and then opened her mouth wide to yawn. 'They've been fighting since Georgie got in from school. They're driving me mad today.' She pushed her hands through her hair. 'Right, you two. Finish your drinks and then it's bedtime. Auntie Jessica and I need to have a chat – in peace.'

The adults moved through to the solace of the kitchen. Jess already felt better being so close to somebody she loved so much. Sensible Phoebe would give her the advice she needed.

'Wine?' Phoebe questioned tentatively.

'Yes, what the hell, I do need a drink.'

'How are you feeling anyway?'

'Really horrid, I'm not sure I like being pregnant actually.'

'How far gone are you?'

'I've literally just missed my period, so probably four weeks that's all.'

Jess relayed the whole 'love' story, from two years ago in the Holiday Inn to that morning. Phoebe listened intently. 'Oh Jess, the good thing is that he knows it was a complete accident, and you in no way, shape or form have tried to trap him.'

'I'd never do that.'

'I know, but it goes in your favour that he knows that.'

'He's adamant he doesn't want me to have it though.' Jess said sadly.

'I think what you've got to think about is what *you*, Jessica Morley, really want. Is it a relationship or is it a baby? Because it sounds like if you *do* decide to have the baby he isn't going to be around very much.' Jess let out a huge sigh. Phoebe put her hand on her arm and continued. 'He is right in saying bringing up a child is hard. It's tough enough with two parents and he is being realistic, in that he does have Evie to think about too. It would be a nightmare for him and also for you, as he wouldn't be able to be around all the time.'

'You know what I'm like though, Phoebes, I've already imagined him moving in with Evie and having a ready-made family.'

'Get real, sis, that isn't going to happen is it? You just told me he was playing the 'mate' card not so long ago.'

'I know, I know. I don't even want to think about that.' Jess screwed up her face in anguish. 'Things have changed since we first met. I haven't said it to him yet but I love him. I *really* love him. In fact I love him more than I've ever loved anyone else – and I'm sure he feels the same now. He's just too scared to admit it to himself.'

'Oh, Jess, I don't want you to get hurt.'

'I know. His friends do rib him about my age, but I'm hoping what we've got between us is enough for him to rise above our age differences. This will make you laugh – I got all excited the other week as he said that one of his mates calls me MrsHarris, and there's me thinking that it's because we spend so much time together like husband and wife, when in fact it's because I'm old enough to be his mother!'

'Oh Jess. I'm not laughing. Sixteen years is a big gap though.' Phoebe stood up. 'Right we're not here to analyse your relationship with him, we're here to establish if you are *going* to have this baby. Let me get the girls in bed and I'll be right with you.' Georgina and Annabel came running through to the kitchen.

'Night, night, Auntie Jessica.' Four-year-old Annabel spouted. 'Can we play with my Plasticine in the morning?'

'Course we can, monkey. Now you be a good girl and get to bed.'

'Auntie Jessica?' It was Georgina's turn. 'Why have you been crying? Has someone been nasty to you?'

'No, darling, no one is ever nasty to Auntie Jessica, and if ever they were, I would tell them that her big grown-up niece Georgina would sort them out!' Georgina smiled and gave her auntie a big kiss. 'Love you both,' Jess said through a watery smile.

'Love you back.' They shouted back in unison, as Phoebe chased them up the stairs.

Jess started to cry. This was possibility the most difficult decision she would have to make in her life.

'So, where were we?' Phoebe poured two more glasses of wine.

'I don't think I can make his life unhappy, Phoebe, I love him too much. What I've got with him is too special for me to muck up. I've been waiting all my life to have a connection like this with someone.' She took a large gulp of wine and announced. 'I'm going to have a termination.' Jess couldn't even bring herself to say the word abortion.

Phoebe nodded. 'Hard as it is, I think that is the right decision to make, Jess. You don't want to be stuck with a screaming baby, if his heart is not in it with you. I can't think of anything more difficult than being a single parent and that is what you would be, if you're honest with yourself.'

Jess wiped her eyes. 'I'll go home tomorrow and get to the doctor. Will you come with me when I have it done?'

'Of course I will, angel.' Phoebe kissed the top of her sister's head. 'Here for you always you know that.'

Chapter Twenty four

Dan potted the black, and staggered back to his seat in the pub. He had already had four pints of Stella and it was only eight o'clock. He fumbled around in his pocket for his mobile, no messages from Jess. He was desperate to talk to her but knew she needed time to think without him. He drafted a text to her, deleted it and called Matt. 'Mate, I'm in the Red Lion, fancy a beer?'

'Alright, Danny Boy. I'm just about to watch a film, but up for one tomorrow'

'Oh come on, mate, just come for the one. I could do with a chat.' Older, wiser Matt realised that Dan had never before 'needed a chat'. 'Alright then. Give me ten.'

Dan and Matt sat at a table in the corner of the pub.

'Fucking hell. No, are you sure?'

'She showed me the test. Two blue lines.'

'Oh mate, what are you going to do?'

'I've told her there's no way I want it. I've just got out of being tied to Alex; I need some time to be me, not another mouth to feed.'

'And how did she take it?'

'She was OK actually. She had a bit of a wobble, said she needed a couple of days to think. Mind you, it's only been eight hours and that already feels like an eternity. If she decides to have it, I really don't know what to do.'

Dan downed his fifth pint. 'I really like her, like her a lot but I can't see a future for us. She's at the settling down age, I'm at the running around stage. I keep telling her that in a roundabout way.'

'Shit, well let's hope she decides it's not right. But

whatever the outcome you must be fair to her, Dan. From what you've told me she adores you.'

'She does, she's filled her fridge with Stella, and the night in London cost her four hundred quid. She's always giving me cards and thoughtful little gifts.' Dan put his hand to his forehead. He was really drunk. 'Oh God, what am I gonna do?' Matt saw tears in his friend's eyes.

'OK, at the moment I don't know what to advise if she keeps it, but one thing I know for sure, is that if she doesn't, you *have* to stop seeing her.'

Fuelled by Stella, Dan opened up. 'I don't want to let her go. She is such a lovely person and I fancy the arse off her. I could go on seeing her like this for years.'

'But you can't, Dan. If you really do think that much of her, you have to let her go. It's not fair on her. She said to you she wants a family and you don't. It's as clear as that. Keep on seeing her and you'll end up breaking her heart.' Dan's elbow slipped off of the table. 'Taxi for Harris,' Matt joked. Dan didn't laugh as Matt continued. 'Come on, mate, time to go.'

Chapter Twenty five

It had been a long couple of days for Jess. She had run through a gamut of emotions. One minute she was sure that in order to keep Dan she would have to get rid of the baby and, to be honest, as she was so in love with him this did seem the right way forward. Then she would swing the other way and worry that this may be her only chance of being a mum. Dan had said he didn't want kids for years and, as she could see herself with no other man, could she just be happy with Evie as a substitute? Part of her thought he may come round to wanting it once he saw how beautiful the baby was, but that was a big risk to take and, if he did decide to leave, it would be a hard and sometimes lonely existence for her.

She talked to her closest friends and not one of them advised she should keep it. This had helped too. Phoebe's decision had sealed it.

Her doctor had been wonderful. Jess matter of factly said that she had found herself unexpectedly pregnant, was sure she didn't want it and what did she have to do.

He had given her the number of a private clinic in London. She had made an appointment for the next day, had had a scan and was all set with a date of two weeks ahead for the procedure. She had wanted to have it sooner but as she was only just pregnant, she had to wait or there would be a risk that they wouldn't be able to conduct the operation successfully. This had actually made her feel better, she had to keep convincing herself that it was just a bundle of cells the size of a pin prick inside her and not a baby at all.

She was already sitting at the table in the restaurant when Dan arrived. He greeted her with a kiss on the cheek. He held his breath when the waitress turned to Jess to ask what she was drinking.

'Large red wine for me please,' she said.

He let out an inward sigh of relief and prayed she had made the decision he wanted to hear. 'I've missed you.' Dan said shakily.

Jess took a deep breath to stop herself from crying. She was sitting opposite the man who she wanted to spend the rest of her life with, and was about to tell him something that she hoped wouldn't affect the rest of her life.

'How are you feeling?' He couldn't come out with what he really wanted to say.

'It's OK Dan. I've booked the termination. All sorted, in true Jessy Morley military style.' Just saying it made her want to burst into tears.

'OK,' Dan said tenderly. 'When for?'

'Two weeks' time,' Jess declared and took a sip of wine. 'I care for you so much, Dan, I can't make you unhappy and I know that this is the right thing to do.' She sniffed. As she said these words, she still wasn't sure if she could go through with it. She was doing it for the sake of their relationship. What mattered to her most at this very moment in time. 'If you turned around to me and said you wanted to keep it, you know I would without hesitation don't you?'

Dan nodded and tears welled in his eyes. 'Obviously I'll be there for you the whole time. If you want me to be, that is?' He was secretly elated that Jess had come to this decision, but he was also pained at how torn his beautiful lover obviously was. He grabbed her hands across the table. 'Jess, thank you, thank you so much. This is the most altruistic thing anyone has done for me in my life.'

'Dan, I want to go home, I don't want to eat. Will you stay with me tonight?'

'Without question,' he replied, knowing he just wanted to hold her close and tell her everything would be alright.

Their lovemaking that night was tender and caring and as he looked lovingly at his sleeping partner, Dan Harris's heart began to argue with his head.

'Love is friendship set on fire.'
Anon

PART 2

Out With the Old

Chapter One

Terminal one, Heathrow airport was its usual chaotic self. Jess picked up some Euros and rushed to the toilet. She could feel the blood coming out of her. Her stomach was cramping. Sitting on the toilet, changing her mammoth sanitary towel, she wished she were anywhere else but here. She was flying to Barcelona to check set up on a big event she'd been arranging. As she was the sole event organiser, she had no choice but to go. She had had the operation a week ago and thought she'd be fine to fly. Evidently it was quite common to bleed like a suckling pig for days afterwards and tampons were a big no-no in case of infection.

Dan had been a complete angel throughout her ordeal. He had met her from the clinic with a huge bunch of yellow roses. Her favourite, and had held her gently that night as she sobbed herself to sleep.

'Don't go to Barcelona,' he'd urged that morning.

'I have to. I'll be fine, don't worry about me.'

She was just about to board when her phoned beeped.

I think you're grand x

Jess knew at the moment this was the nearest she'd get to an 'I love you' from Dan and she smiled. They had become closer than ever over the past two weeks which made Jess realise she had definitely made the right decision. She comforted herself in the thought that in a year or so, when their relationship was even more solid, she would broach the subject of a family again, things would be different then – she was sure of it.

The four day event in Barcelona went without incident. Dan called her without fail every morning and evening and by the time she was due to come home she actually felt much better. She had given Dan a key, so that he could stay at her house on Evie-free nights. She paid the taxi driver and went to put the key in the door. Dan opened it, grabbed her round the waist and kissed her full on the lips. 'God I've missed you. How are you feeling?'

'Bit tired after travelling but generally so much better, bleeding has stopped too.'

'That's a bonus,' Dan smiled. 'Right, well I've run you a nice hot bath and thought we'd get a take-away later.'

'Bloody hell, what's happened to you? I must go away more often.' Jess laughed 'Glass of wine by my bath would be good too, while you're looking after me.'

'I got you a present Jess, here.' He handed her a Jack Johnson CD.

Dan left Jess to relax, and as she was drying herself, she heard the click of the CD player.

'Are you listening Mrs Robinson?' Dan shouted up the stairs as Jack poured out the melody of 'Better Together'.

Her eyes filled with tears at his romantic notion. Dan walked up the stairs. She dropped her towel and hugged him tightly. 'I love you, Daniel Harris.'

'And I think you're grand Jessica Morley.'

Chapter Two

Jess came out of the changing room and did a spin with the Wonder Woman outfit on. Emma could barely talk for laughing. 'That is hilarious. Without question you *have* to get it.'

'Are you sure I look OK? I want to look funny as well as sexy. It is after all only once that you're forty.'

'It's perfect. Great legs, bird. Now get it off and let's go get some lunch.'

Jess had realised that planning her own event was actually quite hard to do. She had wanted everything to be just right. She had decided that fancy dress was definitely the way to go, as it always made parties that little bit more fun. She had booked out the local wine bar and found a cheesy DJ on the internet, who had assured her that he would even be able to get great auntie Constance up dancing.

'What's Dan coming as?'

'I don't know yet, he's being a big cagey about the whole thing actually.'

'Phoebe and co. are coming as the Flintstones. The girls even want to dress the dog up and bring him along as Deano, hilarious!'

'My dad is coming as Nelson. Bless him getting into the spirit of it too.'

Jess got dressed, paid the deposit on her outfit and they headed out into the crisp March sunshine.

'God it's bliss having a couple of hours away from the kids,' Emma exclaimed as their pizzas were put down in front of them. 'It's good to see you looking so well, Jess.

How are things?'

'I feel great actually. Body back in full working order and things between me and Dan couldn't be better. He's even suggested I meet Evie after the party which can only be a good thing.'

'That's fantastic, Jess, definitely a big step forward. From the sound of him he wouldn't just do that on whim, he must be feeling serious about you too.'

'Well let's hope so, he still can't say the three little words yet. I've said them once, holding back now though, don't want to scare him off now do I?'

'Can't wait to meet him at the party. I really can't even imagine what he's like. God you're a lucky cow having someone so young.'

'I have to say the sex is mind-blowing, gets better every time. I think we've got the perfect age combination on that front. It's true what they say about late thirties women, I've never been so horny in all my life.'

'Can I just say, that's another benefit for not having kids, Jess. By the time Mark and I get into bed we are so knackered, a back rub and kiss on the cheek is about all we can muster most nights.' They both laughed.

'He's moving out of the house soon isn't he?' Emma enquired.

'Yeah, Alex has decided to keep it on and is getting a lodger as they have three bedrooms. Not ideal for Evie, but evidently it's a friend of theirs, so it should be OK. Get ready for this – Dan is moving on to a *boat*!'

'A boat?' Emma exclaimed.

'Yeah it's a proper house boat. Big bedroom, shower, toilet and everything. It's moored on the Thames, about half an hour from here. One of his family just uses it in the summer and said he could rent it off them until he gets sorted.'

'That sounds like fun actually,' Emma enthused.

'I can't wait to see it. I've already been on the internet

and got Evie a life jacket as a present, as the thought of a toddler on the water worries me slightly.'

'Jess, what have I told you about being too giving, you haven't even met her yet. Let him worry about her for how.'

'Oh, Em, you know what I'm like, I won't change. I feel like I want to help him.'

'Just don't let him take advantage of you, mate.'

'I won't, I won't.' Jess smiled at her caring friend.

At that moment Jess's phone rang.

'Sorry, Em, it's Dan, do you mind if I take it?'

'Go on, of course not.'

'What's the vibe, Mrs R?' Dan questioned.

'Well I'm jut about to eat a huge piece of vanilla cheesecake, so you've got me for precisely two minutes.' He laughed. 'OK, I was actually just phoning to say I can't make tonight. I'm really sorry, Alex forgot she is on some course and I've got to look after Evie.'

Jess was disappointed but didn't show it in her voice. She knew that tolerance would always have to be in order where a child was concerned.

'Of course that's OK, don't worry. It's my party on Saturday; we can make up for lost time then.'

'Er yeah.' Dan said quietly. Jess thought Dan sounded a bit funny as he continued. 'Let's meet for lunch tomorrow. Can you come to the George and Dragon, as I'll only get an hour 'cos I'm working?'

'Yeah sure, see you one-ish. Hope you have a good night with Evie.'

Jess screwed up her face.

'Everything OK?' Em enquired.

'I don't know. He sounded really odd.'

'Probably 'cos he's calling from work, you know what men are like.'

'Yeah. I guess so.' Jess's voice tailed off. She could sense something was wrong.

Chapter Three

Jess arrived early at the George and Dragon. She was having a bit of a quiet spell work-wise, which actually had been a blessing, as it had allowed her to fully recover from the mental and physical strain of her operation. She parked overlooking the river and watched the swans floating gracefully along. She pondered if she and Dan would mate for life, just like swans evidently did. Just as she was mid romantic thought she was startled by a tap on the window.

'Looking for business?' Dan smirked.

'Get in here now and get those seats back.' She joked, but at the sight of Dan in his well fitted jeans and trendy blue shirt she could quite gamely have gone through with the offer. Dan found a table by the window overlooking the river as Jess ordered drinks at the bar. She sauntered over to him and put on a funny voice.

'A pint of the finest Stella for my immaculate toy boy, and a white wine for the laydeee.'

'You really aren't actually that funny,' he said sarcastically and took a large swig of his lager. He no longer had a smile on his face.

'Dan? What's up with you then?'

'Oh, Jess, I'm not sure how to say this.'

'Try me,' Jess replied nonchalantly.

'When are you going to start looking for a proper boyfriend?'

'What are you on about, Dan, have you been drinking already?'

'I'm serious, Jess.'

It was Jess's turn to take a large slug of her drink as

Dan continued. 'I could go on as we are, well for years in fact, but I sat and thought long and hard last night. Be honest with yourself, Jess. Can you really see me and you working in ten years' time?'

Jess took a deep breath to stop herself crying with shock. 'Woah there, hang on a minute. Where has this suddenly come from? Just a couple of days ago we were love's young dream, what's got into you?'

'Sense, that's what. In ten years' time, I'll still only be thirty-four, a young man. You'll be fifty and wanting to rightly put on your slippers and watch *Newsnight*, whereas I'll probably still be putting on my dancing shoes and going clubbing. We've got to be realistic here.'

'But, Dan, life is for living. Since my mum died I just take every day as it comes, you don't know what's around the corner, let's just have some fun now. It's my party tomorrow, you can't do this to me today of all days.'

'That's another thing: I don't think I'm ready to meet your family and mates. I'm worried what they may think of me.'

'Don't be so bloody ridiculous, Dan. If I'm happy, they're happy. This is about us and no one else.'

Dan wasn't swayed. 'Jess, this can't go on forever.'

'I don't care,' Jess said, her voice beginning to crack. 'I love being with you. It's the happiest I've ever been in my life. You make me…' She was lost for words. 'We're better together that's all.' She couldn't contain her tears any longer.

'Oh, Jess, please don't cry. I love hanging out with you too. But I'm saying this now because I do really care about you. I don't want to fuck your life up, I'm just being realistic.'

Jess felt her stomach lurch. 'I cannot believe that I gave up having a baby for the sake of making this relationship work,' she spat.

'Oh, Jess, please don't say that.'

She continued her rant. 'Good old Jess, get her sorted at the clinic, then I can run along and sew my oats elsewhere.'

'Don't be so melodramatic. It's not like that, Jess, and you know it. I've got to think of Evie too. If I introduce her to you and then we split, it's not fair on her young little head either. I know she'd love you, everybody does and it would be another upheaval for her.'

Jess thought she was going to be sick. 'But if you love someone surely age shouldn't matter.'

'Jess, grow up, get out of your fantasy world. This is real life we are talking about here.'

Jess was taken aback by his sharp comment. 'And what if I say I want to carry on and I'll suffer the consequences?'

'No, Jess, no. It's over.' Dan paused. 'You are the loveliest person, I adore you and really hope we can still be friends, good friends, but that's all I'm willing to offer you.' He stood up. 'I'm going back to work,' He gently put his hand on her shoulder. 'I really hope your party goes well and thank you for helping me release myself from Alex and my unhappiness.'

Jess sat in her car and stared aimlessly at the swans. She felt shocked, hurt, and so unhappy. If she was really honest with herself, the main reason she didn't go through with the pregnancy *was* to make their relationship work. She realised there and then that she had made the worst decision of her life, and there was not one thing she could do to change it. Tears began to roll slowly down her cheeks. 'Thanks for releasing me from my unhappiness,' she mimicked in a baby voice. Fucking bastard! What about her unhappiness now?

Chapter Four

Dan headed back to work with a heavy heart. As much as he cared for Jess, he knew that he was doing the right thing by her and by Evie. It would get too messy if they carried on and he was ready to have fun on his own again now. He was just in the middle of testing a web site, when his desk phone rang.

'Dan, have you got a minute? I'm in my office.'

'Oh, er yeah, sure, Sam. I'll come down and see you.'

Dan walked down to the end of the barn, taking in his funky surroundings and saying hello to various colleagues as he walked passed their desks. He knew he was lucky to work in such a pleasant environment, with such a friendly bunch of people. He tentatively pushed open the heavy pine door to his boss's office. He felt apprehensive and racked his brains to think of any projects he may have cocked up recently.

Sam pushed himself back on his plush leather office chair and put his feet up on his huge antique desk. There were piles of paper everywhere, and Dan noticed a couple of thank you cards on the top of a filing cabinet in a corner of the airy room.

'No need to look so nervous.' Sam laughed . 'Sit down.' He waved his hand at a chair opposite his desk. 'I wanted to give you a pat on the back actually. Here, look.' Sam pushed a marketing magazine over the desk to Dan, and continued. 'Take a look at page four. The recent web site you designed for Silicon Mobile has won an award for design and usability. They are delighted and so am I. It will be such good publicity for Lemon.'

Dan smiled. 'Woah, that's great. I thought it was shit hot!'

'So, well done, Dan. ' He smiled at the exuberance of his youthful employee. In fact, Dan reminded him very much of himself when he was young. Good-looking and cocky, but with enough intelligence to back up his self-assuredness.

Dan stood up. 'I best go and tell those lads in the studio. Daniel Harris, the award winner!' He exclaimed.

'Before you go, Dan. I want you to have this.' Sam handed Dan a cheque. Dan took it and looked at it quizzically. 'Two grand! Sam, I don't know what to say.'

'You actually don't have to say anything. In fact please don't. Keep it quiet from everyone here and thank you again, Dan, great job.'

Dan shook his head in disbelief. 'But you only just gave me a big pay rise a month ago. Thanks, thanks a lot.'

Sam waved his hand in the air, dismissing Dan's comment. 'Now, go spend it on that little girl of yours.'

'Yeah, yeah. I'll do that.' Dan replied, virtually skipping back to his desk.

Chapter Five

'(Is this the way to) Amarillo.' The song boomed out of the cronky sound system. Jess wished she'd vetted the internet DJ. This was the first song he'd put on that had been instantly recognisable. He was pushing sixty and, with his shock of black hair and goofy teeth, Jess wasn't exactly sure that it wasn't Ken Dodd! He was adorned in a flashing, Union Jack waistcoat.

'Jess, where on earth did you find him?' Her friend Hope laughed.

'Don't even go there darling. My usual man I use for events is busy!' Hope was Jess's 'mad' friend. Whenever she went out with her, the night always ended in tears or a gutter as they both had a tendency to drink for England when together.

'Right, I'm going to shake him up.' Hope laughed and pushed her way over to him. She looked stunning dressed as Elizabeth Taylor adorned in a Cleopatra robe. Her tiny little waist and big boobs proved to be a magnet for most men, but alas she had still not found her Richard Burton. She'd had a lot of fun along the way trying to though.

'Is Chris definitely coming by the way?' Jess enquired. Chris was Hope's younger brother. He was just twenty-one and in the army. He was stunningly attractive.

'Oh yes, said he wouldn't miss it for the world, coming in uniform I think.'

'Ooh lovely.' Jess smiled and Hope gave her a don't-you-dare look. She'd always had a bit of thing for Chris but even by her standards she thought him a little bit too young. Thinking of Chris reminded her of Dan with a jolt.

She'd managed to keep it together since lunchtime yesterday, as she'd had so much to organise. She'd had a brief conversation with Emma about it but had managed to remain strong. Today was her day. He had texted her earlier saying, '*Have a good time tonight.*'. Though she wished in a way he hadn't bothered.

She didn't think the friend option was viable. How on earth could she be friends with the man who she had actually thought she may spend the rest of her life with?

Tonight Jessica Morley would be Wonder Woman. No man would ruin her fortieth birthday! She was surrounded by everybody who loved her and if he didn't want to be with her, then more fool him.

'Dad!' Jess squealed. 'You look great.' Her dad gave her a big hug and she nearly knocked off his hat. He had a patch on his eye. 'Nelson, that is so funny!'

'And how's my number one daughter then?'

'She's getting old, Dad, but she's just fine.' Jess laughed. Her dad's partner Maria smiled at her, she had come as the Queen in a powder blue suit with matching handbag. 'Your Majesty.' Jess said curtsying. 'Champagne?'

Phoebe and Glen were the next to arrive as Fred and Wilma Flintstone, hilariously followed by Georgina and Annabel as Bambam and Pebbles. Emma and Mark, expertly made up as Ozzie and Sharon Osbourne, bowled over to Jess with a large, perfectly wrapped present. 'Happy Birthday, darling friend.' Em piped up.

'Pins still looking good, you old bird.' Mark laughed.

'Of course! It'll be your turn next, so watch it!' Jess winked. 'Put the pressies over in the corner, that's cool. I expect a fully laden table later, of course.' Jess joked.

Emma took Jess to one side. 'How you doing?' she asked gently.

'You know me, brave face and all that but I am so not going to let him spoil my night,' Jess said defiantly.

'Good girl, now get on this dance floor and do the Jingo with me!' Emma enthused.

The party was in full swing when the Lemon Events mob arrived. Sam, the handsome MD, was the first to greet her, looking extremely sexy as James Bond. 'Wonder Woman eh? I wouldn't have expected anything less.' He handed her a bottle of Christal Champagne and kissed her on both cheeks.

'Wow, thanks, Sam. That'll be my hair of the dog for tomorrow then.' The party was in full swing when all of a sudden the music stopped and then restarted shakily with 'Waltzing Matilda'. Jess thought the DJ had now gone completely mad, until out of the corner of her eye, walking across the dance floor towards her she saw him. Adorned in an Australian cork hat was none other than her brother. 'Karl, I cannot believe it.' She squealed.

'Couldn't miss big sis's fortieth for the world,' he said in an Aussie accent.

'You have really made my day, what a lovely surprise. You back for good now?'

'Nah, just going get some more money together, then go back to the Gold Coast. Have found myself a cute little Sheila actually.'

'That's my boy. Now, come on, let's get you a drink.' Jess led him to the bar.

Midnight came all too quickly and the revellers made their way home with noisy goodbyes.

'Lunch tomorrow, sis?' Karl shouted back through the door.

'Yeah great. Call me – but not too early.'

Hope and Chris were the last at the bar, as Ken Dodd packed up to leave. 'Are you going to share our taxi?' Hope slurred. Sam appeared from the toilet. 'Share one with me, Jess, I'll help you pack up all your presents.'

'Oh, that's really sweet of you, Sam, thanks.'

'Well we're off, hon, our taxi's here. Don't do anything

I wouldn't do.' Hope winked. She had had her eye on Sam all night. 'Byee.' She stumbled out of the door and Chris picked up her shoe which had gone flying across the pavement. He waved back at Jess.

'Look after her.' Jess shouted. Chris blew her a kiss.

'One for the road, Wonder Woman?' Sam enquired once Hope and Chris were on their way. Jess hiccupped, she really was quite drunk. 'It would be rude not to, Mr Beresford. Large amaretto with ice please.'

'What a fun night and what a lovely family you have.' He stated.

'Your mother was hilarious as the Queen.'

'She's not my mother.' Jess intercepted. She had always worked hard at her relationship with Maria, but knew she would never take the place of her beautiful mum and suddenly felt sad.

Jess looked at Sam, he was around forty-five she thought, and still very good-looking. His salt and pepper hair complimented his deep blue eyes and his crinkly laughter lines accentuated his big character. He had established Lemon Events fifteen years ago, and it had been a resounding success story.

'Happy?' Sam suddenly enquired.

It wasn't until that moment that Jess realised she wasn't happy and all of a sudden started to cry. 'Shit, sorry, Jess.' Sam panicked.

'It's OK, I'm just drunk.' Jess sniffled. Even though her lack of sobriety was evident, Jess knew that she couldn't confide in Sam, re one of his employees. She and Dan had agreed that they would keep what they had together quiet as her working relationship with Lemon Events was so strong, and she didn't want it to affect her business in any way.

Sam pulled his chair in closer and gently wiped a tear from her cheek. 'Want to talk about it?' Sam asked. He was wise man. He had known Jess a long time and knew she wouldn't just cry for any reason, especially after she'd had such a seemingly good night.

'Just man troubles, but it's done with now,' Jess said bravely. She looked directly at Sam, he looked so strong, caring, and kind that she wanted him to put his arms around her and tell her everything was going to be alright.

'Do you mind if we leave now? I don't think I should drink anymore.'

'Of course not, let me get the barman to ring us a cab.'

The taxi rounded a bend and Jess fell into Sam's lap. 'Whoa there honey.' He said laughing, gently lifting her upright. They arrived outside her house and Sam dutifully carried all her presents inside.

'Coffee?' Jess offered.

'No, you're alright, Jess, you get to bed.' He leaned forward to kiss her on the cheek. Just as he did so Jess purposely turned her face and her lips landed right on his. She began to kiss him fast and furiously. Sam reciprocated and then suddenly pulled away. 'Look, Jess, I'm not sure if this is a good idea. You're really drunk. As much as I'd love to do it again I...' Jess now in full harlot mode grabbed him and kissed him again, long and hard. Sam although lost in the moment, regained his senses. His working relationship with her was far too important and his clients adored her. No, as much as he fancied her, he couldn't upset Jessica Morley and lose any valuable company money. He pulled away gently and kissed her on the forehead. 'Hey, tired girl, the taxi's waiting for me outside, I'd better go.'

Chapter Six

Wonder Woman woke up with a banging hangover. She was lying on the top of her bed, still fully dressed complete with thigh-length gold boots. Half asleep, she pulled her clothes off and got into bed. She turned to her right and cuddled her pillow imagining it was Dan. She hadn't really allowed herself to think about Friday lunchtime and the finality of it all. She was amazed at how quickly he could end something so good. That's what really annoyed her about the whole situation. He still had strong feelings for her, yet he had let his twenty-four-year-old head rule his heart. How bloody mature. Why couldn't he be like a normal twenty-something? Why did he have to be so sensible? In questioning this Jess realised why they did get on so well. In essence, he was actually more mature than her. She fell back into a fitful sleep, dreaming about all the characters who'd come to her party. It wasn't until she woke up a second time, the sudden realisation of what she'd done the night before hit her. 'Oh no,' she groaned. 'Oh, shit, how bloody embarrassing.' She continued out loud and then began to sob uncontrollably. Thank God she hadn't taken things further with Sam. If he hadn't been such a gentleman, she reckoned she would have lured him to the bedroom and whipped him to within an inch of his life with her Lasso of Truth.

With such a bad hangover she couldn't seem to see reason and began to question whether she did love Dan at all. If she did, surely she wouldn't even have considered sleeping with Sam? She pushed these thoughts to the back of her head. After all, she had only given Sam a drunken snog. She was being silly. She knew deep down she was in love with Dan; the pain in her heart confirmed that.

Monday morning came, Jess switched on her laptop. She had ignored Dan's calls all weekend. He came on to instant messenger as soon as she logged in.

Dan says:
'Hey, Mrs Robinson, how was the party?'
Jess says:
'Really good thanks.'
Dan says:
'Yeah, Sam said it was great fun.'
Jess says:
'Oh right. Good, glad he enjoyed it.'
She cringed slightly and wanted to end the conversation.
Jess says:
'Dan, I know you wanna be friends but give me some time eh? Bye.'
Dan says:
'Oh er, OK. Take care – bfn Jess xx.'

A week came and went. Jess missed Dan from the bottom of her heart. Even though it was her who had told him to keep away, every morning she hoped he'd call. When he didn't, she literally pined for him. She found herself listening to Heart FM nearly all day long just so she could cry openly without excuse.

She was sitting alone on Saturday night watching some low rate movie, when she couldn't stand it any longer. She had to talk to him.

'Jess, Jess, is that really you?' Jess could barely hear him for the loud music in background.

'Hang on a minute, I'll go outside and call you right back, Mrs Robinson.' Dan said with relief. 'Shit, I've missed you.' Jess curled into herself on the sofa, just hearing his voice made her feel happy again. 'Are you drunk, Dan?' She asked, not caring at all if he was or not. 'I've had a couple. I'm in Reading, come and pick me up. Go on, you know you want to?' Charmed and without hesitation, Jess smartened up her hair and face, sprayed some perfume on her wrists and jumped in her car. I must be bloody mad she thought to herself. Here she was a forty-year-old woman, driving to Reading at 11 p.m. to pick up a young man, who didn't know what he really wanted from life, from a night out with the lads.

She saw him before he saw her, he was sitting in a bus stop kicking his legs backwards and forwards like a small boy and she smiled. She loved him with such intensity, that she knew there and then she would do anything to be with him.

'I'm staying in the spare room,' he announced on arrival at Morley Mansions.

'I've heard that one before.' Jess laughed. Dan pulled Jess towards him. 'I can't do this without you, Jess.' He kissed her tenderly. 'I've missed you more than I've missed anyone before. It's been hell.' Jess kissed him back.

'Let's talk in the morning, eh?'

'Jess?'

'Yes, Daniel.' She replied in her school ma'am voice.

'I think you're grand.' He smiled his big open smile at her.

Dan made love to her with such tenderness that night, it made her cry.

'Jessy, are you OK?' he said with concern as they contentedly lay like spoons.

'I'm more than OK, baby boy. See you in the morning.' She kissed his back gently and fell into the most peaceful sleep she'd had for a long time.

Chapter Seven

Dan got up early. He kissed the still sleeping Jess on the cheek and left her a note on her pillow.

Kingfisher Marina, Thorpe. Gate code: 1585. Boat is called 'Making Waves'. Map open on coffee table with directions. See you at 12

Miss you D x

Jess woke up late. She looked over and noticed that Dan had gone. She couldn't believe she'd missed him and was relieved to see his note. He sorted the move out quickly, she thought. She loved his presumptuousness in thinking she'd be free at twelve and then laughed, as he would have known she'd have changed her plans just to be with him today.

Dan waved heartily as she approached the boat and offered a hand to help her get on. He seemed proud as punch, as he showed her round. He had set out the lounge area with his computer and sound system, and there was a seating area easily big enough for four.

'This is really cool, Dan. Err, not sure about going on a chemical toilet.' Jess turned her nose up.

Dan laughed. 'God you're a posh cow, there's a toilet and shower block in the car park so you don't have to.'

'It's much bigger than I thought too,' Jess said as she took in her surroundings . 'Let's have a look at the bedroom then?' Jess noticed the door to the end of the boat was closed. Dan put his fingers to his lips to shush her. There's a special little girl in there having a nap, you can meet her in a minute. Jess smiled inside. At last she was going to meet Evie.

They climbed up to the top deck where Dan had placed a table and chairs. There was a bottle of wine chilling in a cooler. He laid out packet sandwiches and crisps. 'I know it's a bit cold to be sitting up here today, but I wanted to give you a feel of true boat life.' He laughed.

'I love days like these,' Jess exclaimed. 'Crisp and sunny. And just look at all those lovely swans.' She lay back in her seat and took a sip of wine.

'I'm glad we're cool again Jess,' Dan said softly.

They sat in silence looking at the water for a moment until Jess piped up. 'So why the change of heart?' Dan sighed and continued.

'I guess I realised how much I missed you...' He hesitated. 'Look, Jess, I can't promise you the world but you're right. What we've got is special, and it does seem stupid to not go with it. I will be totally honest with you though, I don't want to *ever* get married, or have any more kids in the near future.' Jess didn't want to think about what he'd said too deeply. All she knew was that she was so happy to be back with the man that she loved. 'Jess, did you hear me? I'm being honest with you.'

'I know you are, Dan, and I value your honesty a lot. It is a tricky one, but I love you. At the moment, that's all that matters to me. You can never tell what's around the corner. Throughout my life, all I've ever done is held my nose and jumped, and I always seemed to have landed in the right place.'

Dan laughed. His free-spirited lover was back right with him and he was glad. Suddenly he leapt up. 'She's awake, stay here until I call you. She'll be grumpy for a couple of minutes while she fully wakes up.'

Jess could hear Dan talking to Evie. Seeing him as a father was really quite alien to her, but he sounded so sweet and reassuring that it made her love him even more. Jess made her way down to the lounge area. Evie was a pretty little thing, her white, blonde hair curled up at her collar, and her big blue knowing eyes looked Jess up and down. Jess didn't think she bore any resemblance to Dan, but guessed at three years-old, she probably wouldn't.

'Evie say hello to Jessica,' Dan urged. The little girl ran behind her daddy's legs and hid.

'No,' she said abruptly.

'Then you won't be wanting any sweetics from my handbag then will you?'

Evie poked her head around from behind Dan's legs. 'Hello Jesska.'

'Pleased to meet you, Evie. I love your Barbie jumper.'

'Right, Evie, we are going upstairs to have some lunch now,' Dan told his daughter.

Jess pulled the life jacket out of a carrier bag. 'I thought she might need this.' She hoped Dan wouldn't think she was interfering. He smiled at Jess. 'You are the most thoughtful person I've ever met.' He kissed her on the cheek and Evie started to cry.

'No, Jesska, that's *my* daddy.' This is going to be fun thought Jess, as she bit into a chicken sandwich.

Chapter Eight

A month passed and Dan and Jess were inseparable. Evie was part and parcel of the package now, and whenever Dan had her at weekends they would all be together. Evie had still not slept at Jess's yet because Dan thought it was too soon. So the two of them would wave goodbye and go and stay back on the boat and then in the morning they would call Jess as soon as they woke up for her to join them. Jess loved staying on the boat when they were alone together. She thought it was like being on holiday. Dan's bedroom looked right out on to the water. It was so peaceful, with the sound of ducks quacking and the comforting whirring of other boats going past.

Evie had had her moments, but in general she was a good-natured little girl and Jess loved having her around. She sometimes ached at the fact that she could have had a little brother or sister for her but then talked to herself harshly saying that she had definitely made the right decision. They were a family now.

Work was busy. Jess had had a meeting with Sam, where she blushed to the tip of her roots and apologised for trying to drunkenly seduce him. Sam had just smiled his crinkly smile and said, 'Seize the carp, Jessy Morley. You're only human!' AG Technology had been so pleased with a recent product launch that she had arranged that they had sent her a bonus cheque for £1000. She certainly was seizing the day and loving every minute of it.

Chapter Ten

Alex felt sick with nerves. Tonight she was going to perform her first stand up as Ali Meadows, comedienne. Since she had split up with Dan, she had got her life together. She had got a new job working as an Account Manager at a local PR company and had recently met Rob at a comedy workshop. Dickhead had upped his maintenance payments and Evie had settled well in to a local nursery.

Dan's confession about seeing Jess had rocked her slightly but meeting Rob had now taken the edge off this, and her relationship with Dan had improved considerably. In fact they were good friends now.

Alex walked purposely into the Windsor and Eton Suite. The booking agent had just told her to ask for Jessica when she got there. Material-wise she was definitely ready. She had attended multiple workshops, and had rehearsed tonight's routine over and over to her audience of Rob, Sal and her new girlfriend, Claire – and of course Evie.

'Ali. Hi, thanks for getting here early,' Jess said in a friendly manner.

'No worries, I like to make sure I know what's what before a gig,' Ali blagged, as if she was a complete pro. Jess continued. 'Here's a running order of tonight's proceedings, you can be as blue as you like, as it's all *men*.'

'Thought as much. I've been rehearsing in front of my daughter, so have had to put a few bleeps in.' Alex smiled.

'That's sweet, how old is she?' Jess enquired.

'She's three.'

A man on the stage put this thumb up to Jess. 'Right, Ali, sound is up, so if you want to go and do a check, Harry over there will mike you up.'

'Cool, thanks.' Alex jumped down from the stage. Her mobile rang.

'Alex, it's Dan, just checking what the plan is with Evie tonight?'

'Oh hiya, I forgot to say earlier, I'm doing my first gig tonight, some corporate do at The Berystede Hotel. I'm *so* nervous. I'm at rehearsals now actually. Sal is going to pick Evie up from nursery, so if you wouldn't mind collecting her from Sal's, at say six, that would be great.'

'Cool, no worries. Break a leg and all that.'

'Cheers, Dan.'

Jess heard her phone and answered it. 'Hi Jess, it's me, how's it going?'

'Fine, fine, Mr Harris. Busy though, just doing sound checks for the event tonight.'

'Oh yeah, I forgot you weren't around later, whereabouts are you?'

'I'm just in Ascot at The Berystede Hotel, which is great, as I shouldn't be that late home.'

'Jess?'

'Yes.'

'Are you having a comedienne at your event?'

Jess was surprised at his question, as he never usually showed such an interest in her events. 'Er, yeah. A new kid on the block, goes by the name of Ali Meadows. She seems really nice.'

'Jess?'

'Yes, Dan.'

'I think you've been conversing with my ex-girlfriend.'

'Oh my God. No!'

'It's fine, Jess, she's been harping on about meeting you anyway, now you're spending so much time with

Evie. Wish I could be a fly on the wall.'

'I wish you could too and I'd swat you good and hard.' Jess laughed.

'Good luck, darling, and defo call me later.'

Alex walked towards Jess to see what time she could do a complete run through before the event kicked off. Jess held out her hand.

'Alex – Jessica Morley.'

Chapter Eleven

'You're not my mummy!'

Jessy sighed, and continued her journey to the comforting row of red wine bottles, ignoring the suspecting glances of weekend shoppers.

'I hate you.' Evie continued her insecure rant, her hair now stuck to her face with tears. 'I want my daddy.'

'Surprisingly I want him too. Now come on, baby girl, let's be friends today shall we?'

'Want chocolate!' Evie screeched.

Jess strapped the still screaming Evie into her car seat and loaded the shopping into the boot. She was in tears herself when she reached Emma's.

Silence at last. The now sleeping Evie looked so peaceful and sweet that Jess could not help but feel a strong surge of love for her. She positioned the car so that she could see when the sleeping child woke up.

'Hello stranger.' Em greeted her. She noticed Jess had been crying. 'What's up, mate?'

'Oh, Em, I really am at my wit's end. I try so hard, but nothing I seem to do is ever right. Daddy this, Daddy that. She just pushes me away all the time.'

'Where is Daddy today then?'

'He's gone to some music festival with Matt, I said I'd have her for the day as it's Alex's birthday and Rob has taken her away for the weekend.'

Emma handed Jess a cup of tea and sat down at the kitchen table, sighing as she took the weight off her feet. 'Bliss – Mark has taken the kids to his mum's for the afternoon. It's so lovely to have a bit of peace.'

'I totally understand where you're coming from now.

This mother lark is not as easy as it looks.' Jess managed to raise a smile and continued. 'Don't get me wrong, I'm chuffed that they've both agreed for me to look after her today, but God I'm finding it hard.'

'At least she feels secure enough to push you away,' Emma piped up. Jess looked confused as Emma continued. 'I remember reading once that if a child feels secure with you they are confident enough to push you away, as they know there is no way that you would ever leave them.'

'Comforting, Em, but sorry at this precise moment, that doesn't make me feel much better.' Jess sighed. 'It's not just Evie, its Dan as well. He doesn't like me disciplining her. She tipped yoghurt all over my carpet on purpose last night and I was really cross. When I told her off, he had a right go at me.'

Emma tutted. 'You spend so much time with her now he can't possibly think he can do all the parenting.'

'I know, I know, but try telling him that. He also says I feed her too much. Surely a child that young knows when she's had enough? I always thought I'd make a good mum, it was probably a good thing I didn't go through with the pregnancy. I feel so useless.' Her voice tailed off and tears welled in her eyes again.

'Oh, Jess, I'm sure it's going to get better, it's all so new, he's only been living with you for a couple of months,' Emma soothed.

'And that's another thing,' Jess continued her rant. 'He worryingly said he felt trapped the other night. He was the one who moved in with me. I didn't ask him to, it just happened. As soon as he knew Evie would settle in my spare room that was it.'

'Look, Jess,' Emma interjected. 'I can see why he did move in. It makes life a whole lot easier for him I should imagine. It can't be easy bringing a young child up on a boat.'

'He's the one who says he feels trapped but, if I'm realistic, I also feel that way. I do, *do* an awful lot. I always get up first and make Evie's breakfast. I play with her until *he's* ready to get up. I cook, clean, and do all their washing. Sometimes I feel that I actually *am* his mother.'

'It's just a blip I'm sure, Jess. Living with someone is hard enough, without a young child in tow. Maybe you should stop doing so much for him though. He does sound like he's laying it on you a bit.'

'It's my own stupid fault; you know what I'm like, ever the pleaser.' Jess exclaimed.

'Yeah, and look where that's got you before.'

'I know, I know but I don't think I'll ever change.'

'How are things when you're alone? Are you still at it like rabbits?' Emma smiled wanting to change the subject.

'It's calmed down a bit now.' Jess smiled back at her. 'A lot of that due to the fact that we are always together on the nights he has Evie, and when he hasn't he tends to go out with this mates quite a lot.'

'Oh. That's not so good.' Emma pondered.

'I'm trying not to moan about it. I love spending time with him and, once Evie is in bed, then we are alone.'

'Alone, but you're not out and about.' Emma picked up. 'I think it's time you and Daniel Harris had a chat.'

'I'm so scared of losing him though, Em.'

'You have to be honest with yourself though, mate. You've got the rest of your life to think of and I don't want you being treated like a doormat.'

'Shit, I better check on Evie.' Jess glanced out of the window, the screaming monster was back. She ran outside. 'It's OK, angel, I'm here, come on inside and I'll get you some chocolate.'

Once inside the kitchen, Emma handed Evie a kit-kat finger.

'No.' Evie shouted and knocked the chocolate out of Emma's hand. 'I want my daddy!'

Chapter Twelve

Alex drove straight to Sally's after the gig. She pushed her way through the door, lit a Marlboro Light, and sat at Sal's kitchen table. 'You will never guess what happened today!' Alex said dramatically.

'You fell off the stage? Your pants fell down? You were spotted by a talent scout?' Sal laughed.

'None of the above.' Alex smiled. 'But, as well as me being word perfect and getting loads of cheers and no heckles, I only met the one and only Jessica Morley.'

'No shit Sherlock, what's she like?' Sal exclaimed.

'I hate to say it, but she's actually *really* nice.'

'No, I mean what does she look like?' Sal asked inquisitively.

'Annoyingly, she's actually really pretty and she doesn't look her age at all. She's really confident and was wearing trendy clothes. I can see why Dan fell for her.'

'So what did she have to say for herself?'

'Not a lot really. She was really considerate where Evie was concerned, said what a beautiful little girl we had, and made a point of telling me that Dan did all the disciplining. I know she said that to put my mind at rest.'

'So, no pistols at dawn then?'

'Not at all, we were both very civil. It's all water under the bridge now. I'm glad I've met her actually. It's strange not knowing who your child is spending so much time with, and at least now I know.'

Sal stood up. 'As much as I love you, Ali Meadows, you are going to have to go now, as I have a hot filly waiting for me in my boudoir.'

'Dirty bitch.' Alex laughed. 'I'll get off then. See ya soon.'

Chapter Thirteen

Jess woke up and looked at her watch. It was 5 a.m. Ever since their seven-month relationship had begun, Dan had always called her to say goodnight. He must have run out of battery she thought and drifted back to sleep.

Chapter Fourteen

Dan and Matt fell wide-eyed out of The Breakhaus. Their ears were still ringing from the club's loud dance music. It was 6 a.m. 'Breakfast, mate?' Matt enquired.

'Yeah, let's go to that little cafe round the corner,' Dan replied woozily.

They slurped on their large mugs of tea whilst they waited for their fry-up.

'What an amazing night,' Matt said sleepily.

'Yeah, Adam Freeland just does it every time doesn't he, he's a legend.' Dan perked up.

'What's the vibe for today then, Danny Boy?'

'Thankfully I haven't got Evie, so sleep it is.'

'Will Jess be cool with that?'

'She actually doesn't even know I'm here. I just said I was out with you.'

'Not like you not to be honest,' Matt stated.

'Yeah well, I haven't been feeling very happy lately. I've sort of moved in and it's all got a bit much. I left Alex because I didn't want to be a married man at my age and now it feels like I've fallen into exactly the same pattern.'

'Shit, so what are you going to do?'

'I don't know, mate, don't get me wrong, Jess is amazing and she is so good with Evie, even though I know she finds it hard. I love the fact that she does look after me. She does all my washing, cooking, cleaning, the lot.'

Matt looked knowingly at him. 'She's not your mother mate.'

Dan sighed as reality hit. 'I think I want to be single again. I haven't really lived yet. I'm not ready to settle down.' He paused. 'It's so hard as I know how much I am going to miss her.'

'When are you going to tell her?' Matt enquired.

'I really don't know. Not today that's for sure, especially on a come down. She's going to be devastated. I'll be taking Evie away from her too. God, what a mess!'

'As I've said to you before, Dan: you've got to be honest with yourself, as well as her. Life's not a game, mate, and the sooner you do it the better for everyone's sake.'

Chapter Fifteen

'Hello gorgeous boy.' Jess greeted Dan at the front door as she heard his key in the lock. She was wearing an outfit she knew he loved, and had had her hair blow dried especially for her night out with him.

'You look great, Jess. I love your new hair.'

Tonight she was determined they were going to work through their problems. There was something too special between them not to make it work. She had let it go that he had stayed on the boat last night. She wanted him to feel that he could have as much freedom as he wanted.

'Do you mind if we don't go out tonight, Jess? I'm quite fancying just chilling out with a couple of beers and a curry here.'

Jess put her hands on her hips. 'Actually I do, Dan.'

Dan was surprised; usually Jess was so compliant to his needs. She managed to keep her voice at a level, even though she could feel the anger bubbling inside of her. 'Look, Dan. We only really see each other when Evie is here, but tonight we haven't got her and I want to go out, just you and me.'

'But I'm knackered, Jess. Had a really late one with Matt last night.' He patted the sofa. 'Mrs Robinson. Come and sit right here.' He cocked his head and smiled at her, he knew he could win her round.

'It's not on, Dan. Can't you think about me for a change? It's not all about you, you know. We're a partnership, or that's what I thought.'

'Stop nagging me, Jess, look – I said I'm tired.'

Jess raised her voice. 'I'm not bloody nagging you. I'm

just stating what I think is right.'

Dan bit his lip. He had never seen Jess angry before. She carried on with her rant. 'I feel like a fucking skivvy half the time. I do everything I can to make life as

easy for you and Evie as possible. I cook, I clean, and do all your ironing.'

'I've never ever asked you to do any of it, Jess.' Dan rightly replied. Then, without thinking, he said the thing that he vowed he would never say to her. 'Anyone would think you were my fucking mother!'

Jess was silent for a minute and stormed to the kitchen. Dan ran after her, realising the harshness of his outburst. 'I'm sorry, babe. That was really out of order. I do really appreciate everything you do for us, but I've never *asked* you to do it.'

'What's happening to us, Dan? Ever since you and Evie have moved in, it's been so hard. I loved it when you were living on the boat and we spent more time together – alone.'

'Evie is the most important person in my life.' Dan stated bluntly.

'I know that, Dan, but I'd quite like to be a close second.' She sighed and raised her eyes to the ceiling. 'Dan. You're my world, you know that. I love you so much.'

And then the knife turned in Jess's heart as he replied. 'And that Jess is the problem – because you're not mine.'

Her lip began to tremble as Dan continued. 'Jess, I'm really not happy at the moment. I need some time out.'

She began to cry. She'd heard this too often before and knew it was the beginning of the end.

'Please don't cry. I got in a rut with Alex. I felt I was too young to be settled down then. It's like I've fallen into that same rut. Don't get me wrong – I love spending time with you but like I've said before I can't see us together in ten years time.'

'You're a fool to not see what we've got together though, Dan.' Jess raised her voice and then softened. 'How about you take a couple of weeks out? Get your head straight, we can work this out, I *know* we can.'

'I think I need longer than that, Jess. I need to spend time on my own. I don't want anyone else, so please don't think that.'

'I don't think I could do any more for you to make you happy,' Jess stated.

'You couldn't, Jess, you are the most generous, kind and loving person I've ever met. It's just not where I see my future lying.'

'Is it because of my age?' Jess asked, not really wanting to hear the answer.

'Being honest with you, Jess, I hate to say this to you, but yes. I told you this before. I'm not ready to settle down yet and you so obviously are. I've still gotta lot of living to do.'

'I love Evie,' she said softly. 'I couldn't bear the thought of not seeing her again.'

'I know you do and that's why this is so difficult too. You made a great mum to her Jess and I mean that, despite it being hard at times. And you will make a great mum to your own child too.'

'But just not with you, hey?' She started to cry again.

'Jess, I'm so sorry. This is the hardest thing I've ever had to do in my life. I am going to miss you so much.'

'Don't go then, Dan.'

'I have to.'

Jess was clutching at straws. 'What if we go back to how we were, you move back to the boat, see your friends, we could see each other a couple of times a week? I'd never stop you doing anything you wanted to do.'

'Jess, no, it wouldn't work. You wouldn't be able to cope with that, I know you. You're an all-or-nothing kind of lady and that's why I was attracted to you in the first place.'

'Tell me you're not attracted to me now.' Jess demanded.

'Jess, I will always fancy the arse of you.' He half smiled.

'So, you love my company, you still want to shag me, isn't that a relationship? I think you're making a big mistake, Dan. I've had a few love affairs in my time but nothing has ever matched the intensity of this. I don't know quite what you're looking for but if you find this again I'll be very surprised.'

'I'm going to go now, Jess.'

'So that's it, you're just upping and leaving me right now?'

'I see no point in me staying, we will go over the same ground again and again and there's just no point.'

Tears were rolling down Jess's cheeks. 'Please stay with me just for one more night.' She pleaded.

'No, Jess, I have do what's right by you and that wouldn't be fair.'

'I haven't even said goodbye to Evie.'

'We're still going to be good mates, Jess, how could we not? You'll see Evie again I promise.'

Jess then realised just how big the age gap was. Dan's innocent, never yet broken heart just didn't get it. How on earth could she be *friends* with him? She loved him far too much to ever just be able to like him.

She sat on the sofa while he packed his things. He even cleared Evie's bedroom of her toys. He came in from packing the car. 'Right, I think that's it,' he said bravely.

He hugged her tightly and they both started to cry. 'Goodbye, Jess, thank you for being so lovely.' Dan didn't look back.

Jess slammed the front door, ran upstairs, and threw herself onto her bed sobbing.

Chapter Sixteen

Not since the death of her mother had Jess felt such sorrow. Jess had always thought the expression 'broken heart' was a myth but the pain she was actually feeling inside made her think that one half of her heart had actually fallen into her stomach. Every other hour after Dan had walked out the door, she had been physically sick. She felt that if she cried any more she would surely have no more tears left for anything else that might upset her.

She barely slept that night and had to call Sam in the morning to say that she was unwell, and that somebody else from Lemon Events would have to head up the conference she was managing for them, at the end of the week. She stayed in bed for two days just venturing out to get water and to go to the toilet. Somehow she felt safe under her duvet. Like the real world was not happening, she could escape and feel safe. She could see no purpose in being there without Dan. Light turned into dark and dark into light. Never before had she loved anyone with such passion, and she felt she would never love again. She began to regret getting rid of their baby. At least she thought she would have something to remind her of Dan and would get to see him occasionally. She felt that a world without Dan was like a world without sunshine.

She had called Emma, but didn't make any sense through her sobbing. Phoebe arrived to try and console her but she just sat there blankly. Being told that time was a healer and that she was too good for him anyway just didn't help. She was in love with him and that was that.

Without him, she could see no light at the end of the tunnel. She could see no point in carrying on.

She found some sleeping tablets in her bathroom cabinet. Maybe if she just took five she would at least sleep for a long time, wake up in a month, and then feel better. She poured herself some water and then the phone rang. She let it go to message. 'Auntie Jessica we love you.' Georgina and Annabel trilled. She threw the tablets down the toilet and started to cry again. At 11 p.m. the tick, tick, tick, of her bedroom clock seemed to mark every second she was spending without him. She got up and ripped it off the wall. She dialled his number. Through stifled sobs she tried to talk to him. 'I, I can't do this without you, Dan Harris. I don't know what I'm going to do.'

'Oh, Jess, baby, you'll be fine in time,' Dan soothed.

'I won't. I can't see any purpose without you. I love you so much.' She hung up.

'Time, fucking time!' she shouted.

Every second felt like an hour. On day three she managed to drag herself out of bed and caught a glimpse of herself in the mirror. Her eyes were like golf balls, accompanied by golf bags. Their sparkle had followed him out the door. Her hair was tangled and greasy and she could actually smell her own body odour. She walked downstairs and suddenly ravenously hungry, she made herself some toast and a cup of tea. She sat in her garden sipping her tea and stared blankly ahead.

Without Dan and Evie the silence of her house took on a silence of its own. Never before had she wanted so much for her beautiful mum to appear in the doorway and tell her that everything was going to be alright. She literally yearned to see Dan. She couldn't even imagine never talking to him again. She felt like he had died and she had died inside. She tried to read a magazine but didn't give a shit about who was zooming who, or who was now a size zero. She tried to watch television but everything she watched just seemed meaningless and trite. In her eyes, without Dan there was no future. She would just exist, that would be it. Go through the motions. She didn't want anyone else but him. She would see her friends and family, eat, sleep, and go to bed, that would be it. She didn't want to go outor ever go on holiday again; her life as she knew it was over.

Day four at the Heartbreak Hotel and Hope appeared. She had been calling and calling Jess and got no answer so had assumed the worst had happened. An unkempt Jess answered the door. Hope kicked off her kitten heels and gave her a huge hug. 'Now, darling girl, I cannot bear to see my gorgeous friend in such a mess.' She ran upstairs and ran a deep bubble bath. She helped Jess up off the sofa. 'Now get up there and get in that bath right now. I don't want to see you until you're squeaky clean.'

Jess did as she was told. While she was bathing Hope tidied up and washed up. Jess felt better for her bath. She threw on her comfiest pyjamas and came downstairs.

Hope had made her a cup of tea and a cheese sandwich. 'Now get that down you,' she said kindly and continued. 'Oh, Jess, I'm so sorry. I'm not going to give you the time's-a-healer shit, because at the moment I know that's not what you want to hear. All I will say though is that if you're missing him this much, even if he's missing you a fraction of that, he's going to be hurting a lot too.' Jess started to cry.

'In a way, that's all I want to know – if he's missing me too.' She sobbed.

'Jess, how could he possibly not be? You are the biggest person I've ever met. You did nothing wrong. It was just bad timing that's all.' Jess blew her nose. 'He told you himself that he adores you and still fancies you. That doesn't happen often when you split up now does it?'

Jess began to shout. 'That's why it's so fucking stupid.

He bloody *loves* me Hope. I *know* he does. He's let his head rule his heart and that really annoys me.'

'Part of him is doing it for you though, sweetie.'

'Bollocks, he's a selfish bastard. I couldn't have done any more for him. We couldn't have had any more fun. Sex could not possibly been any better, what the fuck is wrong with him? Oh, Hope, I'm hurting so badly.'

'I know you are, angel, and if there was anything I could do to take that away I would, I promise you. Shit, I might have to say the time's-a-healer line in a minute.'

They both started to laugh and then Jess started to immediately cry again. 'God I'm a mess.'

'It will get better, baby.' Hope was nearly in tears too.

'But I love him *so* much and I can't ever see that going away.'

'I know you do, Jessy. I'm staying with you all day and tonight darling, you won't have to feel lonely today at least.'

'Thanks, Hope. I'm so desperate to call him.'

'I know you are, but try not to. It's still too raw; you won't have anything worthwhile to say to him. He fell in love with the confident Jessy Morley. He won't be able to cope with you like this. Leave him alone if you can.'

Jess slept fitfully. She woke up at 5 a.m. and smiled at the sleeping Hope next to her. She checked her phone for messages – nothing. She stared up at the ceiling. She wished she was anywhere and nowhere all at the same time. She got up and went downstairs. A letter that's what she'd do. She read somewhere that it was helpful to write feelings down; she wouldn't have to send it. She would type it and re-read whenever she needed to in the hope it would make her feel better.

Chapter Seventeen

Three long weeks went by. She had bravely managed not to contact him. She didn't even send him her heartfelt letter. It had been good therapy to write it, but felt that, as he hadn't even bothered to call her, he probably wouldn't even have bothered to read it. She had thrown herself into a new work project and had managed to immerse herself into a new Carole Matthews novel. She played her Jack Johnson CD so many times that she thought it would wear out. Somehow reading had taken over from hiding under her duvet. She was now hiding behind the characters instead. As long as she was immersed in someone else's life, time seemed to go by faster.

She was just writing an event project plan when Hope called. 'Fancy going away for a few days honey? I've found a good deal to Lanzarote. I've checked the flights. We could go next Thursday and come back the following Monday. Cheap and cheerful but it would be good to get some sun don't you think?' Hope held her breath. She had no idea what her friend would say.

'Do you know what, Hope, that sounds like a marvellous idea. Let's book it.'

'Well done, Jess, I'll come over to you tonight to finalise everything.'

Jess had come out of the major heartbreak hole. She still thought about Dan every minute of the day but managed to hold off the tears most days now. She thought if she had any chance of getting back with him, she would need to disappear. Let the bastard wonder where she was for a change, rather than be so readily available.

Hope wiggled up to Jess who was waiting for her at the Suntours check-in desk. Her denim miniskirt and low-cut top attracted the attention of a ten strong stag party, who were all wearing antlers.

'Hope Adams!' Jess laughed heartily. 'You've still got it, baby.'

'See what you just did, Jess?' Jess looked at her friend quizzically.

'You just laughed out loud.' Hope was right, Jess had not laughed out loud for a month now. She was getting better. She was starting to get over Daniel Harris. 'Daniel who?' Hope would say every time Jess mentioned him on the flight.

The chitter-chattering of excited children, the pit-pat of balls on bats, and the sound of the sea lapping against the shore lulled Jess into a peaceful doze on her sun bed. Hope was next to her, her huge boobs out for the world to see.

'Fanta limon, cocka, massage!' The Fanta man smiled over them, purposely shading their sun.

'No gracias,' Jess murmured from her face down position and laughed heartily. 'Hope, those puppies of yours never fail to get us in trouble. Then, Jess's mobile rang from her beach bag. She lazily reached for it. 'Oh my God, Hope, it's him!' Hope sat upright and listened intently.

'Hello.'

'Hello, Mr Harris,' Jess replied as breezily as possibly. Her hands were trembling.

The long ring tone had alerted Dan to the fact that Jess was abroad. 'Sorry to disturb you, didn't even think you might be working away.'

'I'm not working, Dan. I'm actually lying on a beach with the lovely Hope Adams, it's absolute bliss.'

'That is so random, Jess, whereabouts are you?'

'Say Barbados,' Hope urged.

'Oh just in Lanzarote for the weekend actually.'

'Oh err, well have a good time, Jess, good to hear you.'

'Bye Dan.' Jess sat up on her sunbed, clenching her fists to her mouth in excitement.

'So what exactly did he want?' Hope said.

'He didn't say. He seemed so bloody shocked that I was on holiday he was lost for words.'

'Well good job. He's a fool if he can't see what he's let go, Jess. Let the bastard suffer now.'

'Hope!'

'Jess, don't stick up for him. He will *so* regret leaving you. As time goes on, he will realise you were the best thing that ever happened to him.'

Jess, spurred on by knowing that Dan still obviously did care for her, had a wonderful few days in the sun. She and Hope sunbathed, drank sangria, ate wonderful food, and danced 'til dawn. On Monday morning, they stood in the hundred-deep check-in queue at Arrecife airport.

'You are looking so good, Jess, your face is kinda relaxed and that tan makes you look hot, hot, hot!'

'I really feel *so* much better too. Thanks so much for suggesting we do this, Hope. You've been a complete rock and I really appreciate it.' She kissed her friend's cheek.

'Phone, Jess.' Hope alerted her. Jess scurried around in her handbag.

'Jess, it's me.' She mouthed to Hope that it was Dan again and made a face.

'Sorry, I thought you'd be back, when are you home?'

'Um, later tonight, you OK, Dan?'

'Yeah, er yeah I'm fine, just wanted to say hello really.'

'Well hello, Dan.' Jess replied strongly. 'Look I've got to go I'm at the airport.'

'Well safe trip back and all that.'

'Bye, Dan.'

'So?' Hope enquired. 'What did he want this time?'

'Wanted to know when I was home. He *so* wants me back, Hope.'

'Jess, you don't know that, he may just be being nice, checking you are OK, you know.'

'Hope, he's called me twice, knowing the second time I probably was still away, of course he wants me.'

'We need to discuss on the plane, he can't keep doing this to you. He said he wanted time out and that's what you've got to let him have. Have some more respect for yourself, Jess, please.' Jess knew that Hope was talking sense. She, too, would have given her friend the same warning but, blinded by her love for this young man, all she knew was that she couldn't wait to see him. Just hearing his voice again made her realise just how much she still loved him.

Chapter Eighteen

Tuesday morning, Jessica Morley woke up bright and alert. She checked her body in her bedroom mirror and was pleased at what she saw. Her tan accentuated her now sparkly blue-green eyes and her body looked even more toned than usual, due to her heartbreak, and the one hundred lengths she'd swam in the hotel pool every morning on holiday.

She opened her laptop and logged in. Great – only two work emails. She loved the summer, as it was quiet for her and she could take lot of time out for herself. She had only been online for ten minutes when Dan came on to messenger. Her heart began to beat faster.

Dan says:
Back then?
Jess says:
No, I'm in an internet café, decided to stay ☺
Dan says:
☺ What are you doing later?
Jess says:
Haven't even thought about it yet.
Dan says:
It's just Evie's been asking after you. Do you fancy meeting up after work? Thought we could take her for a bite to eat.
Jess says:
Oh, Dan, I'm not sure.
Dan says:
I'm ready to be friends.

Jess says:
I'm not sure if I am yet.
Dan says:
It'll be fine, Jess, just a couple of hours together and it would make Evie really happy.
Jess says:
Well, OK, then. Let's meet at The Golden Dog at say six? There's a play area for Evie there.
Dan says:
Cool. See you later.

She immediately phoned the hairdresser's and got an appointment for that afternoon.

She had to ring Hope

'Don't tell me off, but I'm seeing him later.'

'Oh, Jess, I'm not sure that's a good idea at all. It will bring all your feelings to the surface and you're doing great now.

'He wants to see me, because Evie is asking after me – nothing more.'

Well, I think he's being selfish. That poor little girl is going to be as confused as you.'

'It's fine, don't worry. I am going to look so damn sexy, be really strong and walk away. I want him to remember me like that, not the snivelling wreck he left a month ago. He's going to get such a burst of the beautiful Ms. Morley today, that it will leave him wanting. Then in a few weeks, 'cos I will be really strong – by then, we can start our friendship, and I can see Evie when I want to.

'I hate to say this, Jess, but I think you're deluded. I really don't think you should go but…'

'Go on… but what?'

'If it was me in your position, I would so do the same. Just keep me posted, baby.'

'I will. Have a good day, darling.'

Chapter Nineteen

Dan handed Jess a glass of rosé. The River Thames sparkled in the evening sunshine and swans drifted gracefully by the side of the boat. It had been so lovely to spend some time with Evie, who had actually run into her arms when she arrived at the pub. Dan was obviously bowled over by how good Jess looked; in fact he hadn't been able to take his eyes off of her. It seemed such a natural thing for her to follow him back over to the boat.

With Evie asleep in the bottom deck, they now had time alone to talk. Jess's feelings hadn't changed for Dan – in fact she felt like she loved him even more. They both took a toke of a joint. The sunset was particularly stunning on this fine summer evening and Jess felt more relaxed and content than she had done for a long time. She lay back on the beanbags that Dan had strategically placed on the top deck and closed her eyes. The next thing she knew was Dan's lips on hers. They began to kiss fast and passionately. Jess didn't need to question her actions – she wanted this man – and she wanted him now. She pulled up her skirt and revealed white lacy panties that accentuated her now golden skin. 'You look so sexy in white.' Dan panted as he ripped off his shorts. Jess pushed him back down on the beanbag.

'*God* I love you, Daniel Harris.' She gasped and sat astride him.

'Woah, slow down, Jessy baby, I want to make love to you *all* night.'

They rocked backwards and forwards tending and teasing each other for what seemed like hours. Then all of a sudden they were again making love fast and furiously, their sweat-drenched bodies sliding against each other. Spent, they lay looking at each other and smiling.

'Mrs Robinson, I've really missed you,' Dan uttered, softly stroking Jess's cheek.

Dan made Jess a make shift bed up on the top deck, and went to sleep downstairs so that he wouldn't miss Evie if she cried.

Jess woke up bright and early, to the sound of ducks quacking and the gentle whirring of other boats going past. She looked up to the sky, smiled, and made her way down to see Dan and Evie. Evie was still asleep, so she snuck into bed with Dan and curled up next to him. He put his arm around her and then suddenly moved it.

'No, Jess.'

'What do you mean, Dan? No!'

'Last night was great, amazing in fact, but I didn't make you any promises.'

Jess went rigid as Dan continued. 'You were flirting so much with me in the pub, and when you said you were cool and we should live for the moment – well I took that as read.'

She gulped and no words would come out of her now dry mouth. Dan's voice brightened. 'It's really weird: I don't get it with us. When I left Alex the last thing I wanted to do was spend time with her, let alone shag her. With you I just still love being with you.'

Jess couldn't believe the stupidity of this naïve young man. She got out of bed, marched up to the top deck, found her scattered clothes, and got dressed. She then stomped back down to his bedroom.

'So last night meant nothing, it was just a good fuck is that what you're saying, Dan?'

'Oh, Jess, I feel bad now, I don't want to be unfair to you. What I said to you when we split up still stands. I still want my freedom. Mates eh?'

'Dan, mates don't make love for two hours like we did last night, that was special and you bloody know that too.'

She was shouting now.

'Shh, Jess, don't wake Evie.'

'Fuck Evie and *fuck* you!'

Jess had totally lost it. Snot was now running down her face but she didn't care. She had to get her true feelings out in the open. 'How could you do this to me? You've been mailing me, rang me *twice* on holiday. *You* were the one who left me to get on with my life remember?' She wiped her nose with the back of her hand. Last night's mascara was now a black river down her cheeks. 'What was I supposed to think? I really thought you'd realised you'd made a mistake. Stop denying your own feelings, Dan Harris. Stop making me feel like this!'

Dan was speechless. Jess didn't recognise her own broken voice. 'I am *such* a strong person but look at the state of me, just look at me!' She pushed her face right into his and hissed. 'You *reduce* me to this weak, pathetic, wreck.'

Evie started crying.

'Daddy, Daddy!' Jess mimicked.

'Stop that this minute, Jess, how dare you!'

'Oh, Dan. I will stop this, don't you worry. Go back to your pathetic life, living on your smelly boat, with your poor insecure little daughter and lesbian ex-girlfriend – I don't want to be part of it anymore.'

She grabbed her bag and ran down the wooden path, flanked by boats, towards her car. And as she vowed never to see Daniel Harris again, she felt the other half of her heart fall to the bottom of her stomach.

Chapter Twenty

Jess was just belting out the chorus of 'Last Christmas' in her car when her mobile rang.

'Hey, Jess, it's Sam.'

'Oh, hiya, Sam,' she replied breezily. She was conscious that since that final day on the boat with Dan, she had not gone into Lemon Events once. She had cleverly avoided it by arranging conference calls or dealing with any issues on email.

'Just wondered how you are doing really?' Sam enquired. 'Long time no see and all that. Was surprised you didn't make our Christmas party last night, not like you?'

'Sam, I'm so sorry I did get the invite but have been so tied up with AG's Christmas event that I forgot all about it.' This was a total lie. She still couldn't face the thought of bumping into Dan.

'Anyway' how about lunch instead? I'm around this Friday, say one at the George & Dragon.'

'Sam, that would be lovely, thanks. See you there,' Jess replied openly. After the second half of her heart was broken by Dan, it had taken Jess a long time to get over him. She still thought about him daily but then pushed all thoughts to the back of her mind and put on a brave face. She had to face it – he wasn't coming back, and if he did he really was wrong for her anyway. They had accepted they were in different places. She wondered what he was doing now and if he was seeing someone else. The thought of that still made her want to cry. She also missed Evie greatly. She almost sent a present on her third birthday and then thought against it. They all had to move on.

Urged on by her friends and family Jessica had joined a Writers Bureau home workshop, and she was actually beginning to enjoy writing articles and getting feedback on them. She also had bravely signed up to an internet dating site but it was a complete waste of money; she was so choosy to avoid getting hurt again that either none of them matched up to Dan or there was something wrong with them. Jessy had nearly worn out her delete key getting rid of unsuitable suitors. She was sure that there would be no one in the world who she would love as much as Dan anyway. So she decided that she would leave it to fate or forever be the spinster of the parish. Hope had laughed, saying that now she was doing this writing course she should dress head to toe in pink and get a fluffy white dog like Barbara Cartland. 'I'd rather be like Joan Collins, thanks,' Jess had replied. 'She seems to have much more fun, plus she nabbed a toy boy who *stayed* with her.'

Chapter Twenty one

Jess arrived early at the George & Dragon. Despite the bad memory of her parting from Dan there, she still loved the welcoming feel of the beamed old pub on the water. She parked facing the river and watched the swans swimming gracefully by. Just as she was worrying about how cold they must be in the icy water, she heard a tap on her window. Sam was smiling in.

'I love swans! Bless them in that cold water,' she announced through the crack in her car window.

Sam laughed. He'd always loved Jess's sense of humour. She got out of the car and he kissed her on both cheeks. 'Hello, stranger. Kissed any unsuspecting 007s recently?'

'Oh God, I'm never going to live that down, am I?' She laughed, blushing.

'Nope.' Sam replied. 'Not often a man gets accosted by Wonder Woman on a dark night.'

Sam went to the bar to buy drinks. She looked him up and down. He really was a very handsome man. He obviously looked after himself, she thought, noticing how pert his bum was. His smart hair cut complimented his designer clothes. She loved the fact that he also was a complete gentleman. Sam put their drinks on the table and sat down.

'Guessing you're really busy at the moment then, as we haven't seen you at the barn?'

'God yeah it's been frantic, but the money will come in handy. Have been saving to go and see my brother in Australia in January,' Jess replied.

'Wow that's fantastic, Jess.'

'Yeah, I can't wait, three whole weeks. I'm meeting him in Brisbane and he's going to show me some of the East Coast.' Jess took a sip of her wine. 'How about Lemon – you busy at the moment?'

'Well it's quietened down a bit for Christmas, but got a big gig coming up for a telecoms company in April that I'm sure we'll need your help on.'

'That's good news, I'll get in touch when I'm back from Oz and you can brief me on it then.' They tucked into their lunch.

'So, have you sorted your man troubles then?' Sam asked out of the blue.

Jess nearly choked on her pasta. Never would she tell anyone about her and Dan, their pact would still remain even now it was over. 'Yes, I have thanks. Picked the wrong one as usual. It was just all a bit raw around my birthday and in the wise words of my father: when the demon drink is in, the wit is out.'

'In your case, it was nearly the whip's out!' He still regretted not staying with Jess that night and was actually amazed that he had resisted. Jess laughed out loud. As she did, she looked closely at Sam's mouth and crinkly eyes. His lips were full and soft. She actually didn't think she'd mind kissing them again. Sam insisted they both have puddings and coffee. By the time they left got out to the car park, Jess could hardly walk for food.

'Thanks so much Sam, I feel like a stuffed turkey.'

'Pleasure, my dear,' he replied. 'Um, Jess, I was wondering if you maybe would like to go out for dinner one night before Christmas?'

'Sam Beresford, I do believe you are inviting me on a date?' It was Sam's turn to blush. 'No just dinner, Jessica Morley.'

'I'd love to Sam but I'm only free this time next week though, loads of events on.'

'Next Friday it is then, be ready for seven.' Sam intercepted immediately. 'I'll send a car to pick you up from home.'

Chapter Twenty two

'He's sending a car!' Jess exclaimed to Emma over a curry on Sunday evening.

'Well that's more like it isn't it? Certainly beats being spun around in a shaky old GTI.'

Jess made a face and ripped off a piece of naan bread.

Emma continued. 'I'm sorry to be brutal, Jess, but we now need to find you a *suitable* man. And from what I've seen, you're now saying Sam Beresford ticks all the right boxes.'

'I don't think I'll ever feel the same electricity as I had with Dan.'

'Yes, but what you will feel is his generosity and kindness. You also said that you actually quite fancied kissing him again.'

'Yeah – he *is* sexy.'

'So, give it a chance – go for dinner, be casual, and just see what happens. It's great you're going on a date. I'm really pleased, Jess. It's about time.'

'I still miss, Dan, you know.'

'No you don't, Jess, you just miss the idea of being with somebody. Once somebody else sweeps you off your feet, it won't be just Hope saying Dan *who*? It will be *you* as well.' Emma refilled her plate with chicken dhansak. 'At least he'll know and hopefully *like* the same music as you. Adam Freefield, or whatever his name is, will soon be a distant memory. Will Young, Robbie, and U2 can be embraced back with open arms.' Emma was on a roll now. 'No screaming two-year-old waking you up at 6 a.m., no having to pay for weekends away. He'll probably even

know what a threepenny bit looks like.'
   'OK, Em, I've got the picture.

Chapter Twenty three

A silver Mercedes pulled up outside. It had been a long time since she'd been out and it had felt good getting ready. She straightened down her black halter-neck dress, re-applied some lip-gloss, pulled on her long black velvet coat, swished a pink pashmina round her and shut the door behind her.

'So where are you taking me then?' Jess cheekily asked the Mercedes driver. 'Bray, madam.'

'Champagne?' Sam enquired as she walked through the door of The Fat Duck.

'Lovely.' She replied smiling. 'Thanks so much for sending the car by the way, I felt like royalty.'

'Well I have to keep my best clients sweet. You know that. I just live round the corner from here anyway, so it made life easier than coming to pick you up.'

Jess had always wanted to eat at The Fat Duck, she'd heard so much about Heston Blumenthal's remarkable menus. She had tried on numerous occasions to get a table for people requesting a restaurant with a difference, but had never once managed to get a reservation. Sam must be in the know to get a table so close to Christmas, she thought.

'How exciting!' Jess exclaimed as they sat down at their table. 'I've always wanted to come here.'

'Good, good, it's difficult to know where to take a lady who's been to most restaurants and hotels with her job.' Sam took a swig of his champagne. 'You look stunning by the way, Jess.'

He seemed nervous, Jess thought. It was strange to see

Sam like this. He was always the confident managing director to her. She hadn't actually thought of him as Sam Beresford, the person, with a life outside events. After they had finished their champagne and were well through a bottle of French red, Sam seemed to relax.

'I've been wanting to take you out since your birthday night actually.'

'I can't believe it's taken you *nine* months to get round to it.' Jess laughed.

'Well you always seemed to be busy when I asked you what you were up to and I didn't want to pry, especially after you told me you had man troubles.'

'Well it was certainly worth waiting for, Sam, the food here is amazing, oh and the company's not so bad I guess.' Sam laughed. 'So tell me about Sam Beresford then,' Jess urged.

'Well I'm a managing director of an event company,' Sam replied. Jess usually considerate, now fuelled by alcohol, wouldn't let him get away with just this.

'Sam! I meant tell me about your personal life, I want all the gore, previous girlfriends, wives, mistresses.'

'Jessica Morley, you're a nosey one aren't you? I shall give you one bit of information and that's it. Yes I have been married, just the once, at twenty-one, we were far too young.' In this context, twenty-one did seem really young to Jess. She suddenly thought about Dan. He was coming up to twenty-five, and it made her realise then, just how young he really was. The man opposite her was twenty years older than him. In fact they could both be his parents.

Sam started to tell his tale. 'We split up amicably after ten years. There was no one else involved. The love just seemed to fade. It was really sad to part, but we didn't want to live a lie. I never regretted a single day of my marriage. Grace is a good woman and our daughter has taken on her spirit and love for life.'

'Daughter!' Jess exclaimed. 'You're a dark horse, I had no idea.'

'Yes, she's twenty now, all grown up. She's a club promoter in London.'

They tucked into their smoked bacon and egg ice-cream.

'God that's delicious! You just wouldn't expect it to be would you?' Jess exclaimed.

'Life would be dull if everything you expected happened wouldn't it, don't you think?' Sam uttered.

'You are so right, Sam Beresford. I can't think of anything worse than knowing what would happen in the future.'

'So where does Jessica Morley see her future lying then?'

'Oh Sam, do you know what?– I really don't know. I always thought that by forty, I'd be settled with kids, doing the school run, making their costumes for the Christmas plays and running in the parents' race at sports days. I wouldn't have to work and would be content with a loving husband, a medium size house, and maybe a cat.' Sam listened intently as Jess continued. 'And look at me, yes I'm a successful businesswoman, got good friends and family, a cool house, smart car, but there is something missing in my life. I miss being in a partnership and I do want a family.' Jess took a sip of dessert wine. She couldn't believe she was opening up to Sam in this way, but somehow it was refreshing being so honest. Once she started she couldn't stop. 'I'm doing this writing course now, I'm quite into it actually, and that is fulfilling me to some level – but it isn't enough. I sometimes do ponder on my purpose if I don't have a family of my own.'

Sam nodded. 'I guess I'm lucky there because I have Charlotte. We've done our best to give her as stable an upbringing as possible despite her living in two homes. But she's flown the nest now. I guess I feel like you. I want a partner, but then part of me is so set in my ways now that I don't think I could bear to share my house with anyone.' Sam was also shocked out how candid he was being. 'You are a very special lady, Jess, and good things happen to good people. Everything will work out for you I'm sure.'

They drank their coffee and Sam settled the bill. He helped her with her coat and walked her out to the waiting Mercedes. It had started to snow. Jess screeched. 'Oh look, Sam! I hope it covers tonight. I just love the crunchy sound and feeling as you take that first step into fresh snow.' Sam smiled at her child-like exuberance.

'Well ciao, bella, thanks for a lovely evening, I'll guess I'll see you when you're back from Oz now?' He kissed her on both cheeks. Jess noticed how gorgeous he smelt. 'Thank you so much, it's been a *real* treat to be brought here.'

'Oh one more thing, Jess, I nearly forgot. Happy Christmas.' Sam handed her a neatly wrapped present.

'Oh, Sam, thank you. Thank you so much. You really shouldn't have though. Dinner was enough.' She could sense his embarrassment.

'Right, I'm off. You take care. Have a fantastic break, Jess.' She waved and smiled from the car window. When Sam was out of sight, she sunk back into the comfortable leather seat of the Mercedes. She really had enjoyed the evening. There had been no heart palpitations. In fact she didn't think that Sam wanted any more than friendship anyway. He had said before it was just dinner and not a date. Sam was good company. It had been a good starter for ten, on her new journey without Daniel Harris. She opened her present, the outer wrapper revealed a small box, beautifully wrapped in red tissue paper. She opened it carefully. Inside was a beautiful crystal brooch in the shape of a swan. Jess said, 'Bless him.' It really was such a lovely present. He had obviously picked up on her swan comment in the George & Dragon car park. Thoughtful went straight to the top of the Sam Beresford tick list.

Chapter Twenty four

Having waved Jess off, Sam then reached for his mobile. 'Hey, Gina, how's my favourite secretary on this snowy evening?'

Gina giggled at the other end of the phone. 'Fine thanks, Boss. What you up to?'

'Oh just finished off at the office actually, and was just wondering if you needed keeping warm on this cold and snowy night?'

'Ooh, Mr Beresford, that's an offer a girl can't refuse.'

'Are you ready for me now?' Sam leered.

'Always ready for you, lover. I shall slip into something a little more comfortable.'

Chapter Twenty five

Jess's head lolling forward from her airline seat woke her up with a start. She wiped the dribble from the side of her mouth and was more than relieved when the captain announced that they were about to begin their descent into Brisbane airport. She found long flights in economy dire. Her boredom threshold was very low and once she'd watched four films, had eaten every morsel of unappetising food off the tray, and ordered the entire magazine of duty free in her mind, that was it, she wanted to get off, usually when there were at least five hours still to go.

'Big sis!' Karl shouted loudly through the chattering throng in arrivals. Jess smiled broadly at her tanned, handsome brother as she negotiated her trolley through the crowd. 'How was your flight?'

'Long!' Jess exclaimed. She noticed a pretty blonde girl at this side.

'Jess, Shelley, Shelley, Jess,' Karl introduced. 'We've arranged a little itinerary for you, hope you don't mind.' Shelley piped up.

'Three weeks isn't long and we don't want you to miss anything,' Karl intercepted.

'Fine by me,' Jess replied. 'I'm so bloody tired though I could sleep for a week.'

'Well I'm afraid, dear sis, you have to stay awake all day today. That's the rules. Your sleeping pattern will be right as rain from tomorrow if you do that.'

She was thankful that day one of the itinerary involved checking into a hotel in the centre of Brisbane and relaxing by the pool. The next few sunny days were a whirlwind. Karl and Shelley were the perfect hosts. Jess experienced the delights of Hastings Street in Noosa, with its tempting boutiques, restaurants and funky pavement bistros. She was delighted to see her brother so happy and relaxed. At twenty-seven, Shelley was ten years Karl's junior. They were completely compatible in every sense and it made Jess wonder why even now in the twenty-first century, it was still deemed more acceptable for a man to date a younger woman rather than vice versa.

After spending a day in Noosa, they then travelled back down South along the Pacific Highway to the Gold Coast for a few days and then spent an amazing day at Byron Bay. Jess was enthralled as they watched dolphins playing in the surf from their lighthouse viewpoint and laughed heartily as they ate carrot cake in The Twisted Sister Café.

She was having a marvellous time, but every time they visited a new place all she could think about was Dan. She wished he was there, to share all these new experiences with her. She was annoyed at herself that she couldn't get him out of her head and kept trying to tell herself that it wouldn't have worked. However, she had a constant niggling in the back of her mind that the love between them was so strong that it was just *meant* to be. She loved him and that was that.

After two weeks Karl and Shelley had to go back to work, so Jess had bravely decided to go off for a couple of days on her own.

The natural beauty of Fraser Island took Jess's breath away as she walked through the impressive rain forest. She craned her neck to try and see the tops of the trees and thought how lucky all the noisy wildlife around her was, to be living in such a beautiful environment. She had never ever seen such a long expanse of bright white sand and clear blue water before. Her tour guide was fun and informed and, as she got back in the red 4x4 with her

Dutch and American travel companions, she felt happier and more relaxed than she had done in a long time.

There was to be a party on the beach tonight, all the other groups who were staying in the same hostel were invited. Jess slung on a pair of khaki shorts and a white vest and closed the door of her dorm. Her room mates, all in their twenties, had decided not to bother showering after the day's adventures and headed straight to the bar. She followed the red glow of the campfire, and as she turned a corner could hear a Counting Crows track drifting across the sand dunes.

'Hey Jess.'

She strained to see who was greeting her and was pleased to see it was Jurgen, one of the Dutch guys from her group. 'Come and join us.' Jurgen was around six-feet-three. The fringe of his blonde hair flopped over one eye and he had a funny habit of flicking it back with his index finger. He had been making Jess laugh all day by mimicking the Americans. Jess had glanced at him on the tour earlier. She loved the way the hairs on his brown muscular legs had turned completely blond in the sun. She'd also for some reason been drawn to his crotch. What was it with her attraction for these younger men?

The music was cranked up and the beer and wine were flowing. Jurgen passed her a joint. She took a big toke and then wandered to a quiet sand dune so that she could just lie and look at the stars. She was in mid-thought about how wonderful it would be if Dan appeared over the hill, when somebody flopped down next to her.

'Mind if I join you?' It was Jurgen.

'Sure,' Jess said dreamily, she was enjoying feeling so floaty and relaxed.

'Having fun?' he continued.

'Yeah, I've had an amazing day.'

He lay down next to her. 'I love the stars.' he announced suddenly. His English was perfect. 'It makes me realise that we are such a small part of this huge universe.'

Jess prayed that he wouldn't start going on about Stephen Hawking or Einstein. She had to admit this was one thing about Dan she didn't miss, his relativity fetish. They lay there in silence enjoying the night sky above.

'Focus on a star, Jess, pick the brightest one,' Jurgen suddenly announced.

Jess looked hard at the sky. 'I've got one.'

'Now concentrate hard and make a wish,' Jurgen continued. 'Next time there is a full moon your wish will come true.'

Jess laughed and wished with all her might that Dan would come back to her one day. 'You should be Italian not Dutch coming out with romantic notions like that, young man.'

Jurgen sat up on one arm and looked intently at her in the moonlight. The waves were crashing on the shore in the distance. 'Jess, do you mind if I kiss you?'

Jess, slightly stoned and drunk, giggled. Without waiting for a reply, he leant down and kissed her tenderly. His lips were soft and warm, and she enjoyed the thrill of his tongue gently exploring her mouth. He gently lifted her vest and began exploring her breasts. Jess squirmed at the pleasure of this physical contact, after not having any for so long. She could feel his excitement beneath his shorts. He gently undid her zip and slid his fingers inside her. They writhed around on the sand exploring each other's bodies.

'I want to fuck you.' Jurgen suddenly said bluntly. He rolled on top of her and tried to push himself into her.

'No, *stop*!' Jess shouted, pushing him off and jumping up.

Jurgen raised himself up on his elbow, shocked at Jess's outburst. 'Jess what, what is it?'

'I can't do this.' She started to cry.

'It's OK. Don't cry. I'm sorry. I just got caught up in the moment. I thought you wanted to as well.'

'No, Jurgen, I'm the one who should be sorry. You're great, it's just I'm really raw from a recent break up that's all.' She wiped her eyes with the back of her hand and whispered. 'I still love him.' She felt foolish that she had got herself in this position and was pleased that Jurgen had acted like a gentleman, or heaven knows what would have happened.

He put his arm on hers gently. 'Jessy, you can't stop a river flowing to the sea. If it's meant to be, he'll come back to you.'

'Thank you, Jurgen, that is so sweet of you.'

He got up off of the sand, kissed her cheek softly, and slowly walked back to the group.

Jess lay on her hard dormitory bed sobbing. How could she have so little self-respect and so readily give herself to another man, especially when she was so in love with Dan. She knew that it was madness, but she felt like she was betraying him. She didn't want to sleep with anyone else in case it dulled the memory of the wonderful lovemaking she had experienced with him on the boat on their last night.

Chapter Twenty six

It was snowing heavily when she landed at Heathrow. She pushed her trolley sleepily through the green channel and wished she'd pre-booked a taxi. Half asleep she suddenly noticed amongst the drivers rallying for position, a board with her name on it and approached the driver. 'Jessica Morley, that's me. Strange, I didn't arrange a taxi.'

'Lemon Events arranged the booking, madam.'

Dan instantly came into her mind but he didn't even know that she'd been going away, then she realised it must have been Sam. She hadn't actually thought of Sam at all since she'd been away, but smiled to herself at the thoughtfulness of the man. Once in the warmth of the car, Jess switched on her mobile. Beep, beep, beep, the text messages came flooding in. Em, Hope, Phoebe, her dad, even Karl, checking she'd landed safely. She prayed that Dan might have tried to contact her but nothing.

She was unpacking her case when the phone rang. 'Jess, hi, it's Sam, good time?'

'Hey, Sam, it was great. Thanks so much for arranging the taxi by the way. It was such a pleasant surprise.'

Sam continued. 'No worries, I know what it's like after a long haul. Anyway I won't keep you now as you must be shattered, but I do need to talk quite quickly with you about the Telecoms project that's come off. How about a breakfast meeting at my house tomorrow, say 8 a.m.?'

'Yeah, that's fine, can you mail me over your address. Let's hope this snow lets up or I'll be coming to you on a sleigh.'

At 8 a.m., Sam greeted her at his front door with a kiss

on both cheeks.

'Jeez, I wish I'd said a lunchtime meeting now. I've been pacing the floor for hours in the night. Bloody jet lag!' Jess exclaimed.

Sam laughed. He'd always loved her honesty. She shook the snow off of her boots and made her way into Sam's cottage. The décor was funky but homely at the same time. There were statues and pictures everywhere. A big open fire roared in the dining room. She also noticed an array of thank you cards on his bookshelf – ever the generous, Jess thought.

The delicious smell of fresh coffee filled the room. Out of the corner of her eye she noticed a table in the kitchen, laden with all sorts of scrumptious-looking pastries.

They ate their way through the pastries and chatted about Jess's adventures in Australia. Sam nearly choked on his croissant when Jess relayed her tale of nearly wetting herself as she thought she was being chased by a dingo on Fraser Island, when in fact it was a cat from the hostel. They discussed the upcoming Telecoms project and Jess was relieved that Dan hadn't been put on the project team for this one. Two hours flew by and Jess got up ready to go.

'Oh I can't believe I feel stressed, and I haven't even been back a day yet,' Jess sighed.

'We can't have that now, can we?' Sam replied. He took her by the hand and led her towards the back door to the garden. The snow was falling heavily again. 'Now shut your eyes and take a big step,' he urged. Sam held her hand as Jess's feet sunk into the fresh, crisp snow with a loud crunching noise.

'Oh my God, fresh snow! I just love it!' She screamed and ran down the garden, making snowballs and throwing them around as she went. Running up to the back door and gave Sam a big kiss on the lips. 'Sam Beresford, you are going to make someone a very happy woman one day.'

'If you love something, set it free. If it comes back, it was, and always will be, yours. If it never returns, it was never yours to begin with.'

Anon

PART 3

Ten Years Later…

Chapter One

'I'm sure he's having an affair, Em.' Jess took a big slurp of tea and ran her fingers through her sleek bob. She kicked off her trainers and relaxed back into the kitchen chair. She still looked far younger than her years and, despite giving birth at forty-five, had still managed to restore and maintain her trim figure. 'It's my bloody fiftieth birthday party on Saturday too. I really can't be bothered with it, all that playing happy families shit.'

Suddenly, there was a scream from the garden and Emma's daughter Laura came running in. She was now twelve, going on twenty-two, and loved mothering five-year-old Freya whenever Jess came round to see her mum. 'Freya just fell off the swing.' Laura panted.

Freya appeared at the back door with a tear-streaked face. Her nose was red from the cold March air. 'Mummy, I hurt myself.'

'Let's have a look at you, darling girl,' Jess said calmly.

Freya was very pretty, with dark brown wavy hair and the biggest blue eyes. Jess and her husband had been the happiest people alive when they found out she was pregnant. And, when their little bundle of loveliness appeared, she suddenly felt she was now complete as a woman. Motherhood suited her.

Plasters in position and an orange squash later, silence in the kitchen resumed.

'Now where were we?' Jess continued.

'Ah, just the slight issue that you think your husband is having an affair,' Em replied. 'It amazes me that it's even in your head. In my eyes, you and Sam have always seemed to have the perfect relationship.'

'Perfect. I bet you never thought the words perfect, relationship, and Jessica Morley would ever go together, did you?' Jess smiled.

Emma laughed at her matter-of-fact friend. Jess had always had the wildest of relationships, so when Sam Beresford had proposed she was as happy for Jess as Jess was herself. Sam was a good man. He was thoughtful and kind and offered Jess the friendship and respect that she so rightly deserved. 'So come on what's changed? You both seemed fine when you came over for dinner last month,' Emma enquired.

'We haven't had sex for two months. I mean, we usually only do it about once a month anyway, but well I had a few wines and started coming on to him the other night and he literally pushed me away. Said he was tired.'

'Oh, Jess, if that's it I really don't think you need to get a private detective yet. If I was given a pound for the times Mark said he was tired, I'd be a millionaire by now.Aand we're not getting any younger; he probably *was* tired.'

'I think I was born horny.' Jess laughed but then continued in a sombre tone. 'Every Sunday morning now as well, he says he's going off to get the papers and is gone for around two hours. I question him when he comes back and he says that he wanted to enjoy the morning air and had gone off for a long walk.'

'Again, Jess, maybe he did go for a walk! Where on earth is he going to go for hot passion on a Sunday morning? Be realistic.'

'Yes I suppose. He just seems to be acting a bit odd lately that's all. He stays late a lot more with work than he used to, and he is away at least one weekend a month.'

'Jess, he has always been like that. You know the nature of the events business, you worked in it yourself for long enough. You're just noticing it more now as you're feeling sensitive.'

'I guess you're right, Em. It has never been the conventional nine to five relationship in that respect. He hasn't surprised me for a while either.'

'You've just been spoilt, Jess, it's not as easy to be whisked away for romantic weekends with a little one in tow, you know that.'

'I know. Maybe I am being silly. I was going to talk to him but you're right, it does seem ridiculous. Sam wouldn't hurt me. I've never known anyone love me like he does.'

It had taken Jess a long time to realise that Sam was the man she had wanted to spend the rest of her life with. He had wined and dined her and showered her with gifts. It had been a year-long courtship, before she had even slept with him. Mainly because she was so used to turmoil in a relationship, the balance with Sam actually threw her off kilter. Her age old commitment phobia came to the fore, but in the end it was a classic case of love being friendship that's been set on fire, and Sam delightedly won her over. There had never been any real passion, just a slow-burning love that eventually Jess realised would offer her the contentment and family she so desperately had craved for. There had not been a day in their eight year marriage that Sam had not made her feel special or wanted.

They shared a beautiful cottage in the Berkshire countryside and, since having Freya, she no longer had to work. In fact her childhood dream of living in a rose-covered cottage with a perfect family had been fulfilled, Aapart from having a cat as Sam was allergic to them.

'It's hard to swallow but, as time goes by, it's not all passion and red roses.' Em continued.

'God, I wish it was though,' Jess replied. 'I love Sam and I love being a family with Freya, but sometimes I have to admit I do think *is this it now*? It's like there is still something missing, like I'm looking for something else but

I don't know what it is.'

Emma sighed. 'Do you know what? I feel like that some days too. Mark goes off to work, I get up do the school run, go to my part-time job, do the school run again, cook dinner for the kids, wash up, cook dinner for us, clear up, and go to bed.' Jess smiled knowingly. 'But do you know what Jess. I wouldn't change my life for the world. I adore our kids and even though he annoys the arse off me sometimes, I wouldn't want to be with anyone but Mark. Anyway, let's cheer up; we've got your party to look forward to.'

Jess groaned. 'You know what Sam's like. Everything has to be perfect. We've got a huge marquee arriving today, which is to be attached to the conservatory, big heaters the lot. The hugest glitter ball you've ever seen and the cheesiest 80s band.'

'Sounds great!' Em interjected.

'Yes I suppose it will be. He's excited too as he says as well as being my birthday, it's the anniversary of us. I couldn't work out why, then suddenly remembered our drunken snog on the night of my fortieth.'

'God, do you remember that?' Em piped up. 'Ken Dodd the DJ, he was hilarious.'

Jess laughed. 'I was so in love with that whippersnapper Dan then. Isn't it funny how time changes everything? I never thought I'd ever get over him. Bloody hell I was crazy about that boy though. I do have to say that nothing has ever matched the passion I had with him. It was electric.'

'I can't remember now if you ever saw him again after you split?' Emma questioned.

'No, never did. I was so relieved that the year Sam proposed Dan evidently moved to London to work with a firm of web designers there, so there was never any awkwardness at Lemon.'

'That's right. Have you ever mentioned it to Sam?'

'God, no. I didn't think there was any need. I mean can you imagine him knowing that I was fraternising with one of his junior staff? I don't think he'd have dealt with it too well, you know what a proud man he is.'

'Isn't it funny when you think back?' Emma laughed and continued. 'And going back to your concern, I think it's highly unlikely your lovely husband is having an affair. I mean look at the effort he's making for your birthday. He loves you, mate, so stop worrying.'

Freya came charging into the kitchen. 'Guess what, Mummy?'

'Tell me, Freya Beya?' Jess scooped her precious daughter into her arms.

'I love you a million thousand dollars.'

Jess tickled her daughter's tummy playfully. 'And I love you more than pink milkshake.'

Chapter Two

'You have to tell her Sam. It's me or her now. I'm sick of being the bloody mistress. A quick Sunday morning shag and the odd night is just not enough for me anymore.'

Sam sat up in bed and ran his hands through his hair. 'But Cherry.'

'No bloody buts, this has been going on for too long now, two years too long in fact.' Cherry took a drag on her after-sex cigarette. 'I mean surely there's no comparison. I'm twenty years her junior. It must be like shagging a bit of leather.'

Sam cringed inwardly that his young lover could be so harsh about Jess. He still loved his wife very much, but when Cherry joined Lemon as a new account manager, he had fallen for her blonde, brassy charm, and short mini-skirted apparel. He had questioned his actions, many a time, but had just put it down to a mid-life crisis. He couldn't however imagine life without his vibrant, charming Jess and beautiful little Freya. Undoubtedly, sex with Cherry was amazing. He had reached raw highs with her that he had never experienced with Jess. But he still adored being close to Jess too. When he made love to her, he did just that. He tended to her body with gentle compassion.

Sam knew he had to give Cherry some sort of answer. 'OK, I hear you, baby. It's Jess's party at the weekend. I want it to be special for her. Let's get that out of the way and we can talk again.'

Cherry huffed. 'I want it to be special for her,' she mimicked in a baby voice.

'I bet that's bloody costing you the earth and we haven't been away together for weeks now.'

Sam got out of bed and sighed. He was still a very fit man for fifty-five. Cherry looked him up and down and then smiled at him. 'Baby, you know how I much I love you.'

'Yes I do,' Sam replied wearily and opened his wallet. 'Look, here's £500. Go and get yourself a nice outfit. I'll come round Monday and you can show it off to me then.'

Cherry smugly took the money. She knew just how to play Sam Beresford.

Chapter Three

The morning of Jess's party arrived. It was a beautiful crisp March day. The good weather was a relief to Jess, as she imagined everyone having to wear woolly scarves in the marquee, despite the heaters that Sam had organised. Much to sociable little Freya's delight, an array of people had been backwards and forwards all day with catering supplies, band equipment, decorations, and flowers. She ran around the marquee amongst them, chattering furiously to anyone who would take the time to stop and talk to her. She was going to stay with a friend in the village tonight, so Jess could let her hair down without having to worry about getting her to bed at a reasonable hour.

Jess made herself a cup of tea and sat in the cottage's pretty window seat, and began looking through tonight's guest list. Her whole family were coming. Even though her dad was now in his eighties, he and Maria said they wouldn't miss it for the world.

She smiled when she thought about her dad and Maria. It had been hard on all counts when her mother had died, however, despite teething difficulties Maria was accepted into the fold. She had proved to be the mainstay of the family and most importantly had made her dad very happy. Karl and Shelley were coming up from Brighton, and Phoebe and Glen had probably already left their house. Phoebe was so excited to have a weekend away from the girls. Sam's daughter Charlotte, now thirty, was also coming with her new boyfriend, whom Jess and Sam had yet to meet. Charlotte was now a successful marketing manager in the music industry. Sam was really proud of his daughter, and Jess had been more than happy that she had accepted her and the arrival of Freya so openly. But that was Charlotte all over, she had a zest for life and always went out of her way to help and please people.

Sam walked into the living room and smiled. He put his arm around his wife and kissed her on the top of the head. 'So how's my favourite birthday girl then?'

Jess smiled and turned to face him. 'I'm actually really looking forward to tonight now.'

'Good, good. It's going to be great and you will no doubt be the belle of the ball.'

'Just don't let me jump to the floor when 'Oops Upside Your Head' comes on.'

Jess laughed. This was her renowned party piece, which ended up with everyone seeing her knickers and her usually ruining whatever she was wearing.

'Daddy!' Freya rushed in and jumped into Sam's arms. 'I didn't tell Mummy about the car I promise.'

Sam put his fingers to his daughter's lips to try and hush her and beckoned Jess to the front door. 'You'd better follow me, Mrs Beresford.' Sam flung open the front door and Jess shrieked with delight, as there sitting on the drive, adorned with a huge pink bow, was a stunning, mint condition, dark blue, Mark II Golf GTI convertible. She had mentioned to Sam a few months ago that she had had one in her twenties, and it had been her favourite car ever. Sam was delighted at his wife's reaction. 'It's obviously very old, Jess, but with a bit of love and care it will keep on going for you for years to come.'

'Bit like us then hey?' Jess laughed and threw her arms around her thoughtful husband. 'God I love you, Sam Beresford,' she said loudly and hugged him tight.

'Mummy, can we go for a drive now, pleeeease?' Freya urged.

Chapter Four

Sam waved his beautiful wife and daughter off of the drive. Tears stung his eyes at the nature of his betrayal. What on earth was he thinking? How could he possibly even think of leaving this wonderful woman, adorable child, and settled life behind? And for what? Hot, hard sex with a younger woman who, he was certain, only saw him as a future bank balance anyway. He realised then that he shouldn't have kept his affair with Cherry running for so long. It had been easy with all the others. They were just passing flings and luckily had never reached ultimatum status. He made a decision there and then, that this was it. He knew now where his heart would lie forever. He would be a one-woman man. Monday night he would finish it for good with Cherry and he would never again have another affair.

Chapter Five

'You look *so* handsome in black tie,' Jess enthused to her preening husband. 'In fact that is exactly what you were wearing on the night of my fortieth. You didn't look half bad then either.'

'I should have got you a Wonder Woman outfit for later,' Sam said. 'God I fancied you then, I can't believe it took me so long to unleash my own Lasso of Truth and tell you.'

Jess wriggled into her cocktail dress. The silky fabric accentuated her curves and the plunging neckline showed off her ample bosom. She had chosen electric blue to highlight her eyes, and had had her hair blow-dried especially for the night's festivities. In short, she looked simply stunning. Sam kissed her gently on the cheek so as not to smudge her lipstick. 'You look beautiful darling. In fact you still easily pass for forty.'

Guests started to filter in through the back gate: a plethora of penguins and fancy frocks. Blue flares lit a pathway down the garden, to the entrance of the marquee. A jazz band had started up in a corner, while chattering partygoers mingled over their first glass of champagne, and nibbled on elaborate canapés. Jess radiated happiness. Here she was surrounded by everybody she loved, at a party just for her. She had made sure her dad and Maria were comfortable at a table near the bar and had a laugh with Phoebe about not believing how old they both were. She was in mid conversation with Karl and Shelley about whether they would ever take the plunge to have kids, when Sam walked over to her.

'All OK?' Jess enquired. Sam put a loving arm around this wife.

'Fine, fine. Charlotte just called though, the babysitter let her other half down. He's trying to find another one but she's definitely going to be late.'

'No worries, they are staying over anyway aren't they? So we'll have plenty of time to catch up with them over the weekend,' Jess replied.

The 80's band suddenly came to life belting out a Duran Duran favourite. 'Her name..' Hope sang, as she shimmied over to Jess. 'Darling girl, you surely can't possibly be fifty, you look *so* young.' They both laughed out loud. Hope actually looked about thirty-five now. Her recent boob job, collagen-pumped lips, and regular botox injections made sure of that.

'Nice frock, love,' Jess exclaimed. 'Did you leave the other half of it in the shop?' Hope laughed again.

'Darling, if you've got it flaunt it, I say. And if you haven't when you get to our age, you should bloody flaunt it anyway. Now are there any potential men here for me, honey? I'm feeling hungry.'

'Hope Adams, you are the most insatiable woman I've ever met.' Jess smiled. 'However, I've actually got somebody in mind for you though.' She pointed over to the left speaker. 'In his mid-forties. He's a complete Jack-the-Lad but has a big heart to compliment yours.'

Hope ogled across the dance floor. 'Hmm, check him out. Let's hope everything else is big on him too.'

'Hope!' Jess exclaimed.

'You love it really,' Hope chuckled and walked seductively towards her prey.

The dark-rooted blonde heading up the band launched into 'Call Me' by Blondie and Jess caught Emma's eye as she to her side. The two friends began to dance wildly, mouthing all the lyrics that they had both learnt off by heart in Emma's parents' bedroom, when they were just thirteen years-old. They breathlessly walked to the bar and got themselves a large wine each.

'Jess, you look stunning, mate. I saw the Golf on the drive too, what a cool present.' Emma panted.

'I know I feel thoroughly spoilt. I do really love Sam you know. I also had a good think about what you said, and you're right. There is no way on earth he would have an affair.'

Sam waved over to them both from the other side of the marquee. Jess smiled widely, and blew him a kiss. By 11 o'clock the party was rocking, Madness, The Police, The Jam, Prince, and Wham aided the celebrations. Suddenly, the music stopped with a groan from the revellers. However laughter soon resumed, as Sam appeared carrying a magnificent cake in the shape of a star, ablaze with fifty candles. He cleared his throat and addressed his audience.

'Now I'm not one for speeches and I know you want to carry on enjoying yourselves but, before you do that, I just wanted you to join me in wishing my beautiful wife a very happy birthday.' The audience looked on happily. 'Jessica Beresford has been a shining star in my life for the past ten years and I hope she will be until eternity.'

Sam certainly wasn't renowned for his outpourings of affection, and a tear fell down Jess's cheek. An 'ah' resounded around the marquee, before a drunken rendition of 'Happy Birthday' commenced.

'Three cheers for Jess,' Sam shouted

He didn't notice the mini-skirted blonde staggering across the marquee towards him. 'Hip hip bloody hooray,' Cherry angrily spat in his ear. 'You better be leaving her on Monday.'

Sam, now white with shock, ushered Cherry quickly outside of the marquee. 'What the fuck do you think you are doing here? Turning up at my private home, to my wife's special party. How dare you!' Cherry was clearly very drunk.

'I was sat on my own at home and thought fuck it, if he's having a good time then

I should be too.'

'I'm ringing you a taxi now,' Sam said sternly. 'And on Monday we shall talk as I promised.' He physically marched his mistress to the front gate. 'Now you wait here until the car arrives.'

Cherry fuelled by alcohol saw no sense or reason. In witnessing Sam's outpouring of affection to his very attractive wife, she realised that the chance of him ever leaving her, were probably very remote indeed. She burst back into the marquee and marched straight over to Jess. Jess, who was now mid conversation with Hope was oblivious to what was to come. Culture Club's 'Do You Really Want to Hurt Me' filled the air.

'Happy birthday, Jess. Really pleased to meet you.' Cherry held out her hand in greeting.

'Hi there and thanks,' Jess hesitated as she looked Cherry up and down. 'Sorry to be rude, but I'm not sure if we've met before?'

'No, Jess, we haven't. My name is Cherry and I'm having an affair with your husband.'

Chapter Six

Jess opened her eyes. Her head was pounding. She rubbed her face, stretched and then, as if she had been hit on the head with a rock, suddenly realised the terrible truth from last night. She looked around her unfamiliar surroundings. Where was she? That's right she had decided to go and stay with Hope. She felt such a fool. Her hunch had been right all along. The man she had been sharing her life with for eight years was having an affair, with a girl young enough to be his daughter.

Hope appeared at the bedroom door. 'Tea?' She enquired gently.

'Yes please, angel.' Jess replied weakly. 'Hope, please tell me that no one else realised what was going on. I was so drunk I can't remember everything that happened now.'

'Well only Jack-the-Lad as he shared a taxi back here with us,' Hope replied.

Jess managed a smile. 'Is he still here?'

'Obviously,' Hope shrugged. 'Jess, honestly don't worry. I will gag him not to say anything. You were ever the professional. You acted as if you were running your own event. You kept your smile on until midnight and said goodbye to everybody with grace. Nobody had a clue, darling, honestly, I promise.' Jess breathed a sigh of relief.

'The last thing I wanted was a big scene with everyone there, especially Dad and Maria. That would have been terrible.'

'I can't believe you were so calm with Sam. It was like something out a movie Jess,' Hope exclaimed. 'You just said through gritted teeth, "You pick up Freya in the morning. I am going to stay with Hope, and we shall talk tomorrow." If it had been me, I would have completely lost it!'

Jess's eyes filled with tears. 'That's the whole thing with me and Sam. I am really angry with him, but it's weird. I'll go home later and we'll probably discuss this, like we discuss putting the recycling out.' Just then her mobile rang.

'Jess, it's Sam, I'm *so* sorry and I really can explain.'

'Isn't that what all adulterers say?' Jess replied wearily and continued. 'Well I guess there's no point screaming and shouting, when can we talk? I obviously don't want Freya to hear. Is she OK by the way?'

'She's fine. Charlotte arrived really late last night, thought we could maybe all have lunch today to make up for her missing your party. Why don't I get her to look after Freya instead, and we meet in The Royal Oak at say one 'o' clock?'

'OK.' Just as Jess had assumed, it was as if they were having a normal conversation. 'What's Charlie's new man like by the way?'

'He's joining her later on, only just managed to get a babysitter,' Sam answered.

'Did you tell her?'

'Yes I did.'

Jess showered and borrowed some of Hope's clothes. She luckily managed to find something fairly conservative, amongst the leopard skin and fur. She got a taxi to the pub and waited for Sam.

He looked ashen as he walked over to her. 'Jess, let me have my say before you say a word, please.'

Jess sat in silence and looked at the man opposite her. She *did* love him. He had been her life for the past eight years, and she couldn't bear to imagine life without him in it. He was her rock.

'I met Cherry at work, she's an account manager. I

guess I was flattered by the attentions of a younger woman.'

Jess could no longer remain silent. 'So in true middle-aged style, the man sees the short skirt, the blonde hair and decides he wants to fuck her!' She said bitterly.

'Jess, shush, we don't want the whole pub to know our business.'

'How long has it been going on?' Jess hissed.

'Two years.'

'Two years! Two years!' Jess repeated not quite able to believe what she was hearing. 'You disgust me, Sam, how can you be having sex with someone and then get into the marital bed with me for two bloody years! By the look of the slag, I could have all sorts of diseases.'

Sam sighed. 'Oh, Jess, I really am *so* sorry. I now realise it was a terrible mistake. I've never stopped loving you – you know that. It was just kind of different with her.'

'What *passionate* you mean?' Jess looked to the sky. 'It was sex, Sam. That was all. Not making love, just pure filthy sex. I think I'd rather you'd had a quick one with a whore if that's what you were looking for.'

'You're not going to leave me,' Sam demanded. 'I was actually going to go and see her Monday and finish it for good.'

'Oh nice,' Jess said sarcastically. 'Keep wifey happy with the birthday party and then trot round to Fanny Ann's and tell her it's over afterwards. Great! Well do you know what – I'm glad she had the balls to tell me, because you never would have!'

'And if you'd never have known. Everything would still be perfect Jess. Like it was yesterday, and the day before that. I know now it is *you* I truly love. I was just stupid – blinded by the excitement of it all.'

'So have you spoken to her?' Jess enquired.

'Yes I have, I've told her in no uncertain terms it's

over.'

'And how about when you go into work? When she's flashing her young pins and those baby blues at you, how exactly are you going to resist her?'

'Jess, I've said it's you I love and I don't want to ever see her again like that. I *promise* you with *all* my heart.'

'So where do we go from here?' Jess said practically.

'We go back home and see our beautiful baby girl and we start afresh. I will do anything, and I mean anything to make you happy, Jess.'

'Oh God, Sam, I can't believe you've done this. I've never felt happier and now I feel so betrayed. It's worse because I've always trusted you. I did have my suspicions just recently but then thought that you would never, ever be capable of doing something like this. Look, Sam, I'm not ready to go home and start playing happy families. I need some time to think about what is best for me and especially Freya.Freya adores you, but I'm not sacrificing my happiness just for her.'

'Jess, please don't talk like this. I don't see why you should have to leave me. We've got so much history; we *can* and *will* work this out.'

They go into Sam's Mercedes, in silence. Jess had agreed that they would go back home, and she would pack a bag for her and Freya. The pair of them would then go and stay with Phoebe for a few days.

'Mummy!' Freya ran out to the drive to meet her. 'I missed you. Did you have a luverley party?'

'I did, angel. Are you OK?'

'I'm fine thanks. I've been playing hospitals with Charlotte.'

Charlotte walked through to the kitchen to greet her. She gave Jess a kiss on the cheek and gripped her hand in a supportive, womanly way. 'Happy belated birthday, Jess.' The doorbell rang. 'That'll be my wayward boyfriend.' Charlotte stated.

'I'll get it,' Jess insisted, and on opening the front door, her legs suddenly turned to jelly. Because, there, standing right in front of her was none other than Mister Daniel Harris.

Chapter Seven

'Oh my god, Jess, what did you do?' Phoebe opened her eyes in amazement at Jess's revelation, as they sat at the kitchen table.

'Well I was so shocked to see him just standing there in front of me, after all those years, I blushed to the tips of my roots, and started to stammer like a teenager.'

'Did anyone notice?' Phoebe interrogated.

'Luckily, I don't think so, I pretended to drop the tea towel I was holding on the floor and managed to recover myself.'

'Did he look the same?'

'Well he's put on a bit of a weight. His hair is cropped closer to his head as he's receding a bit but apart from that it was the same old, or should I say young Daniel Harris.' Jess hesitated and continued. 'Of all the chances of him meeting Charlotte though, isn't that the weirdest thing?'

'So did you find out how they met and everything?' Phoebe should have been a CIA agent!

'God no, I was so shocked to see him, plus, I was still reeling from Sam's confession that I was actually quite rude. Sam went into overdrive about Lemon, as he obviously knew Dan from old. So, I just sneaked upstairs, packed a bag for me and little miss, and here I am.'

'What, you didn't even say goodbye?'

'I just said it was good to see them and I hoped we'd meet in better circumstances next time, and that was it. It was weird though, as Dan actually didn't seem that shocked to see me.'

'Well you know what he's like – nothing fazed him

before did it? He probably thought nothing of it.' Phoebe chipped in and continued. 'Oh, Jess. What a shocker of a weekend, poor you.'

'I know, I could be front page in the tabloids today. Husband sex betrayal shocker with young office nymphet. Ex toy boy of wife now dating adulterer's daughter.'

Phoebe laughed. 'It actually really is quite unbelievable. Anyway how you feeling about Sam? I'm so sorry.'

'Oh, Phoebes, I'm just so hurt that it's been going on for so long. I feel *so* betrayed. It's worse, because really, Sam isn't like that. He's never been a womaniser. Part of me realises it was my fault in a way. He's so gentle, and the fact that he succumbed to that dirty bitch... well it makes my stomach churn.' She took a slurp of tea and carried on. 'And if he says he's never going to do it again, I actually will believe him. You know what he's like, Phoebes. He will keep his word I know he will. God, it's so difficult!'

'You really have to weigh up the pros and cons here, Jess. You've got a lovely home and Freya adores you both.'

'I know, I know. But somehow if I stay with Sam I do think I'll be settling. I know I'm fifty now, but I'm a young fifty. I'll meet someone else I know I will. But, I want the *passion* back Phoebes. We've never had that, and do you know what, now this has happened, I think it gives me good reason to take the chance, and find complete happiness – without Sam.'

'Jess, please don't be rash. You'll be in effect a single parent. Sam is a good man. I'm sure you can work it out. Look why don't we get an early night, we're all tired and emotional today. You can think again in the morning.'

Jess walked slowly up the stairs and peeped in at Freya, who was sleeping soundly on a camp bed next to Annabel. She got herself ready for bed, feeling completely torn. She lay awake for hours, worried not by her precarious future with Sam but instead by the intense feeling that she'd had at the sight of Daniel Harris.

Chapter Eight

Dan lay awake. He was sorry that he had upset Charlotte. It was the first time in their month as a couple that they had stayed together and he had not made love to her. She had been confused, as he hadn't been able to give her a good enough reason as to why he didn't want to. He remembered back to when they first met. He had spotted her on the dance floor at The Breakhaus, and was enthralled by her free-spirited exuberance as she threw back her head and danced, as if no one in the world was watching her. It was an added bonus that she was the marketing manager for a group of clubs in London, one of them being The Breakhaus, and he now could gain free entry to them all.

He'd been adamant that he wasn't ready to meet her family yet. She had however been insistent that she couldn't miss her step-mother's birthday party and it was an ideal opportunity for him to 'grow-up' and 'mingle with the fold'. It wasn't until they had had a conversation on Friday night that he had even bothered to ask about her father.

'What, Sam Beresford who used to run Lemon Events?' he had exclaimed.

'Yeah why, do you know him?'

'I used to work for Lemon about ten years ago, how random is that?'

'You may know his wife then, as she used to work a lot for Lemon too back in the day. Her name's Jess, I think her maiden name was Morley.'

Dan had nearly choked on his Stella. 'No, no, I don't

recognise the name,' he had lied.

Since he had left Jess it had taken Dan a lot longer to get over her than he thought it would. He's had a couple of long-term relationships and, during each one, he had always remembered Jess's words that he would find it hard to match a passion like they had. She had been right. He had been happy, but had never felt completely fulfilled. He had kept her email address and mobile number for years but, when about four years ago he had decided to see how she was doing, both no longer existed.

'So, now you know who you are going to visit, you have to come,' Charlotte said smugly.

Dan had smiled. 'Yes, Charlie, I do have to come.'

Chapter Nine

Sam paced the garden waiting for Jess and Freya to return from Phoebe's. He heard the distinctive engine of the Golf and literally ran to the front door to greet them.

'Daddy!' Freya ran into his arms.

'Hello, angel, did you have fun with Auntie Phoebe and the girls?'

'It was great, we went swimming and to the park and to feed the ducks.'

'Well that's lovely. There's a little surprise for you in your bedroom if you want to go up and look.'

Freya dropped her coat on the floor and ran upstairs. Sam had bought her a painting set, and had laid it all out on a plastic sheet in her bedroom. He knew it would occupy her for a while so that he and Jess could talk in private.

'Wow, thanks, Daddy,' She shouted down to him.

Jess attempted a smile at Sam.

'I've made some tea,' he announced. 'And got you some carrot cake.' He knew that was Jess's favourite. Sam flitted around Jess, not quite sure where to put himself.

Jess broke the silence. 'Look, Sam, this is all lovely thanks, but come on let's sit down and face the issue shall we?'

They took their tea through to the living room and sat looking out over the garden. Jess took in the surroundings of their lovely home and took a deep breath. 'Look, I've been thinking long and hard and,' her voice faltered, 'I need more time to think Sam. I'm going to go away for a while, just to clear my head. I do love you without question. But what's happened has rocked me to the core. I don't know if I will ever be able to trust you again.'

Sam's eyes filled with tears. 'Jess, I will do anything, and I mean literally *anything* to make you stay. I promise faithfully that I will *never*, *ever* betray you again.'

Jess looked at the kind and thoughtful man opposite her. She could actually even forgive him for what he had done. He had obviously also felt the lack of passion in the relationship that she had done, the only difference was he had acted on it. She knew that he meant what he said, but there was something in her that knew she wasn't prepared to settle right here, right now, for what she had already.

'Oh, Sam, I'm not saying this is goodbye forever. Let me just get my thoughts together. Everything is just so raw and I don't think I could bear for you to even kiss me at the moment, let alone touch me.' The physical reality of what Sam had done suddenly hit her and she felt repulsed.

'Where are you going to go?' Sam enquired nervously.

'Well, I think it makes complete sense for me to go down to the Cornwall cottage. I'll be alone, it won't cost us anything, and I can't think of a better place for me to sort my head out.'

'So far away,' Sam stated.

'We couldn't be much further away than we already are,' Jess said sadly.

'And what about Freya and school?'

This was the hardest part for Jess. 'Well...' She faltered and then spat out the rest of her words at a hundred miles an hour. 'I hope you don't mind but I thought that you could look after her for a couple of weeks, so that she doesn't miss any school, and then it will be the Easter Holidays. If I'm not ready to come back then, she can come and stay with me at the cottage.'

Sam actually seemed relieved. With Freya staying with him, he didn't feel that all was lost. Jess would have to come back. 'I know I won't be able to stop you, Jess, so

OK. I'm more than happy to care for Freya. I will make sure I always take her and pick her up from school, so she doesn't feel that her life is too disrupted. Now shall you tell her or shall I?'

'Let me pack first, and then we can sit down with her together.'

'So you're going today?' Sam said surprised.

'Yes,' Jess replied strongly.

Freya walked down the stairs, covered in paint.

'Just look at you,' Jess said and laughed. 'Now go back up there and wash your hands, and then come back down. Daddy and I need to talk to you about something.'

Freya sat fidgeting. She was a wise little girl and Jess knew that they would have to tell her the truth.

'Now, Freya. Mummy and Daddy need to spend a little bit of time apart.'

'Why?' Freya twiddled with her hair.

'Because we aren't friends at the moment and if we spend some time apart then we will be again.'

'What like Lucy at school's mummy and daddy you mean? She told me they weren't friends because her daddy kissed her mummy's sister.'

'Well not quite like that,' Jess half smiled at Sam.

'Her mummy told him to go away and never come back again and he did as he was told.'

Jess raised her eyebrows at Sam and continued. 'So I'm going to Cornwall for a couple of weeks and we will see each other in the Easter Holidays.'

'Cool. Does that mean I miss school then, Mummy?'

'No darling,' Sam interjected.

'Mummy's going to Cornwall and Daddy is going to look after you here until Mummy comes home.'

A look of defiance struck Freya's face. 'But I want to go to Cornwall.'

'You can't, darling. Mummy needs time away and you need to go to school.'

The little girl started to cry and Sam pulled her towards him to hug her. 'Now kiss Mummy goodbye, Freya.'

'I hate you!' Freya screamed at Jess as she struggled from Sam's arms, ran upstairs, and slammed her bedroom door. Jess went to run after her.

'Leave her, Jess, I'll calm her down,' Sam said softly.

Jess picked up her case, tears now streaming down her face. 'Goodbye, Sam.'

'Call me when you get there.' He managed a smile, even though he was dying inside.

Chapter Ten

It was raining and dark when Jess arrived in Looe. She pulled up alongside the harbour wall, wound her car window down slightly, and felt soothed by the sound of the waves crashing on the beach in the distance. The cottage smelt musty as she pushed open the heavy door and she shivered with cold. She wished she'd called ahead to Mrs Treboric to get things ready for her arrival. But she'd left in such a hurry that it would have been too late. She switched on the hall light and immediately turned the heating up high.

The drive down had seemed to take forever. She felt distressed at leaving Freya in such a state but knew she had to do this. All of their futures depended on the outcome of her decision. She called Sam to let him know she'd arrived. Freya had settled and gone to bed. The little girl had told Sam that she'd been sorry for what she'd said and would talk to Jess in the morning. Relieved at this news, Jess ran herself a deep bath and lay back and relaxed. She loved it here. She immersed herself in the soothing, warm bubbles and suddenly felt sad. She vividly remembered the day that she and Sam had viewed the cottage, to buy it. They'd been so excited, just a month into their marriage to find such a perfect, romantic retreat for the weekends. Once it was theirs, during the summer, they would leave work on a Friday night and meander their way down to the south west. Heady days would be spent whiling away hours at various beautiful beaches. They would then stock up with all their favourite food and drink and spend the evenings on their terrace overlooking the sea, chatting about everything and nothing. Jess thought back fondly to these times. They were good times. In fact, she thought, there had never actually been any bad times with Sam, until now. Life was always constant. Not a rollercoaster of regret, like she had so often experienced in her twenties and thirties. She ran in some more hot water and lay back, comforted by the silence. Here she was though, at fifty-years-old, actually craving to get back on that rollercoaster, or was she?

'Oh I don't know,' Jess said out loud. 'What is it that I want?'

After a good sleep, the next day she awoke to the sound of gulls and the sun streaming through her bedroom window. It was really quite lovely not to have to worry about anyone but herself for a change. She drifted back to sleep for an hour, got up, dressed, and walked down the steep hill to the shops to get some supplies.

She felt refreshed as she sat back on the terrace, eating her scrambled eggs on toast and supping her tea. Freya had called to say sorry and that she was looking forward to the Easter Holidays. She knew that her mummy would never leave her and that was enough for her now. Just as she was washing up, Jess's mobile rang.

'Hey, Jess, it's Charlotte'

'Hiya, Charlie. Look, I'm so sorry about Sunday.'

'Don't be silly, Jess. I totally understand. Of course my loyalties lie with Dad, but really I don't know what on earth he was thinking.'

'Well, yes.' Jess wasn't quite sure what to say.

'Anyway, I'm calling because I want you to know I'm thinking about you.'

Jess was desperate to mention Dan and then thought against it.

Charlotte continued. 'I will help Dad out with Freya when I can, although I'm going out to LA for a few days with work tomorrow.'

'Ooh get you, international jet-setter and all that,' Jess joked.. 'He's not a bad man, Jess, and he does love you dearly.'

'I know that and I'm sure we'll be fine but I just need this time out.'

'I totally understand. You take care now.'

'I will, thanks for your kind words. Oh, and have fun in LA.'

Chapter Eleven

'Matt mate, it's Dan, how's it going?'

'OK, mate, all good. Just putting the twins to bed, they've been driving us mad, hang on.' Matt shouted up the stairs. 'Sara, be back up in a sec, just going to have a quick word with Dan.'

'Don't let me forget their birthdays will you?' Dan stated. 'You really shouldn't have chosen me as their Godfather; you know how I always forget everything.' Matt laughed as Dan carried on. 'Mind you, I bumped into Jessy Morley at the weekend, I remembered her for sure.'

'Jess, remind me?' Matt scratched his head. 'Oh God yeah, the older bird from years ago. How come?'

'Spookily, she's now married to Charlie's old man!'

'Bloody hell, how random is that, what's she like now?' Matt asked with interest.

'Still fit actually.'

'And would you still?'

'Actually mate I can't believe how I felt about her when I saw her. It was weird. Like it was only ten minutes ago, not ten years.'

'But surely you wouldn't go there again? I mean from how you talk about Charlotte, I thought she was your perfect match.'

'She is a great girl, but there's just something about Jess, it's hard to explain. Charlie's old man had just been caught with his pants down, so it all kicked off at the weekend.'

'You do pick 'em, mate. Shit, Sara's shouting for me, I'd better go and help her. How's Evie by the way?'

'Thirteen going on twenty-three, you know what she's like. Anyway, you get on. I'm over your way in a couple of weeks. I'll drop by.'

'Be good to see you, mate. Laters.'

Chapter Twelve

Jess finished watching the lunchtime news, wrapped herself up warm and put on her walking boots. She loved the walk across the cliffs from Looe to Polperro. In fact she knew the path like the back of her hand as she and Sam had followed this route hundreds of times. She stopped periodically to sit on benches along the route, taking in the magnificent views of the ocean as she did so. Gulls winged overhead and she noticed a myriad of colours in the hedgerows, as flowers started greeting the spring sunshine.

For the first time in a few days she felt calm. It had been the best thing she could have done, to remove herself from the situation at home totally. She admitted to herself that she and Sam had fallen into a comfortable rut. She realised that the lack of passion in their relationship wasn't just down to him. Since Freya had been born, no longer did she seduce him. More often than not she was so tired, that she would just pull on her old pyjamas, grab her book from the bedside table, read, and go to sleep. However, this still didn't excuse the fact that he had betrayed her. She wished that they had talked, before he had decided to stray. She didn't even realise he was feeling frustrated, but that was Sam all over. He would go with the flow. If she had asked him to make love to her he would have done, but damn maybe he should have tried to instigate it for once, rather than go elsewhere. She cringed at the thought of him sleeping with Cherry. But on the other hand was quite relieved. From first impressions, Cherry didn't seem a particularly nice person. At least she could be comforted that he had gone with her just for sex and nothing more. It almost seemed more acceptable somehow.

She walked down into Polperro harbour, relishing the quietness and picture postcard beauty of this pretty village. She adored Cornwall out of season. In a week, she knew this would all change. The Easter throng would be among them and you would have to almost push your way through the streets, amass with ice cream wielding children and would-be surfers. She walked slowly around the tiny streets, marvelling at the pretty little cottages with their tiny front doors and different coloured window frames. She moseyed amongst the many gift shops with their meaningless trinkets and checked out fleeces in a surf shop. It had seemed like years since she could actually just be her. Jessy Morley, independent woman and not part of a family. Although she already missed Freya, she had to admit she liked the feeling.

She bought a freshly made pasty and a cup of tea and wandered to sit up on a high bench, overlooking the harbour and the ocean. She looked down and noticed a good-looking lad tending to a fishing boat. He must have been in his mid-twenties. He was weather beaten and very handsome. The same age as Dan when she had met him, she thought. She had tried to push recent thoughts of Dan to the back of her mind. When they had split up all those years ago, it had taken her a year to get over him properly. Sam's attentiveness and love had obviously helped. Throughout that year, she would wish with all her might for him to come back into her life. In fact, she would have done literally anything to just spend one more night with him. She had been so completely head over heels in love with him then. The only time since she had really thought about him was when she fell pregnant with Freya. She realised then it was how it was supposed to be, with a supporting loving husband and secure environment for a child. She also did think with sadness that she would have had a brother or sister for Freya if she hadn't gone ahead with the termination. But in fate's path, Sam may not have even entertained seeing her if she had somebody else's child. Who knows how her life would have panned out then? Yes, Dan had made her heart flip when she had seen him last week, but she had now put that down the shock of it. She probably wouldn't even see him again now. Charlie was always so busy and, with the relationship being so new, anything could happen. If things developed, she would worry about it then. In her eyes, she had no unfinished business with Daniel Harris. He had been the love of her life but that was that. He was history. It was her life, here and now, that she needed to address.

She walked down through the gloaming, from her hilltop viewpoint, and decided to have a drink in The Blue Peter. A fire was roaring as she entered the cosy pub and it brought back memories of her and Sam snuggled together, drinking Scrumpy and finishing many a Sunday paper crossword in here. For old times sake she ordered a pint of the strong cloudy cider and found a comfy seat in the corner, in which to read her acquired newspaper. There were just a couple of ruddy-faced locals drinking at the bar, and a flea-bitten black Labrador lying down in front of the fire. She relished in the anonymity of it all. It was eight o'clock by the time she had finished her second pint of Scrumpy and she actually felt quite drunk. She shakily walked to the bar.

'Another?' The young Dutch barman enquired. Jess in her drunken haze thought that she recognised him, then realised he looked very much like Jurgen whom she had met all those years ago in Australia. 'No', she laughed. 'I'd better not; you'll be fishing me out of the harbour; that cider of yours has gone straight to my head.'

'Oh go on, it's nice to have some fresh female company this time of year,' the Jurgen lookalike urged.

Jess could sense him flirting with her and it flattered

her greatly. 'Maybe another day.'

'Do you live here then?'

Jess could feel herself looking the young man up and down.' No, I've got a cottage in Looe, just having an extended break.' She went to walk out of the door and suddenly turned back. 'Look at me, I came up to the bar to ask if you had a taxi number and off I go wandering out the door.' The charm of the young man had thrown her off kilter slightly. It was wonderful to feel fancied and fancy free.

'I'm doing a split-shift tonight, I could give you a lift at nine if you like?' the young man offered.

Jess hesitated. 'That's really kind of you but I really better be going.'

She got into the taxi. He could only have been late twenties she thought, and was oh-so *very* handsome. She smiled to herself, delighted that she still had what it took. If Sam wasn't to be her future, she knew damn well that the next best thing would be just around the corner.

She lay back in the taxi, feeling slightly woozy. The full moon lit up the harbour. The tide was way out and boats precariously listed, awaiting their watery support. She thought fondly of her trip to Australia and Jurgen. He had been such a gentleman amidst her trauma, and she had never forgotten the romantic words he had said to her as she had walked away from him: You can't stop a river flowing to the sea.

She got out of the car at the bottom of the hill to the cottage, thinking the walk in the fresh air would clear her fuzzy head. As she turned into her quiet lane, she noticed a car parked right behind hers with the lights on. She approached nervously as it didn't seem right somehow. She had a torch in her handbag and held it at the ready. She bravely approached the car and as she did so she heard classical music drifting out from the half open window. In true Charlie's Angels style, she shone her torch right into the would-be offender's eyes.

'Jess, Jess, it's OK, it's me.' Her heart leapt into her mouth.

'Dan? What the fuck are you doing here?'

Chapter Thirteen

Sam lay awake. He found it difficult to sleep without the reassuring warmth of his loving partner. He missed Jess to the core. It wasn't until she had left, that he realised quite how much he loved her and was terrified that she wouldn't be able to see past what he had done. Thank God this was the only affair she had found out about. Why-oh-why had he been so stupid? Jess had been right: sex was sex. It could never compensate for the long lasting love between two people who had grown together. Gaining affections from other women did give him a buzz, but now was the time to break this addiction. He knew he would never be found out about any of the others. He had to start afresh and make a life for just the three of them: Jess, himself, and their beautiful little girl.

He heard Freya stir and got up to check she was OK. He quietly walked into her bedroom and pulled the quilt snugly up to her angelic, sleeping face. She looked so like Jess and had acquired the same determination and feisty spirit of his attractive wife. Tears sprung to his eyes. What if Jess did decide to leave him? His life would be so empty without her. And as for even contemplating not being able to see his growing daughter every day, that was just too much to bear. It had been hard enough to be a part-time parent to Charlotte, without having to go through that pain again.

He went downstairs and poured himself a brandy to help him sleep. He replaced the decanter on top of the drinks cabinet and went to his study to recline in his comfy leather chair. Soothed by the brandy and reassuring thoughts that everything would be OK he dozed off.

A loud crash woke Sam with a start. 'What the hell was that?' he said aloud. He jumped up and was alerted to the sound of somebody running fast across the gravel drive. He ran to the front door to see what was going on and suddenly felt a searing pain in his foot. He switched on the light, blood was pouring from his heel and he was standing in a pile of shattered glass. The porch window was smashed to pieces and lying in the hallway was a brick.

'Daddy, Daddy!' Freya began to cry. He quickly wrapped a tea towel around his foot, soothed Freya with the pretence she had had a bad dream, and debated whether he should phone the police or not.

Chapter Fourteen

Jess opened a bottle of red wine, grabbed a couple of glasses, and walked into the sea-facing lounge. Dan was lying down on the couch. 'Make yourself comfortable,' she said sarcastically, but with smiling eyes. 'Here.' She handed him a glass of wine. 'So, what brings you all the way down to the depths of Cornwall then, Mr Harris?'

Dan sat up and took a slurp of wine. Without flinching he automatically replied. 'You do.'

Jess looked directly at him. He was undoubtedly still a handsome man. She shifted in her armchair and as much as she didn't want to, she had to admit that she still fancied him.

Dan looked his former lover up and down. 'You look great, by the way, Jess. Not a day over forty. Thought you might have let yourself go a bit, what with being married for all these years.'

Jess lifted a cushion as if to throw it at him. 'God, age hasn't mellowed you has it, you're still a cheeky bastard.' She stood up and walked over to the window, the full moon lit a pathway right across the sea. With her back to him she blurted. 'This is too weird, Dan, I'm not sure if I like it.'

He walked behind her and gently put his arms around her waist. The same electric current from all those years ago, went right through her. Frightened by the strength of her own feelings she snapped. 'No, Dan, get off me.' She pulled away from him and sat back down on an armchair. 'How did you know I was here anyway?'

'Charlie told me. She's in LA at the moment. She'd

mentioned the name of the cottage and that it was in Looe, so I figured all I had to do was get here and ask some local where the cottage was.'

'Very clever of you,' Jess uttered. She was secretly bowled over by the fact that he'd made such an effort to come and see her.

Dan continued. 'I thought this was the perfect place for us to meet. I knew you didn't have Freya, Charlie is away, and Alex has got Evie all this week.'

Jess softened at the mention of Evie. 'Bless Evie, how is she?'

'She's great. A little madam but then she always was. She's kept her lovely blonde hair and is a clever little thing, well not so little now. I can't believe she's at secondary school. Here, I have a photo of her on my phone.'

Jess looked at the smiling Evie and felt sad. 'Do you know that I missed her more than you as time went by? I imagined her going through the different stages of her life, starting school, making friends – everything in fact.' She took a slurp of wine and then said candidly, 'You can't imagine how much you hurt me, Dan. I actually thought I'd *never* get over you.'

Dan bit his lip. 'I was so immature then. Now I am older I really can't believe I was so insensitive. To keep coming back to you when I was never sure what I really wanted, I realise now how hurtful that must have been for you.'

'So please tell me it was worth my pain. No disrespect to Charlie, but you obviously have yet to find what you were looking for?' Dan lay back on the sofa.

'I had a wild year after we split up. I hit the drugs hard, when I didn't have Evie obviously. I found it hard to strike up a relationship for a while. Anybody my own age couldn't hack having a toddler in tow at weekends and I didn't want to find anyone who wanted to settle down, as that wasn't what I wanted at all. He smiled at Jess and continued. 'Do you know what as time went by, I also was aware that I never ever said I loved you? You were so right, after I'd had a couple of long-term relationships I realised that I actually did love you. I loved you very much, Jess.'

Jess pushed her hands through her hair and let him continue. 'What we had was really special. I just didn't see it at the time. And now here I am, ten years on and who's the fool? It's certainly not you. Just look at you, Jess, you are simply beautiful. You have a gorgeous daughter and a dream country cottage. You won't ever have to work again. Your life is sorted.'

'Let's not forget the little matter that my loving husband has just had an affair with someone young enough to be his daughter though,' Jess quipped.

'I thought I wouldn't mention that,' Dan replied.

'Well there's no point in not, that is the reason why I'm here after all,' Jess said indignantly. Dan continued. 'And how are you feeling about it, it must have been quite a shock?'

'Look, Dan, I don't wish to be rude but I actually don't want to discuss it with you. But no my life is not sorted. In fact I'm at a major crossroads in it.' She stood up again, and then blurted out of the blue. 'God, this is surreal. You're sleeping with my husband's daughter. You shouldn't be here, Dan. It's not fair on anyone.' Dan was not perturbed by her outburst.

'That's all it is, Jess. I'm sleeping with her. I can't see a future for me and Charlie. She is so ambitious and at last I feel I'm ready to settle down. I want to create a proper home for Evie. She's been pushed from pillar to post for so many years. It may be too late, but I owe it to her to offer her stability throughout her teens at least.'

'Well all I can say is you better tell Charlie how you feel sooner or later. She's a great girl, and I won't have you hurt her. There's no point stringing her along and it's certainly not fair on Evie. Time goes so fast, Dan, you'll blink and suddenly *you'll* be fifty!'

Dan didn't reply, just lay back on the sofa again and flirtily asked, 'So did you do any more drug taking, Mrs Robinson?'

Jess smirked and replied almost insolently, 'No.'

'Are you sure?' Dan cocked his head to the side and smiled.

'I didn't actually. It was weird I always associated them with you and I never ever felt the urge to take them again. It was like it was our fun and I didn't want to share those feelings with anyone else.'

'That's sweet,' Dan replied.

'Well don't flatter yourself too much,' Jess continued. 'I wasn't in a crowd who'd ever even consider taking Class As. So even if I'd wanted to I wouldn't have had a clue where to get any anyway.'

'There goes my feisty Mrs Robinson, glad you're still you, Jessy Morley.'

'I'm still the same bloody person, Dan. Nobody can change that much surely.' She stood up to walk to the toilet and missed her step. 'Whoa, I'm a bit tipsy.'

'You've only had a couple of glasses,' Dan said surprised.

'Actually, I had two pints of Scrumpy in the pub earlier. By the way, do you still like Stella?' She suddenly enquired.

'Oh yes indeedy. Why have you got some?'

Jess shook her head and laughed, suddenly remembering their first encounter. 'Did you notice my car by the way?' she asked.

'I can't believe I didn't mention it – it is class, Jess. I'd love to have a go in it tomorrow, if that's OK?'

'God, remember that first time you took me to the pub in that old GTI of yours. I thought I'd die of fright.'

Dan laughed. 'I can't believe you didn't say anything.'

'I didn't want you to think I was acting my age now did I?' Jess smiled.

'My driving was appalling then. I actually had an accident soon after we split, nothing major, but Evie had been in the car and it did make me realise that I had to slow down.'

'Thank goodness for that,' Jess added.

'Remember the Soho Hotel too?' Dan continued reminiscing. 'Jess, all I can say is that was a young boy's dream. Bling hotel and a sexy older woman. Gave me years of masturbating material that did!'

'Daniel Harris, what are you like?'

'Shit sorry, Jess, that was rude.'

'I like rude,' she replied without hesitation. Then in realising just what she'd said, she darted off to the loo.

On her return, they finished the bottle of wine and pulled the sofa forward so they could both see the sea. 'I take it you've booked a hotel?' Jess questioned, knowing full well he hadn't.

'I was err, hoping I could crash here if that's OK with you, I take it you have a spare room?'

They both laughed and Jess continued. 'Yes I have a spare room and you are sleeping in it tonight, without question.' His leg touched hers by accident and the same old electric current buzzed between them both.

'Did you feel that, Jess?'

'Feel what, Dan?' She lied and moved down to the end of the sofa.

'Oh nothing, it must have been a spider of something running over my hand.' Dan lied.

Jess laughed to herself. He had been so honest up to now. She knew that she couldn't let her heart rule her head. She had to be realistic. And, despite Sam's betrayal, she was still a married woman, and Dan was seeing Charlie. There were so many people's feelings at stake, people who she really cared for. They sat in silence for a while, taking in the moon-drenched vista, until Dan piped up.

'Have you got any more wine?'

'I have but I shouldn't, I'm drunk already.'

'Oh go on, Jess, have another glass.' Dan urged.

Here we go again Jess thought and prayed again that there were no gas ovens around!

'Let's play scrabble,' Dan suddenly suggested catching sight of the battered box on the bookshelf.

'I never thought I'd see the day.' Jess laughed. 'Daniel Harris, playing scrabble! I've got dominos for after too if you want,' she said and got up to get another bottle of wine from the kitchen.

She returned minutes later to find Dan, lying on his back and snoring loudly.

She moved the coffee table back to allow room for the duvet she had placed over him and, as she did, she saw the Scrabble letters he'd arranged on the board: *I think you're grand x.*

Chapter Fifteen

Jessy awoke early and after phoning to check if Freya was OK, immediately dialled Emma's number. 'Oh my god! I don't believe it,' Emma exclaimed. 'What on earth are you going to do?'

'I'm going to do nothing, Em, absolutely nothing. There is no way he is going to walk right back into my life after all these years.'

'But how do you feel about him now, Jess? It must be really strange to see him again.'

'I still fancy the arse off of him. He still excites me. He still makes me laugh. It's as if he's never been away, but I can't play at life anymore, Em. I've got to think clearly about where I see my life heading. It's not a bloody dress rehearsal anymore. At my age I'm not prepared to go into anything lightly and make a mistake.'

'And how are you feeling about, Sam?'

'Oh, Em, I don't know. I do love him, but having this time out and seeing Dan again has made me realise that my relationship is actually quite dead.'

Emma's sensible voice soothed Jess. 'But, you could make the decision that Sam isn't who you want to spend the rest of your life with, and not find anyone else who offers you the passion you are craving?'

'I've thought about that too, but I'm not prepared to accept a life of mediocrity I want more.'

'Oh, Jess, I hope you are making the right decision. I really think you should take some more time to decide. And if you *do* leave him, what about Freya?'

'She will come with me of course.'

'Oh, Jess, that will break Sam's heart and Freya's for that matter.'

'Em, don't even go there, I feel all confused again now.'

Emma swiftly changed the subject. 'So is Dan going home today?'

'I've got no idea; he fell asleep before we discussed that.'

'And, Jess, what if he hadn't fallen asleep, do you think you'd honestly be in bed alone now?' Jess went silent for a minute. 'Oh, I don't know. I'm so glad he did fall asleep. I have to resist him, Em. I have to.'

The friends said their goodbyes, just as Dan came bounding up the stairs. He knocked on the door and Jess pulled the covers up to her neck. 'Enter,' she said humorously.

Dan poked his head around the door and grinned. 'Morning, Mrs Robinson, can I take a shower?'

Chapter Sixteen

Jess shrieked with delight as Dan drove her car, roof down, around the tight country Cornish Lanes. She felt like Grace Kelly, in her makeshift serviette scarf. Dan had pulled on her favourite pink beanie hat. They kept glancing at each other and laughing out loud at their tasteless apparel, as the wind whipped their reddening faces.

'Where are you taking me?' she shouted above the engine.

'Wait and see.' Dan smiled.

They drove for what seemed liked ages and arrived in the seaside town of Polzeath. They parked up and walked towards the sea. The rugged, sweeping beach was amassed with surfers in wetsuits enjoying the first rays of spring sunshine.

Dan took Jess's hand. 'This way I think.'

They started to walk along the coastal path towards Daymer Bay.

'I just love everything about Cornwall,' Jess exclaimed. 'Just look at these views. It really is something else.'

They stopped along the way to take in the beautiful vista, chatting and laughing as they went. Dan had decided that he was going to go home the next day as Charlotte was flying back from LA. Jess too would leave, as Freya was breaking up from school and she wanted to be there to pick her up. Although Freya would have loved to come down to the cottage, Jess wanted to speak with Sam face-to-face, sooner rather than later.

'So what are you showing me?'

'Look over there.' Dan pointed to their right.

In the distance she could see a beautiful little church that looked like it had almost sunk into the grass. Jess smiled broadly. 'You are so clever remembering that I like old churches, Dan.' Dan began to reel off some facts about the church.

She'd forgotten that he always seemed to know something about everything, and she was impressed. 'This, my dear Jess, is St Enedoc's Church. Evidently in the 19th century it is reported that the church was almost completely swallowed by the sands of Daymer Bay. Apparently the only way into the church was through the roof! And because of this the church gained the nickname of Sinking Neddy.'

'You should be a tour guide not a web designer.' Jess laughed.

'Follow me.' Dan carried on. 'I've got something else to show you.'

They went through the old gate to the churchyard and Dan pointed to his right.

'Oh my God, I don't believe it. I didn't know John Betjeman was buried here!' Jess shrieked. She looked at his ornate black headstone with interest.

'Jess, stop blaspheming, we are in the Lord's garden,' Dan said with mock authority and they both sniggered like school children. 'Betjeman was renowned for saying his biggest regret was not having enough sex, how terrible would that be?' Dan smirked at Jess. He then proceeded to climb a grassy bank, and begin his recital.

'Love-forty, love-fifty, oh! weakness of joy,

The speed of a swallow, the grace of a boy,

With carefullest carlessness, gaily you won,

I am weak from your loveliness, Jessica Ann Morley.'

'Pot Pouri from a Surrey Garden!' Jess exclaimed laughing out loud at his clever interpretation. 'I cannot believe you just remembered that, Dan Harris.'

'I doctored it especially. I know how much you love your poetry, and especially Betjeman.'

Jess looked at him and bit her lip, there were tears in her eyes. She took his hands in hers, looked up at him, and their eyes met. They kissed passionately and Jess melted into his embrace. After what seemed like for ever, Jess broke away.

'This is the most romantic moment I have ever had in my life,' she said softly.

Dan put his hands on her shoulders and looked her right in the eyes. 'I love you, Jessy Morley.'

They ran up the path to the cottage, like excited school children. As soon as the door shut behind them Dan grabbed Jess and began to kiss her passionately. She pulled away.

'No, Dan, let's not.'

'Why, Jess, it seems like the most natural thing in the world? I know now that I love you. I love you with all my heart. In fact if I'm honest with myself I actually don't think I've ever stopped loving you.'

'Dan, I still feel for you too, I fancy you to the core, but it's just not the right time now.'

'I don't understand, Jess, I really don't.'

'Look, I'm still married.'

'Jess, your marriage is a farce; your husband has been having an affair!'

'Yes I know that, but two wrongs don't make a right, Dan. I have to talk to Sam. I need to do what's right by him and Freya, and I don't want us jumping into bed with each other on a whim. It will cloud my judgment.'

'So you might stay with him, is that what you're saying?' Dan asked quietly.

'I need to talk to him,' Jess said, not wanting to admit to herself or Dan her final decision, of which she now actually wasn't sure of. 'And *you* also need to decide if you really don't want to be with Charlie,' Jess stated.

'I made my mind up on that, the minute I set eyes on you at your house the other week,' Dan instantly replied. 'Jess, *it* makes sense, *we* make sense. We're *better* together.'

'Dan, please give me some time and respect, to sort my feelings and my life out.'

Dan took a deep breath. 'OK, Jess, I will do anything to make life easier for you and I mean that.'

They slept in the same bed, cuddling up closely all night. Ten years ago this was all that Jess had hoped for. Ten years on, she now wasn't sure if Daniel Harris was the man to make her life complete.

Chapter Seventeen

The next day Jess waved Dan off, vowing she would get in touch with him when she had sorted everything out. She began her long drive home. She couldn't deny that she loved being with Dan. They had funand there was a massive attraction, but she felt she had almost been cheated by him too. After the way he had broken her heart. She felt it was too easy for him to just walk right back into her life after all this time, and pick up where he had left off. Ten years was a long time. People changed, and just because hewas ready to settle down with her now, it didn't mean that she was.

She pulled into the familiar drive of Fern Cottage. The shrubs seemed greener than when she had left, and daffodils sang their yellow praise all over the front garden. And, there, swimming in the large pond to the right of the house, she suddenly caught sight of two swans. It was at that split second she made her decision.

She could see Sam hovering behind the glass in the front door. As soon as she opened her door he came running out and gave her a tentative kiss on the cheek.

'Good to have you home. Freya is more than excited that you are picking her up from school.'

'I can't wait to see her,' Jess enthused.

Sam carried her case in and made her a cup of tea, so obviously wanting to avoid the subject of them for as long as he could. He had decided not to mention the broken window incident for fear of worrying her. The police had done as much as measure the footprints and said they were small, so had just put it down to a childhood prank.

'Cottage in good order?' he questioned.

'Yes, all was fine. It really is so lovely down there.'

'Maybe we should spend the summer down there? You know how much Freya loves it.' Sam looked at Jess questionably.

She looked at her caring husband. She *did* love him dearly. Passion, or no passion, this man had given her so much, including the child she had always longed for. She took in her surroundings. They had worked hard to build this home together, and she soaked up the comforting familiarity of it all. She had been offered sex on a plate by Dan and had decided not to take it. Maybe it wasn't passion she longed for after all. Maybe Dan Harris had been the catalyst for her this time. The catalyst to make her realise that Sam Beresford actually *was* the man she wanted to spend the rest of her life with.

'You didn't answer my question, Jess.'

'Sorry what did you say again?'

'About going to Cornwall in the summer?' Sam reiterated.

Jess got up from the kitchen chair, walked over to him, and placed her arms around his neck. 'How long have we got until I pick Freya up?' She questioned.

'Couple of hours,' Sam replied. Jess took his hand. 'Let's go upstairs husband.'

They made love, like they had never made love before. With Sam leaving Jess panting for them to do it all over again.

'Wow,' he exclaimed as they both lay back exhausted on the bed.

'Sam Beresford, I love you, and yes we can go to Cornwall for the next fifty summers if you want to!'

Chapter Eighteen

Jess set off alone to collect Freya from school. She called her sister from the car. 'Phoebes it's me, I'm back. It's just a quickie as I'm on my way to collect Freya.'

'Hiya, have you seen Sam then?'

'I'm staying with him, Phoebes.'

Jess heard Phoebe's obvious sigh of relief at the other end of the phone. 'I am so pleased, Jess. I didn't want to be too blatant, but I did think you would be a fool not to. To start again at your age wouldn't be a picnic, I'm sure of it.'

'I am going to make this work, sis, I *really* am. We actually just had the most amazing sex. I think one of us needed to have an affair to shake us both up.'

'I am so happy for you, Jess.'

'Right I better pick up little madam, I have missed her so much.'

'OK, catch up soon.'

'Mummy!' Freya came charging out of the school gates. 'I love you more than a trillion million dollars.'

Jess caught her in her arms and swung her around. And I love you more than Barbie's pink car.' Jess enthused.

Once Freya was safely strapped in the back seat, she piped up, 'Are you going to stay at home now? Daddy cried once one night. He said he had a fly in his eye but I know it was because you went away.'

'Yes, angel, Daddy and I are going to stay at home forever and ever now.'

They all ate Freya's favourite tea of fish fingers and chips, then played whatever games she wanted to play until she fell asleep in Jess's arms on the sofa. Sam looked at Jess and smiled. 'All our own work that one. I think we did a good job don't you?'

Jess smiled back at him. 'Yes, Sam Beresford, I think we did.'

Jess lifted Freya gently, to carry her up to bed.

'Shall I follow you up?' Sam winked.

'I think it would be rude not to,' Jess whispered and smiled.

Jess's coughing woke her up. She opened her eyes and realised she couldn't see. She felt a burning in the back of her throat. She sat bolt upright in bed, then screamed in realisation of what was happening.

'Oh my, God, Sam the house is on fire!'

They both leapt out of bed and rushed to the door to go and get Freya. Their bedroom was filled completely with smoke. They were both coughing violently.

'Jess, quick as you can, dampen some clothes, we need to put them over our faces.'

Sam dialed 999. Jess did as she was told. She was even more filled with panic when she heard Freya was shrieking in the next room. 'Oh my God, Sam,' Jess screamed. 'Quick!'

Sam ran out into the landing. Flames were furiously licking against Freya's door.

'No!' Jess screamed. 'No!'

'Freya, stay where you are darling, Daddy's coming to get you. Lie flat on the floor, angel, don't panic, it's OK.'

'Daddy, I'm frightened!'

Knowing he couldn't reach his screaming daughter from the inside, Sam ran back into his bedroom and leapt out of the window, on to the flat roof of the kitchen and then down to the ground. He rushed to the shed, grabbed the ladder and extended it to reach Freya's room. Jess ran into the en suite bathroom, put a damp towel against the door, opened the window, and stuck her head out. Sam smashed Freya's bedroom window and lifted the terrified child onto his shoulder. The fire engine belted into the drive, a fireman leapt out and ran up the ladder to meet Sam and the sobbing Freya halfway. 'My wife,' Sam wheezed. 'Back window.' He could barely speak.

On hearing Jess's screams, another fireman had already run around the back of the house with a ladder and whisked her down on his shoulder. With sirens blaring, an ambulance arrived. A group of villagers crowded outside the drive.

'Anyone else in there?' The leading fireman asked.

'No, we are all out,' Sam shakily replied. He was ashen. He looked back at their once perfect cottage, and saw that the flames were now licking out of the roof. He knew that it would be a shell by the morning. He walked slowly over to the now sobbing Jess and Freya, who were being tended to in the back of the ambulance.

'My beautiful girls, it's OK we are all safe. I love you both so very much. Everything is going to be just fine.' He then suddenly grasped his chest and fell to the ground.

'Sam, oh no! *Sam!*' Jess screamed. 'Somebody do something!'

Chapter Nineteen

Jess felt like she was having a really bad dream and in a minute she would wake up. The doctor said that it had been a massive heart attack and there was nothing more anyone could have done to have saved him. Jess knew this was true as the ambulance men had done everything possible at the house, and on the way to the hospital, to try and revive him.

Jess and Freya had both been checked out in case they had inhaled too much smoke, but were both fine. Phoebe and Glen had come immediately to collect Freya, and had booked into a local hotel so that Jess could be with her as soon as she left the hospital. Karl was going to drive up in the morning.

'Can I see him?' Jess asked the kind young doctor.

'Of course you can,' he replied softly.

Glen motioned that he would wait outside for her. Sam was still in a cubicle in Accident and Emergency. She was glad that she didn't have to go to the mortuary. She didn't want to even imagine her loving, warm husband in such a cold, austere environment. A nurse held her hand as she walked over to him.

He looked so peaceful, beautiful in fact, like a sleeping child, as if all the stresses and strains of the past few weeks had just drifted away from him. Jess kissed his cheek.

'Goodbye, angel. Thank you for making me so happy for the past ten years.'

Silent tears fell slowly down her face. She didn't want to leave him. The thought of never seeing him again made her go weak at the knees and the nurse helped her to a chair. She too had tears in her eyes. 'I'm so sorry,' she said. 'Can I get you a drink?'

Jess, now in complete shock shook her head. Glen walked in, took her arm, and gently said, 'Come on, Jess, let's go and see Freya now shall we?'

Chapter Twenty

The next week was a complete blur for Jess. Karl, Phoebe and Glen helped with the formalities that follow a death and set about arranging the funeral. Hope's large sprawling house, a pay-off from one of her three marriages, was in the same village that Jess lived. She had gamely turned it into a base to save them all staying in a hotel. Emma had brought a case of Laura's old clothes for Freya and, as they were the same size, another case of her clothes for Jess. Jess's dad and Maria had come to visit. They were both devastated, saying more than once that they wished it had been one of them, as Sam still had so much life to live. Charlie, who too was completely inconsolable, had also stayed over for a couple of days to assist.

The day before the funeral Jess said she felt strong enough to go and visit the house. As Karl drove tentatively into the drive Jess began to sob. Her beautiful home was now a charcoaled wreck. Blackened roof struts pointed to the sky and the acrid smell of smoke still seemed to linger in the air. Police tape banded the whole of the outside, so Jess could not even have gone into take a look inside if she wanted to.

She walked around the back of the house and was strangely comforted to see that Sam's precious study and the kitchen had been barely touched by the fire. As she walked back around the front of the house, a police car pulled into the drive. Karl made the officer in the passenger seat aware who they were. Then quickly, whilst Jess was out of earshot said, 'She doesn't know there's an investigation going on, mate, so be gentle with her.'

The policeman nodded knowingly. 'We do have to speak to her though, sir. Mrs. Beresford is obviously key to our enquiries. We will contact her straight after the funeral.'

'Madam.' The driver of the car addressed Jess. 'We are so sorry to hear of your sad loss.'

Jess smiled weakly. 'Thank you.'

As the police car pulled out of the drive Jess began to cry again. Karl held her. The realisation of what had happened hit her, and through rattled sobs she tried to unravel the events of that night. 'Oh, Karl, I've just remembered something so, so terrible.'

'What, darling? Whatever it is, it's OK.'

'It's so not OK, Karl, I remember taking the battery out of the smoke alarm for one of Freya's toys about a month ago and forgot to replace it.'

Karl held her tightly.

'It's all my fault,' she wailed. 'If I hadn't been so stupid, we would have awoken earlier, the house would have been saved and Sam probably wouldn't have died.'

She became hysterical and dropped to her knees on the gravel, holding her head in her hands. 'It's all my fault, it's all my fault.'

Karl gently lifted her up and held her close. He couldn't bear to see his dear sister in such a mess. He had to release her guilt. 'Jess, darling Jess, it wasn't your fault. The fire brigade had to call in the Fire Investigation Team. They think the fire was caused deliberately.'

Jess suddenly stopped crying. 'What do you mean? Arson? Why? Who would do such a thing?'

'They've reason to believe that something containing petrol was pushed burning through the letterbox,' Karl advised. 'Even if the smoke alarm had gone off, the blaze would have taken hold so quickly it probably wouldn't have made that much difference.'

'God, this gets worse, Karl, I really do feel like I'm living a nightmare. Who on earth would want to harm any of us?'

'I really don't know, Jess. Now, come on, let's get back to Hope's. There's nothing we can do here at the moment.'

As Jess walked to the car she kicked something with her foot. She looked down, it was the pretty wooden Fern Cottage sign, that she had had made especially for Sam the week they moved into the house. It was only slightly burnt on the corner. She picked it up and held it to her chest. 'Oh, Karl, I am going to miss him so much.'

Chapter Twenty one

Hope had to park miles back down the church lane as there were so many cars parked on verges. She had been making last minute preparations to make sure that her house was perfect for when everyone arrived back there for the wake. Jack-the-Lad had stayed behind so that there was somebody there when the first mourners arrived.

She kicked off her black stilettos, put them in her hand, and ran as fast as she could, laughing to herself that she would probably be even late for her own funeral. As she breathlessly reached the church gates, she noticed a lone figure standing there, crying.

She recognized the mini-skirted blonde from Jess's fiftieth. 'What the fuck do you think you are doing here?' Hope spat.

'I had to say goodbye, I loved him so much,' Cherry sobbed.

'Well I suggest you turn right around and say your goodbyes somewhere else.'

Hope was furious and continued venomously. 'How dare you even think of coming here, when my beautiful friend is about to bury her husband.'

Cherry saw red. 'Well maybe you want to tell your beautiful friend that I wasn't the only one. It's common knowledge at work that he'd been shagging half of Berkshire before he ever set eyes on me.'

Hope was incensed. 'You are one sick slag, now piss off and go and crawl back under the rock you came from.'

'You'll see,' Cherry shouted after Hope as she ran into the church. 'You'll see.'

Chapter Twenty two

Jess looked beautiful in her black fitted-suit and veiled pillar box hat. Her swan-shaped crystal brooch caught the light and glistened momentarily as she strode confidently to the front of the church. She held her head high and cleared her throat.

A swan swam across my heart today
I felt its beautiful wings touch my soul
It's going to nest there now
A loving creature to draw strength upon

Her voice began to wobble. 'Sam, you are and always will be my swan.'

She walked back to stand with her family and held Freya's hand tightly. She had to remain strong for their gorgeous little girl today. She even managed to belt out Sam's favorite hymn 'Jerusalem' at the top of her voice.

Hope ushered everyone in through her large hallway to her spacious living room. Jess had been strangely comforted at just how many people had been at the church. She knew Sam was a popular man, but the number, mainly women, who attended his funeral, surprised even her. It seemed weird that just a short time ago, most of these same people were here celebrating her birthday, and it made her realise again just how precious life was.

She wondered who on earth would have a grudge against them, enough to endanger their lives. She tried to put this thought to the back of her mind. She had to get through today and then she could worry about that.

She could then also concentrate on the massive decision of where she and Freya would live. Sam would obviously have made sure they were insured but, with an investigation going on, she had no idea how long it would take to get the money through and the house rebuilt.

Hope had taken control of organising the wake, ably assisted by Jack-the-Lad. Young male waiting staff dressed in smart black T-shirts and trousers attended everybody's needs.

'Only Hope could manage this.' Jess smiled to herself. She poured herself a large glass of wine and looked for Freya. She was happily playing outside with Annabel and Laura. She noticed the nosey village set, eating their way through the buffet and gossiping in the corner. One of them apprehended Charlie as she walked by. 'Your poor mother, such a dreadful loss.'

'Yes, we are all going to miss my dad very much,' Charlie answered. She walked over to Jess and put her arm around her shoulder. 'Hey, Jess, how you holding up?'

'I'll be glad when everyone goes home to be honest,' Jess replied weakly. 'Don't they say that once the funeral is over you can start moving forward?'

'I'm missing him already,' Charlie said bluntly. 'He should be here, charming his guests as usual.' Tears pricked her eyes.

'Is Dan here?' Jess enquired. 'I didn't notice him in the church.'

'Yeah, he's here. He stood at the back. I said he was stupid, but he said he didn't feel right standing with the family. He's just parking his car up the road, as the drive is so packed.'

This was the first time that Jess had actually thought of Dan since she waved goodbye to him at the cottage. She was so glad that she had made the decision to stay with Sam, and that the last night she had had with him had been so loving. He would have died knowing that he was forgiven and she wanted to be with him. She wanted his eldest daughter to know this too. 'I made peace with your dad before he died, Charlie. I realised that I did want to spend the rest of my life with him. Sod's law, his big bloody heart had to give out.'

Charlotte smiled through her sadness. 'I'm so pleased, Jess. You must feel better for that?'

'I do. Are you staying tonight by the way?'

'Yes, I can actually stay for as long as you want me too. I've taken a week off work, so if you want me to hang around until you've sorted yourself out a bit I'm happy to. Dan and I came in separate cars, as he has got to leave early for work in the morning.'

'Thanks, Charlie, I appreciate that. Now go and get yourself a drink.'

Jess took a deep breath as she saw Dan approaching her. She noticed how handsome he looked in his black suit and tie. He gave her a kiss on the cheek and she was sure she noticed tears in his eyes.

'Hey, Jessy, what a shitter.'

She laughed quietly at him. 'Only *you*, Dan, could come out with something like that.'

'I'm here for you, Jess,' he hesitated. 'As a friend that is, and I mean that.' He lovingly put his hand on her shoulder. Jess was touched by his sincerity. She thought it was weird, the different reactions death caused. It did make everything else pale into insignificance. She had always been a fixer of the attitude that there was a solution to everything in life. But death was one thing that not one person had any power over. Sam was gone, gone forever. No second chances to say goodbye. De nada. Nothing. Extinct. Obsolete. Gone.

'Come and see us soon,' her dad said as he started walking to the taxi that Jess had arranged for him and Maria. Even though she had already said goodbye once, she ran over to him again and gave him a big hug and a kiss. 'I love you both very much, now look after yourselves.' She gave Maria a kiss on the cheek.

'We will do,' Maria replied shakily.

After about three hours, everyone, apart from the main crew who were staying at Hope's had left. 'I'm exhausted,' Jess said, and flopped down on one of Hope's big sofas.

'Let's get drunk,' Karl suggested.

'Oh I'm not sure,' Phoebe added sensibly.

'Yes, let's,' Hope retorted. 'There's loads of wine left.'

'Have you got any Stella?' Dan piped up which made Jess smile. She stood up.

'I'm just going to check on Freya and then I'll be right down. Can someone pour me a large glass of red please?'

She walked slowly upstairs. She had put Freya to bed earlier, and tried to explain again that her daddy had gone to see the angels. She pushed open the bedroom door quietly. Annabel was reading quietly with a torch under her covers. Jess mouthed hello and smiled at her. She kissed her sleeping child on the cheek. Freya stirred and said sleepily, 'Is Daddy still seeing the angels, Mummy?'

'Yes he is, darling girl. Now you go to sleep ,' she whispered.

Jess closed the door behind her, stood on the landing, and began to sob until she didn't think she could possibly cry anymore. Phoebe, realising Jess had been gone a long time, went up in search of her. 'Oh, Jessy darling, come here.' She took her grief-stricken sister in her arms.

'What am I going to do?' Jess wailed.

'It's OK, we're all here to help you,' Phoebe soothed. Everything is going to be alright, I promise you.'

'God, I wish Mum was here,' Jess said quietly, almost crushing her sister.

'So do I.' Phoebe was now crying too.

Jess, suddenly back in fixer mode, pulled herself together. 'Right, well we're not going to get anything done grizzling our eyes out on the bloody landing are we?' She grabbed her sister's hand. 'Now, let's go downstairs and get pissed.'

Between them Jess, Phoebe, Glen, Hope, Jack-the-Lad, Karl, Shelly, Charlie, and Dan managed to polish off ten bottles of wine. After their seventh rendition of 'Angels' they all decided that bed was the only option and staggered up the stairs. Jess bumped into Charlie outside the bathroom. She kissed her stepmother on the cheek. 'Dad would have been very proud of you today, Jess.'

'Thanks for saying that, Charlie, you weren't half bad yourself.'

'Goodnight,' they both slurred in unison.

Jess had been in bed about half an hour when she heard a light tapping on her door. Despite being drunk, she had so much running through her mind that she just couldn't sleep.

'Yes,' she said quietly.

'Budge up, Mrs. Robinson.'

The room was pitch black, but she instantly recognised the delectable smell that was Daniel Harris.

'What about Charlie?' Jess whispered.

'She's sound asleep,' Dan whispered back.

He found her lips and Jess kissed him back passionately. Her breathing fastened. They explored each other in silence, bringing each other to heights that only they could reach together. Jess felt no guilt. To make love to someone, whom she knew now loved her so much, seemed somehow right at this moment in time. Life was short.

Chapter Twenty three

The next morning Hope dished out painkillers with coffee as everybody's heads were throbbing. Jess was thankful that Georgina and Annabel were keeping Freya amused, as she couldn't bear to have to deal with her child's matter-of-fact questions this morning.

Charlie appeared in the kitchen, her eyes were red from crying.

'Oh, Charlie, darling, come and sit down,' Jess said caringly.

'God, why is life so unfair,' Charlie cried. 'He was such a good man.'

'I know, angel, I know.' Jess held her to her chest.

Hope looked on. She had been bothered by Cherry's comments at the church gates. Yes, a woman scorned would be angry but why should she lie about Sam's other indiscretions. She looked at Jess's tortured face. She had never kept anything from her friend in her life, but this was something she would never be able to tell her. She knew Jess's heart was breaking anyway. What good would it be to drag up even more hurt? She decided at that moment that Sam Beresford's sordid secrets would remain buried along with him, the bastard!

Everyone ate their toast and then milled off to their respective rooms to pack. Jess and Charlie sat alone at the kitchen table in silence until Charlie put her head in her hands. 'Oh, Jess.' She started crying again.

'It's OK, darling,' Jess soothed, suddenly feeling complete guilt, for her actions of the night before. 'I told Dan it was over this morning,' Charlie wept.

Jess felt a sudden surge of relief and panic at the same time. Last night had felt so right with Dan. However, in her sobriety she realised the enormity of what she'd done in sleeping with him. She knew she wasn't Charlie's actual mother, but the devastation of her actions could have been huge.

'Dad's death just made me realise that I can't just play at life anymore. Dan's a great guy and we've had amazing fun together, but there is just something missing. If you asked me what that missing something was, I wouldn't be able to tell you but what I do know is that he's not the one.

She looked directly at Jess and questioned. 'You just know don't you, if they are the one I mean?'

'Yes you do,' Jess said quietly. 'You really do.'

Chapter Twenty four

Freya was insistent that she spent the rest of the Easter holidays with her cousins. Phoebe gladly agreed. She knew her dear sister needed time alone to sort her affairs and, if Freya was kept busy, she wouldn't think so much about Sam not being around. Jess was just sitting quietly at Hope's having a cup of tea when there was a sharp knock on the door. It was the police. 'Mrs. Beresford, we'd be really grateful if you could come to the station with us.'

Jess obligingly agreed. She wearily got into the police car and thanked the officers for giving her some time, before the obvious questioning had to ensue. She sat in their dank interview room and felt desperate. Who'd have thought that her life would come to this? Her husband dead, her home burnt down. She was now, at fifty years-old, a single parent.

'Can you think of anyone at all who would have a grudge against you or your husband?' The older of the two policemen asked matter-of-factly. He had a large moustache that moved as he talked and it actually made Jess want to giggle.

'No,' she replied immediately. 'I still think it must be a terrible mistake. My husband and I lived a quiet, normal existence.'

The policeman was stony-faced.

'My husband was a good man,' she added, suddenly for some strange reason, feeling guilty herself. He placed some folders in front of her on the desk and then held a key up in front of her. 'Do you recognise this key, Mrs. Beresford?'

She took it from him and fingered it.

'It was in a folder marked 65 Eastern Street,' the Policeman added.

'Eastern Street, I'm not aware of that address and a key is a key to me. But I guess it could be an office key. The barn where Lemon Events is situated had lots of doors,' Jess stated.

The policeman looked at her with pity and produced yet more folders. 'I really don't like to do this to you, Mrs. Beresford, but we went to the Eastern Street address. It was indeed an office, rented by your husband. We recovered the following from one of the filing cabinets there.'

He put a bright pink folder in front of her. 'Take a look.'

Jess quizzically opened the folder. It was full of greetings cards. She curiously looked inside one of the cards.

Darling Sam, you were so right Gay Paris is all it's cracked up to be. Thank you for a wonderful time. All my love Sabine

And then another.

If this is just a starter as you implied, I cannot wait for the main course. Kisses Julia

She was white by the time she read the third one

Sam Beresford, Monte Carlo and me! Let's live the dream! Love always Susie xx

'It's fine everybody has a past,' she said nonchalantly, wanting for some reason to stick up for her obvious philanderer of a dead husband.

'I'm so sorry, Mrs. Beresford, but some of the cards were in envelopes, the postmarks go back over the past six years. We also found a numerous receipts for hotels and restaurants around Europe.' The moustache continued moving.

'He always travelled with work, that's why you found

those,' Jess replied, not wanting to believe what she was hearing.

The first policeman continued. 'We are obviously making enquiries with all of the ladies concerned. We have reason to believe that your husband's philandering could well have led to the incident at your house.'

Jess felt sick. She sighed deeply in disbelief. The second policeman, who was young enough to be her grandson suddenly piped up. 'I'm afraid we have more bad news for you.'

Jess sunk into her seat, how on earth could she possibly hear something worse than her husband being a serial adulterer?

'Due to the serious nature of the incident at your house, we obviously had to go through all of your husband's paperwork and computer files. I'm afraid it's come to light he didn't renew the buildings and contents insurance for Fern Cottage this year.'

Too busy bloody shagging probably, Jess thought. Then, realising the seriousness of what they were saying, she tried to think clearly. 'OK, but I know he had life insurance policies. He did always joke saying that if something ever did happen to him, I would be more than fine. These policies will cover the house rebuild, I know they will.'

The policemen looked at each other and Jess could tell there was worse to come.

'What? What now?' she spat. 'Please don't tell me they were invalid too?'

'Not invalid, Mrs. Beresford, but it has also come to light that your husband had a tendency for gambling over the internet. He was in a lot of debt, so much so that his company is now in liquidation. Whatever money he did have will go to pay his debtors. I'm so sorry.'

Jess thought she was going to be sick. Not only did she now not have anywhere to live, she had no money to live on. Angry that these two total strangers had delivered such devastating news in such a cold fashion, she jumped up and slung her handbag over her shoulder. 'Take me home please.'

Chapter Twenty five

Hope was waiting for her on her return. She could see the look of pain on her friend's face. 'Come on in, angel, tell me all about it.'

'I need a drink, Hope.'

'Tea?'

'No, something much stronger!'

Hope poured Jess a large scotch, and they made their way out to sit in her rambling garden. It was a beautiful sunny April day. Hope's youthful, bare-chested gardener was down by the orchard on a sit-on mower. Jess laughed momentarily. 'Only you could pick a gardener like that, Hope Adams!'

Jess began to enlighten her friend about the events at the Police Station. 'No wonder there was no bloody passion in our relationship, Hope. He didn't just have that one indiscretion. The bastard has been shagging around for years. Good old quiet Sam, I really can't believe it. But I saw it today, the evidence right in front of my bloody eyes. Hundreds of thank-you cards from women sucked in by his charm.'

Jess took a large gulp of her drink. 'How could I have been so stupid, Hope?'

'What a complete bastard,' Hope stressed and continued, her voice softening.

'Jess, I have something to tell you and I really don't want you to be cross that I've kept it from you.'

'Hope, nothing will ever shock me again, what it is?'

'I bumped into Cherry at the funeral.'

'You *what*?'

'You know I arrived late, well she was outside the gates crying. Anyway she spat out that she hadn't been the only one, and Sam was renowned for having affairs.'

Jess sat back and closed her eyes, Hope continued.

'I hope you're not cross at me for not telling you, Jess, but I think sometimes there are some things that are better left unsaid. I knew you were hurting anyway and I just didn't see the point in making you feel worse.'

Jess waved her hand in the air. 'Hope, I'm not cross with you, don't be silly. I know now anyway don't I? I am bloody furious with him! Not to mention the embarrassment of everyone at Lemon knowing what he's been up to and little old wifey at home has had no fucking idea, for years! I am stunned, Hope. In fact I am so upset that I never thought I'd ever say anything so awful, but I'm glad he's dead! How dare he? How dare he put me and Freya through this?'

Jess stood up and starting pacing around the garden table. 'The police said that they think that the fire was probably started as a result of his philandering, and this makes total sense. One of these women must have eventually snapped. They saw him coming back to his beautiful home and family without fulfilling any of his empty promises to them.'

'Or it could have been one of their husband's or even brother's, you just don't know?' Hope added.

'God I didn't even think of that. Just how many lives did Sam Beresford ruin I wonder? It just is too disgusting to think about. I cannot believe I could misjudge somebody so greatly. Hope, I am never ever going to trust a man again.'

'Oh, Jess, I'm so sorry.'

'And it gets worse, in fact the women issue shouldn't be top of my list, I am also stony broke.' Jess continued with tears in her eyes. 'The bastard was not only spunking our money up the wall on all of his whores. He also was evidently gambling our hard earned cash on the internet.' Jess sat back down. 'I am dumbfounded, Hope, completely blown away that I could live with a man for *so* many years and have no clue of this at all. I thought I was an intelligent woman.'

'Oh, Jessy, you *are* an intelligent woman. He was just a scheming rat. I really can't believe it of Sam either though,' Hope replied amazed.

'Well they say the quiet ones are always the worst.' Jess attempted a smile.

'Shit, Jess, what are you going to do?'

'Well I can sell his Mercedes as I'm more than happy to trot around in my old GTI. I've got a bit of my own money but not enough to live on for more than six months. I'm going to have to get a job.'

'What about the Cornwall cottage?'

'I'm assuming that will have to go as well. The situation is dire by the sound of it. I called Jonathan, our solicitor, before I got here, to see exactly where I stood. His hands are tied, until the police release all Sam's files of course. He said it may take up to two weeks.'

Hope put a supporting arm on her friend's leg. 'He must have had a will surely?

Jess shrugged. 'I guess so. I'll know when I meet with Jonathan. It will be interesting to see just what he intended to leave, if anything.'

'You know you can live here for as long as you like, Jess,' Hope piped up.

'I'm so grateful for that, Hope, but I actually need to get some independence again. I was going to look at renting a small place in the village if I can, just for six months, and then see where life takes me.'

Hope lowered the parasol and they sat in silence for a while. Jess began to mellow as the whisky took effect. 'Hope,' she said quietly. 'There's something I haven't told you either.'

'Go on,' Hope urged.

'I slept with Dan on the night of the funeral.'

'No way, Jess!'

'So I'm just as bad as Sam really. My husband is barely cold, both his daughters are asleep next door, and there I am shagging another man: his eldest daughter's lover!'

'Oh, Jess, don't beat yourself up about it, you were both drunk.'

'That had nothing to do with it, I wanted him, Hope. I wanted to feel close to someone when everything else seemed to be ebbing away in my life.' Jess drained her glass of Scotch.

'Anyway,' Hope tried to pacify her friend. 'Charlie dumped him the next day anyway, didn't she? So actually there is no harm done.'

'I suppose. Dan really loves me now you know. It's so weird how the tables turn over time isn't it?'

'How did you leave it with him?' Hope asked.

'I didn't. We did the deed, both of us woke up with a start at 4 a.m. and he scurried back to Charlie's room. We didn't have time to talk.'

'And how do you feel about him now?'

'I guess I do love him, but I'm just not in love with him anymore.' Jess tipped her head back and rested it on the garden chair. 'I'm knackered. This afternoon has really taken it out of me. If you don't mind I'm going to go up for a nap.'

'Of course, darling, you go up,' Hope said kindly.

Jess headed up to her room and flopped on the bed. Tears filled her eyes and she looked up at the ceiling for what seemed like hours, furiously mulling over how on earth Sam could have got away with all that he had done, for so many years.

Chapter Twenty six

Freya was back at school. Despite asking every other day if Daddy would ever come home from where the angels were, she had actually dealt with Sam's death remarkably well. Jess on the other hand wasn't coping so well. Her emotions were so mixed that sometimes she actually felt like she was going mad. She missed Sam. But the Sam she missed was the person she had fallen in love with, not the person he had become.

She felt deep anger that he had betrayed her so greatly and had in effect got away with it . She wished nothing more than for him to walk through the door so she could ask him what on earth he had been thinking. She wanted to punish him, shout at him, and beat him with her fists. She would have left him for sure if she had found all this out, and that would have been the biggest punishment of his life. She was right to forgive the one affair thinking that maybe it was half her fault, but countless affairs, that was just inexcusable. And, as to leave her and Freya in financial dire straits, that was even more unbelievable.

She was just about to ring the letting agent in the village when her mobile rang.

'Jess, it's me.'

'Oh hiya, Dan.'

Dan continued. 'Just phoned to see how you're coping? I would have called before but thought you would need some time for reflection?'

'I'm not coping well actually, Dan. It's not every day you find out your husband is a serial philanderer and one of his ex-lovers or their associates tried to kill you in a fire.' She tried to joke but her voice was cracking. 'I don't want to go into detail now, Dan, but he's also left me with no money or home. The house wasn't even insured.'

'*Fuck*, Jess, that's terrible. I am *so* sorry.'

'I guess you're OK about splitting with Charlie?' Jess was happy to change the subject from her woes.

'You know I am. I knew it wasn't right before she did.' Jess heard him take a breath.

'Jess?'

'Yes.'

'I was wondering if we could meet. I really want to see you?'

'Oh, Dan, I've got so much going on at the moment.' Dan went silent and Jess gave in. Maybe a bit of light relief was just what she needed. 'When were you thinking?'

'This weekend actually. Alex is going on holiday with Evie, so I'm free as a bird. Is that OK with you?'

Jess went on. 'Perfect actually. Freya is going to stay with Emma and Mark for the weekend. They thought I could do with a break.'

'Are you still staying with Hope?'

'Yes I am, until I sort out renting a place.'

'OK, pack a bag and don't forget your passport. I will pick you up at ten. Jessica Morley, I am taking you away!'

'But.'

'No buts, just be ready.' Dan hung up.

Chapter Twenty seven

At exactly 10 a.m., Jess heard the crunch of tyres on Hope's drive. She looked out of her bedroom window and saw Dan's brand new Golf GTI. She checked herself in the mirror. Her dark jeans and a crisp fitted white shirt accentuated her figure. She was glad that despite the entire trauma she had been through she still looked passable, albeit a little tired. Dan greeted her at the front door.

'Hey, Jess, you look lovely.'

'Thank you. Now just where are you taking me, baby boy?'

They smiled at each other and Dan felt like he had been whisked back ten years. 'It's a surprise, so please don't ask me again.'

Jess settled back in the comfy leather seats of Dan's new car. She thought back to the time he had picked her up in his old boneshaker all those years ago and laughed to herself. The banging rant of Eminem had been replaced by Classic FM, and there wasn't even a sniff of marijuana. They drove through the Berkshire countryside until they hit the M4 and headed London bound. Terminal Two Heathrow Airport was its usual chaotic self, but as usual with Dan by her side she felt completely at ease.

'I'm so excited,' Jess enthused and squeezed Dan's hand as the plane roared into the sky.

Jess loved Prague. She had run an event there before Freya had been born, and was enthralled then by the buzz of the Old Town Square at night and the cobbled streets with their beautiful architecture. They checked into a hotel just off of the Old Town Square, dumped their bags and set out to explore.

'We have to go to Charles Bridge,' Jess exclaimed.

'Whatever you wish, Mrs. Robinson,' Dam smiled.

It was a beautiful sunny day and the Vltava River twinkled in front of them.

Dan took Jess's hand as they began their stroll across the bridge. She marveled at the impressive statues that lined the route. They mingled among the various stalls that were selling jewelry, pictures, and various keepsakes After a while Dan broke their silence.

'Now, did you know?'

'Probably not, so go on tell me an interesting fact, Mr. Harris. I know there's one coming.'

They both laughed as Dan continued. 'Well the bridge's construction started in 1357 under the auspices of King Charles IV and it wasn't finished until the beginning of the 15th Century. It was originally called Stone Bridge or the Prague Bridge but has been the Charles Bridge since 1870. There are 30 statues on here in total.'

'Dan, sometimes you worry me, I really don't know where you store all of that useless information you come out with.'

They found a bar at the end of the bridge and sat outside taking in the vista.

'What's your poison, Ms Morley?' Dan took Jess's hand.

'Well if they do Stella it's got to be that – don't you think?'

She smiled broadly. Jess took a sip of beer from her pint mug and for the first time in a long time felt really relaxed. 'I haven't got a lot of money for this weekend, Dan.'

'Shush.' Dan lifted his hand up to stop Jess saying anymore. 'I said this weekend was my treat and I won't have you even mention it again.'

Jess felt like a scolded child, but secretly *loved* the fact that Dan wanted to look after her. 'OK, well thank you. I really do appreciate it.'

They finished their beers and Dan leaned across the table and clasped both of her hands in his. 'Has anyone ever told you, you really are quite beautiful, Jessica Morley?'

'I've lost count.' She laughed.

Dan got up to go the toilet. Jess studied him as he returned to his seat. He hadn't really changed that much at all, apart from a slight beer belly and his hair receding. He still had his youthful exuberance but did look his thirty-four years. She had to admit that she still really did fancy him. The sun set over the bridge and Jess felt like she was sitting in the middle of a picture postcard.

'What a lovely way to spend a Saturday night,' Jess stated after a while.

'This is so not it though, Ms Morley. Come on let's go, I've booked us a restaurant for dinner.'

They sat at a table overlooking the river in the exquisite eatery that Dan had chosen. The waiters, smartly dressed in black, tended to their every need as the delectable cuisine was served course by course. Jess finished the last mouthful of her main course.

'That was to die for. Well done, Mr. Harris, on your choice of venue, I might have to employ you to run some events for me.'

Dan laughed. 'It's a pleasure, Ms Morley.' He then became more serious. 'Look if you don't want to talk about anything regarding home then tell me, but what exactly are you going to do? – Will you have to start working again?'

'I will, but in a way I'm quite glad. What with Freya being at school and me now being alone I really could do with something to stimulate my mind. I was actually thinking of putting the writing course I did when we split up to good use.'

'Cool, well that's positive. What sort of writing do you think?'

'Do you know what? I haven't even thought about it, but maybe initially I will just send some topical articles off to various magazines and see if any of them are interested. I'm not really sure how it works. I need to research it and see what sort of living I could make.'

'Maybe you should write a novel?' Dan questioned. 'I can see it now: Jessica Ann Morley, international novelist!'

Jess laughed. 'I hadn't even thought of that. Maybe I should do an autobiography. The world and God's dog all seem to be writing about themselves at the moment.'

'Good idea,' Dan replied.

Jess continued. 'I've got quite an interesting life story if you think about it. Older woman meets toy boy, he breaks her heart, she meets a serial philanderer, her house burns down and the toy boy comes back.' She paused, laughing.

Dan looked intently at her and said softly, 'And then the toy boy asks her to marry him.'

'How funny would that be?' Jess carried on laughing oblivious to Dan's intentions. Suddenly boosted by the thought of her future, which after two pints of lager and half a bottle of wine suddenly seemed quite bright, Jess felt jubilant. 'Let's go dancing!' she announced loudly, then leaned over and kissed Dan full on the lips.

At midnight they were still only halfway up the queue of Prague's trendiest club.

Every time a bouncer opened the door to let people in, they heard the dance music belt out into the busy street. Behind them was a rowdy stag party.

'Hey mate,' one of the stag party slurred to Dan. 'Good on ya, bringing your mother.' The group all sniggered in unison. Dan's face turned to stone.

'She's not my mother!' he snarled.

Jess was mortified. Near to tears, she grabbed Dan's

hand and marched him back down the street, away from the taunts of the perpetrators. She began to shout at him.

'Whatever you think of me, however good you think I look, face it, Dan, I am still fifty years-old! Maybe you were right all those years ago, how could this possibly work?'

She pulled her hand out of his. 'I want to go back to the hotel.'

'But, Jess, you wanted to dance.'

'No buts, Dan. I have never been so embarrassed in all my life.'

She opened the hotel door and went straight to the bathroom. The reflection looking back at her, if she was really honest, was not that of a fifty-year-old woman, but she had to face it: that is what she *was*. She was middle-aged and yes, she was old enough to be Dan's mother.

Dan was lying on the bed wearing just his boxer shorts, when she eventually appeared from the bathroom. 'Drink?' he asked and smiled.

'I'll have a whisky please,' Jess took off her jeans and lay next to him in her white shirt and sexy white cami-knickers. Dan looked at her and let out a loud wolf whistle.

'Jessica Morley, you are the sexiest woman I have ever met and I mean that.'

'Really?' Jess felt in need of reassurance.

'Yes, you are.'

'Oh, Dan, I always prayed something like that would never happen.'

'Jess, they were just drunk lads and thought they were being funny. You *do not* look like my mother, how many times do I have to tell you that?'

'Oh I'm sorry, Dan. All my life I have always been so self-assured, but finding out about Sam being unfaithful , so many times, has knocked the stuffing out me. I guess it's made me think – what on earth is wrong with me? In fact the same feelings I felt when *you* left me.'

Dan bit his lip. 'Oh, Jess, I'm so sorry I hurt you so badly. I promise to make up for it now.' He leaned over and kissed her tenderly. The electric current sparked between them and she wrapped her legs around his. 'Dan, just hold me.'

Suddenly, Jess started to sob. Dan held her tightly. He pushed her hair out of her eyes, dabbed her face with a tissue, and kissed her forehead.

'Shush now, let it all out, Jess, just let it out. Everything is going to be all right.'

Jess cried herself to sleep with Dan holding her as if she was the last woman on earth. When he could hear her breathing shallow, he leant up on one arm and looked down at her. Without question this was the woman he wanted to spend the rest of his life with and, as he began to drift off to sleep, he started to plan a proper proposal.

Chapter Twenty eight

A week later, Jess nervously pushed open the front door to the solicitor's office. She walked tentatively up the creaky stairs. It always amazed her, that even with the fees that solicitors charged in general, their offices were usually dark and dank with a dying plant in the waiting room. Bennett, Howard and Oswaldson was no exception to this rule. Jonathan Bennett, the Beresford family solicitor, held out a reassuring hand as Jess got to the top of the stairs and greeted her. He was short and slight for a man, standing around five foot eight. He bore a perfect dark ring of hair around his head like a monk. Jessica noticed that he always wore immaculately tailored suits and smelt of a pleasant musky aftershave.

'Take a seat, take a seat.' Jonathan urged in his eccentric manner, as he ushered Jess into his office. His large green felt-covered desk was strewn with papers, and his red velvet curtains had seen better days. Shaking his head, he continued. 'Terrible business, Jess, terrible business regarding Sam, I am so sorry.'

'Yes it was, and still is, Jonathan.' Jess took a deep breath. 'Thank you for your condolences.' She sat down. 'There's no room for sadness now though,' she stated in a matter of fact manner. 'I'm here to sort out my affairs and begin a future for myself and Freya.'

'Yes, yes of course,' Jonathan replied. He sat down opposite her as Jess continued. 'So, were the police telling me the truth? Is it right I have no money to come from Sam?' The solicitor ran his hands over his balding head and replied softly, 'I'm afraid so, Jess. Sam was in a lot of debt and for some reason he stupidly didn't insure the cottage.'

'Too busy doing other things,' Jess said bitterly, cringing at the thought of what those other things might be. She pulled herself together and continued. 'And what about the Cornwall cottage?'

'Now, for some reason I didn't actually deal with the purchase of that one. I have no records,' Jonathan replied. 'Would you like me track down the deeds and any other necessary paperwork?'

'Yes please,' Jess said. 'I think from memory we did have a solicitor in Looe. Sam always used to deal with everything and I would just sign if I had to. I have no recollection of which firm though, I'm afraid.'

'No problem, Jess, no problem at all. Leave that with me.'

'Thanks, Jonathan. That would be great.' She sat back in her chair. 'By the way, did he make a will? It was amazingly something we didn't talk about. In hindsight with a young daughter, I should have insisted.'

Jess could almost see the man opposite her sink under his desk. His left eye began to twitch.

'Are you OK?' Jess enquired.

'I was hoping you wouldn't want to see it.' Jonathan squirmed.

Jess screwed up her face, not knowing what on earth he meant. The troubled solicitor suddenly began to continue really fast, as if what he was about to reveal wouldn't seem quite as bad if he spat it out in one go.

'But legally as executor, even though there is no money at this stage to give to you, of course you must, yes, you must see it.' Jonathan jumped up and pulled an envelope from a filing cabinet.

'Sam was my friend, Jess, but really I don't know what he was thinking. I tried to talk him out of it but he would have none of it.'

Jess was now really puzzled. With trembling hands, the solicitor handed over the last will and testament of Mr. Samuel James Beresford. She read slowly. On reaching the second line her hands began to shake too.

I bequeath sixty-per-cent to my wife, Jessica Ann Beresford. The remaining forty-per-cen, to be split equally between my three daughters – Charlotte Grace Beresford, Freya Ann Beresford and Evie Alexandra Meadows.

In a complete daze, Jess walked down the stairs of Bennett, Howard and Oswaldson's. It was incomprehensible; Sam was the father of Dan's child. How could that be?

She was fumbling around in her handbag, looking for her car keys, when she heard somebody call her name. She looked up with a start.

'Jessica, can we talk?' Jess didn't recognize the greying-haired lady with elfin like features who stood in front of her.

'Sorry, do I know you?'

'It's Alex, Ali Meadows. Please, we really do need to talk'

Chapter Twenty nine

Jess cradled a cup of steaming tea in her hands. She looked around her, and made sure that she didn't know anyone in the village coffee shop. The last thing she needed was anyone knowing any more of her business than they did already. Alex nervously fingered the fake-flower table decoration. Despite her elfin-like features, at forty-three she hadn't aged well. Her now shoulder-length dark hair was streaked with grey. Her frown lines were evident and her lips wrinkly; not helped by a decade or two of cigarette smoking, Jess thought. She wore faded unfitted jeans and a plain black sweatshirt.

'Quite a coincidence, me bumping into the mother of my dead husband's second daughter, just as I'm given his will,' Jess said sarcastically.

Alex shifted in her seat. 'I pretended I was your secretary,' Alex confessed. 'Said I wanted to reconfirm your appointment. I knew you'd be here today.'

Jess raised her eyebrows. 'Quite the mistress of deception, aren't you, Ali Meadows, if that is still your name?'

Alex shook her head. 'No, it's not. I got married. I'm Alex Hargreaves now. Had two boys since we last met.'

'Right,' Jess replied. 'Nice for Evie having two brothers and two half-sisters now.' Jess carried on venomously. 'Well, for your information, Alex Hargreaves, there is no money left for your lovely daughter.'

Alex ignored Jess's comment and brushed her hair back off her forehead. 'Jess, do you mind if I start from the beginning?'

'I'm all ears,' Jess replied.

Alex took a swig of hot chocolate, cleared her throat, and began to tell her story. 'Thirteen years ago, I got a three-month contract to work at Lemon Events. The company was small then and Sam interviewed me. He was flirtatious from day one. In fact for the first two weeks, every evening just as I was packing up my desk, he would ask me to go for a drink with him.'

Jess nodded and said, 'Go on.'

'Well, in the end I relented, went for a drink, got very drunk and slept with him without a condom. Hey presto. Four weeks later, one very stupid pregnant lady.'

Jess actually felt sad. Condom or no condom she knew too well the feeling of finding out you were unexpectedly pregnant.

Alex continued. 'I'd always wanted children and thought at thirty it was a good time to go with it. I knew Sam had money and I would always be all right.'

Whether it was right or wrong, Jess understood why Alex had made her decision. 'And?' Jess urged Alex to continue.

'Sam didn't want to know. He was furious. In fact, he couldn't believe I had been so stupid. My it-takes-two-to-tango speech fell on deaf ears and he was adamant that I shouldn't have the baby. He thought that his reputation as a managing director would be ruined and he didn't want to upset Charlotte or his ex-wife. He said if I did go through with it he would never support me, as he already had to give money to support Charlie. I think he thought that by offering me zero security, I would change my mind and not go through with the pregnancy.'

'Poor you,' Jess softened. 'It makes me realise that he was more of a bastard than I'd ever imagined.

'Anyway,' Alex continued. 'The month I found out I was pregnant, Dan joined Lemon. I really did fancy him and him me. We went on a couple of dates and after that short time I could really see a future with him.'

Jess took a deep breath, not really wanting to hear what Alex was going to say next.

'I told him, that I must have been one of the unlucky 0.1%, or whatever it is, of pill users, where a pregnancy occurs, and he believed it. He actually seemed quite delighted. He was only twenty-one so I guess it all seemed like a bit of a novelty at the time.'

'And what did Sam say?' Jess enquired.

'I told him what I'd done and he said it was a master plan on my part that I could never tell anyone the truth, especially Evie, as he didn't want her thinking he was a bastard. He changed his mind about the money too, knowing that as he was now relinquished of full responsibility he would help me out.'

'Did he ever want to see his daughter?' Jess asked.

'No, my contract ended at Lemon after the three months anyway, so he had no reason to see me. Dan was still contracting for various companies, so Sam actually didn't even know when Evie was born. It was only when Dan decided to go back to Lemon permanently that he started asking questions. He got my mobile number somehow through Dan I suppose, and arranged to start paying £500 a month into my bank account.'

'Poor, Dan,' Jess stated . 'He loves Evie to the core.'

Alex sighed. 'I know he does, Jess, and in my eyes Evie *is* Dan's daughter.

Together or not together as a couple, he is still a brilliant father to her. I guess you know that already?' Alex said knowingly, taking a sip of her now cooling chocolate and went on. 'I was so angry when Dan left me, Jess. Even though I knew our relationship wasn't perfect. With the anger of a woman scorned and all that, I actually did nearly tell Dan about Evie.'

Jess bit her lip and stated, 'I'm sorry you felt pain,

Alex, but Dan did tell me it was over with you before we actually got together. I would never have been party to an affair. These things sometimes happen you know, in the big scheme of relationships and life.'

'I know they do, I'm not stupid.' Alex paused. 'You must think I'm a calculated bitch the way I trapped and lied to Dan though? I know he didn't deserve to be lied to, but I think if I tell him the truth now, it will break two hearts: his and Evie's. With Sam out of the way, no one will ever need to know. My husband isn't even aware. It's just you and me now, Jess, and I really hope I can trust you enough not to tell Dan.I thought you would find out through the will reading today, as Sam had always said he would leave her some money if anything ever happened to him. I wanted to be the first person you saw before you could tell anyone else.'

Jess was upset with Alex for deceiving Dan but actually could see why she had made her decision. She put herself in Alex's position. If the same applied with Freya and her, could she have confessed to Freya that the person she had known as her father for her whole life actually wasn't her father? Her answer would be no. She would not ruin the equilibrium of her daughter's life. There really would be no point.

'Another cuppa?' Alex enquired.

'Yes OK,' Jess replied, wondering why Alex wanted to prolong the agony of her revelation.

'I've something else really serious to discuss with you, Jess, and woman to woman, mother to mother I really hope you will understand.'

Jess wasn't sure how many surprises she could take in such a short time. She took a deep breath and exhaled loudly. 'Just tell me, Alex. I really don't think there is anything that can shock me anymore.'

'I started the fire at your house,' Alex said quietly.

'You what!' Jess exclaimed. She jumped up, scrabbled

for her purse and banged a £10 note on the table to cover their bill.

'Come on, let's go for a walk, I can't talk to you openly in here,' Jess spat through gritted teeth.

Alex dutifully followed Jess out of the coffee shop as she started to rant. 'You are telling me that you put a burning cloth through my letter box? You in effect killed my husband and could quite easily have killed me and my daughter?'

'I honestly thought you were still away,' Alex said, her voice now wavering. 'It was Sam I wanted to hurt, not you, and of course not your daughter. When I say hurt, I don't mean that literally. It was just supposed to be a warning. I threw a brick through the window the week before and he did nothing. I thought that a few flames in the porch would make him realise I meant business. I had no idea that the whole house would go up in smoke.'

'I really don't understand your motive, Alex, please explain: what do you mean by business?'

'I was angry with him, Jess. My husband, Rob, is an entertainer. Work isn't always great. With three children, even with my part-time salary, we live constantly on the breadline. Rob thought I had savings, that's how I got away without telling him about my allowance from Sam. Anyway, the past year, Sam gave me no money at all. He said he was completely broke. Stated it was up to me, after thirteen years, to have sorted my life out. He thought that my husband and Dan should be looking after me. Well, I didn't believe that he could have no money. He lived in that beautiful house and had two beautiful cars. I knew he had thrown the elaborate party for you for your birthday, as Dan had mentioned it.'I was also annoyed that Dan was seeing Charlie. Not, of course, because I was jealous in any way, I love Rob very much. It just almost seemed incestuous somehow, that he was dating Evie's half-sister, and neither myself nor Sam would be able to say anything about it.'

They walked as far as the park and took a seat on a bench.

'Oh, Alex, I can see why you were angry, but do you realise the implication of what you've done? It's arson. It's a really serious offense. You've burnt my beloved house down. You brought on Sam's death. The charge would be attempted murder I'm sure.'

'I know, I know,' Alex began to cry. 'I threatened him and said if he didn't give me any money then I would make it known to you and Freya just what a bastard he was. It was just a warning, Jess, that's all. If I'd have known the fire would spread, there is no way I would have done it.' There was panic in Alex's voice now.

'He actually was telling you the truth for once,' said Jess. 'He didn't have any cash flow to talk of at all. He was living off his last bit of credit. Unbeknown to me, he'd been shagging everything that moved, taking countless women away on exotic weekends and gambling his way through his mid-life crisis.'

'Shit, Jess. I am so sorry for you. I knew he was a bastard but I honestly thought that you had calmed him. That it was an idyllic marriage.'

'Let's start selling those rose-tinted glasses shall we? We'd make a fortune.' Jess managed a smile.

'Oh God, if I had thought for one minute he was telling the truth I never would have behaved so rashly. I can't tell you how sorry I am.' Alex continued weeping.

'His many indiscretions didn't come to light until after the fire, so maybe you did me a favour,' Jess said reassuringly. 'I would still be living a lie now and imagine how awful that would be. At least now I've got a chance to find real happiness again.'

'With Dan?' Alex asked quietly. Jess realised that Dan must be a lot closer to Alex than she realised.

'I don't know,' Jess replied and immediately changed

the subject. 'So about the fire, Alex. The police are swarming over everything. If they find out Evie is Sam's, I'm sure they will question you. Bear in mind that my solicitor knows the truth too.'

Alex put her head in her hands. 'I can't have Evie, my family or Dan find out. It would be too much to cope with. What if I go to prison? I cannot bear to think of Evie and my boys without a mum to bring them up.'

Jess felt tears prick her eyes. Her mum had died when she was just thirteen, and she knew how tough life had been, growing up without her around. She took a deep breath and before she said what she was about to say, she made it clear in her own mind that she was doing this not for Alex, but for Evie, Dan and Alex's boys. She cleared her throat. 'Although it is very doubtful – because Sam I'm sure had a lot of enemies.' Jess paused. 'If it does come to the crunch, Alex, and the finger is pointed at you.' She paused again. 'I will make sure you have an alibi that will stand.'

Jess could almost see the relief pour through Alex's body. Alex went to speak and Jess raised her hand to shush her. 'I want to hear no more on the matter. I'm doing this for Evie and Dan, because I love them both, and not for you. I can't condone what you've done, but I'm a human being and I couldn't bear to see any child without their mother, and the man I care about, suffering because of it.'

Jess stood up and brushed down her skirt. 'Now let's go shall we?

'Jess,' Alex said quietly.

'I said no more on the matter,' Jess replied sternly. Alex ignored her and put her hand on Jess's arm. 'I can see why Dan fell in love with you.'

Chapter Thirty

'Welcome to my new abode.' Jess gave Emma a welcoming kiss. She had come round for a coffee and natter while the children were all at school.

'Come on then show me round,' Emma said excitedly.

Jess glanced sidelong at Emma. She did love her friend dearly and, at that moment, was sorely tempted to tell her about her tête-à-tête with Alex and about Evie being Sam's, but managed to hold it back. She knew for all concerned that she just had to keep it a secret. Nobody would ever need to know. Two weeks after her meeting with Alex, Jess was delighted to have found a mid-terrace two-bedroom cottage in the same village as Fern Cottage. It was within walking distance to Freya's school and reminded her very much of Morley Mansions, where she used to live before she met Sam.

'Some of the furniture is a bit questionable I know, but it made sense to rent furnished. I can add in my own bits and pieces as time goes on. Just didn't want to blow the little bit of money I have got saved just yet.'

'It's lovely, Jess, I just love all the fireplaces in every room and it already has a really homely feel to it.'

'Bit smaller than I'm used to I know, but plenty of room for me and little missy. She loves her bedroom, mainly because the walls are pink.'

Emma was delighted to see her beautiful friend so buoyant. Jess continued with enthusiasm.

'I'm all set up on broadband now so even have a link to the outside world. I've felt like I've been in a bubble for the past couple of months but I'm ready to start afresh now.

'I'm so pleased, Jess, it's good to see you getting yourself sorted. Have you thought what you are going to do work wise?'

'Well the writing idea has gone out of the window for now. I think to be honest I'm going to stick to what I know and do some freelance event jobs. I don't want to take too much on because of Freya. I've found out the day rates from an agency I've worked with before and they are really quite good.'

'Well that's positive. Maybe you can look at your writing as a hobby and see what happens?'

'Yes, I did think that. Make it fun rather than relying on it. Every little bit of extra cash will help.'

Just then the phone rang. 'Sorry, Em, I'll just quickly take this.' It was Jonathan, her solicitor. 'OK, right, understand. Is there anything I need to do?' Jess fiddled with her hair as she listened intently.

'Oh, Jonathan. That is the best news I have heard in quite some time. Thank you so much for making my day.' She hung up, grabbed Emma around the waist and danced around the kitchen with her. 'You'll never guess what!' Jess was beaming. 'The Cornwall cottage was solely in my name. We bought it outright all those years ago. I never even knew. It's mine, Em, and nobody can touch it!'

'Oh, Jess, that is just fantastic.'

'What a complete relief.' Jess almost sang. 'Seagull Cottage is mine, all mine.'

She ran around again like an excited child.

'Right, tea and carrot cake to celebrate.' They settled at the kitchen table.

'Now, Jessica Morley, I want to hear all about Prague.'

Jess liked to be called by her maiden name now. She had decided she would keep the name Beresford for Freya's sake but, as soon as she could, she would change it back to plain old Morley.

'Prague was fine. It seems like eons ago now.'

'Fine? What sort of description is that, Jess?'

'Well OK it was more than fine. Dan was a complete angel. He treated me like a princess actually: paid for everything, booked the best hotel and best restaurant. He couldn't have done anymore to make the whole weekend special.'

'I can feel a but coming on though, Jess?'

'Something awful happened actually. It was my own stupid fault really. I said I wanted to go dancing so we queued outside a nightclub for ages.'

Emma began to chuckle. 'I can't even imagine going into a nightclub at our age, Jess.'

'Well, I know that now, but you know what I'm like. I was really drunk and didn't care. Anyway, some young lads behind us implied that I was Dan's mother. I can't tell you how mortified I was, Em.'

Emma couldn't help but laugh. 'Look, Jess, I know I shouldn't laugh – but it is quite funny in a way.'

Jess started to laugh too. 'I know, but on a more serious note, Em, the age gap is big. Dan adores me and says is doesn't matter, but I think now it does matter to me. When I'm sixty, he will be just forty-four and we both know that is still young. Hope assures me that Botox will save the day, but I want to grow old gracefully, Emma.'

'Wasn't it you who always said that age had no boundaries in the name of love? Emma prompted. 'And I think growing old disgracefully will be much more fun!'

'Well OK yes.' Jess laughed and hesitated. 'Maybe I just don't love Dan like I used to.' She sighed and took a mouthful of tea.

'Don't get me wrong, the same old electricity is there. I could eat him sometimes. It's just he's not on my mind the whole time like he used to be all those years ago. He's not my world anymore.'

'But, Jess, we are older now. Maybe you are just

approaching your relationship in a more sensible fashion. Face it, you were so hedonistic in your late thirties.'

Jess smiled. 'And my goodness what fun it was!'

'Anyway he's coming over this weekend to stay with Evie. It will be really odd to see her again after all these years but I am really looking forward to meeting her. It's amazing to think she's thirteen now.'

'God I remember when she was just three years-old and you came round mine, tearing your hair out as she was such a little madam.'

'Yes I remember that too. She did used to lead me a merry dance.' On realising the time Jess jumped up. 'Right, school run time, we'd better get going.'

Chapter Thirty one

'Evie, this is Jess. A very good friend of mine.' Evie looked shyly at Jess. Her hair was still very blonde and cascaded down her shoulders. Her big blue eyes took up most of her pretty little face.

Dan smiled at Jess, it had been an effort to get Evie to come and visit, she would have much rather stayed at home in London chatting to her friends on Facebook.

Freya came downstairs. 'You're name's Evie isn't it? Do you want to play with my dollies?'

'No thank you,' Evie replied politely.

'Oh.' Freya seemed stunned at her refusal.

'Freya, why don't you take Evie outside and show her your new swing?' Jess piped up and smiled at Evie. 'Is that OK darling?' She couldn't believe how grown up she was for thirteen, with her trendy hipster jeans and funky T-shirt. Evie nodded and happily followed Freya out to the garden.

Jess was almost startled at coming face to face with a being whose almond-shaped blue eyes and perfect teeth, so closely resembled those of her dead husband's. She took a deep breath. There was no mistaking that Evie Meadows was from the loins of Mr Sam Beresford.

'Penny for them?' Dan smiled and kissed Jess on the cheek.

'Kids eh?' she said knowingly.

'Gets harder as they get older,' Dan agreed.

Jess sank back into her chair. Here she was happier than she'd felt for a long time:in her new garden with her beautiful daughter and a man she loved, but with one big problem. The man in question's daughter was her own daughter's half-sister and not his child at all, and she could never ever tell him that. She was usually so honest with Dan that she wasn't sure if she was strong enough to keep up the deceit. Jess recovered her thoughts and smiled. 'I thought we'd just stay in and have a barbecue if that's OK with you?'

'Perfect,' Dan replied. 'The house is lovely by the way, Jess. In fact, it reminds me a lot of Morley Mansions. Do you have a spare room by any chance?'

They both laughed.

'Actually no I don't, our daughters are in it tonight!' On saying these words, she realised a third little person could be running around her garden and a look of sadness crossed her face.

Dan, ever perceptive, put his arm around her.

'Not a year goes by without thinking what would have happened if I'd had the baby, you know,' Jess said softly. 'I think now how perfect it would have been for Freya to have an older sister or brother.' As she said these words, she realised that in fact Freya was now playing with her older sister and openly shook her head at the bizarreness of the situation.

Dan bit his lip. 'But Jess, it was the right decision at the time, and who knows what path your life would have taken if you had gone through with the pregnancy.'

She walked over to the kitchen window and watched the girls playing on the swing outside. With her back to Dan she continued. 'It's bitter sweet you coming back into my life, Dan.' She turned to face him. 'It really pains me to think that if I had gone ahead and had the baby then you probably would have come back anyway, so I went through all of that torment for nothing.'

'Never look back, Jess,' Was all Dan could muster. 'Life is a rollercoaster, if we all lived on ifs and buts then we would never move forward with anything.'

'Oh I know that, but it was one of the hardest decisions I had to make and I feel it was the wrong one now.'

'Only regret the things you don't do, Jess, and just think you may never have had Freya.'

'That is a good point, Dan, and I could never imagine life without her.' She also realised then that it was actually Dan who had lost out. If she chose to spend her life with him, although he would of course never ever know it, it would be him who would never have a blood child of his own.

Dan lifted the somber mood. 'Now come on, Jessy Morley. Let's get out in that sunshine. I'll help you light the barbecue.'

Freya and Evie, now bored with the swing, were making a camp out of an old table, they'd found down the bottom of the garden, and some dust sheets from the shed.

'Bless Evie for humouring Freya, I'm sure she'd much rather be with kids of her own age,' Jess stated, craning to see if there were any more resemblances.

'She's a good girl,' Dan stated.

'Does she remember me do you think?' Jess enquired.

'I don't think so now. It was weird, because when we did split up she did ask if she could come round and see you on numerous occasions. That was really hard to deal with actually.'

'I used to miss Evie terribly. God that whole time was just awful. And now look at us, who'd have thought it,' Jess replied and poked Dan playfully in the stomach with her finger.

Dan smiled. 'Poor you, I can't believe how I treated you. I was so young then that I didn't think things through logically. In hindsight, we did move in together far too quickly. I didn't even think of poor Evie's feelings. My great big male ego got in the way I guess, and I selfishly just thought of myself.'

'Oh it's OK, Dan. I was so blindly in love with you that

I didn't see sense to put a halt to it anyway.

Dan took a gulp of his wine and looked at Jess intently. 'And are you blindly in love with me now, Jess?'

Before Jess had time to answer there was a scream from down the bottom of the garden. Freya came charging up to the patio area where Jess and Dan were sitting.

'It bit me!' Freya cried.

Evie soon followed. 'I think it was a wasp, Jessy,' she said in a matter of fact voice.

After administering ice cubes and sting relief cream, Freya calmed down and went off to continue her camp building with Evie.

'Right, Daniel Harris, be a man and get that barbecue lit please. I shall open some more wine.'

The afternoon sped by. The evening drew in and Evie and Freya, already the best of friends, went upstairs to watch a DVD. Jess and Dan sprawled on either end of the sofa, Jess's legs resting on his lap. 'Have you heard from Charlie lately?' Jess enquired.

'Just a really quick call, to see how I was doing and that was that,' Dan replied. 'I know I won't hear from her again. We are history now. You?'

'She made a flying visit to Hope's just before I moved in here. She seemed fine, albeit in denial about Sam's actions though. She really can't believe he was such a bastard.'

'So will you tell her about us?' Dan said.

'Dan, there really isn't anything to tell at the moment, is there?

Dan shifted on the sofa and breezed over Jess's comment. 'No, no I guess not,' he spluttered.

Jess carried on. 'Let's just enjoy each other for now and see what happens eh?'

'That sounds like a plan to me, Jessy Morley.'

'What time do you have to head back tomorrow by the way?'

'Probably around lunchtime. Alex is having Evie for the next couple of days and I need to drop her to her.'

'How is Alex by the way?' Jess asked breezily.

'She's good actually. She married Rob. The guy she met straight after me and they've got two boys together now. Evie loves him and her stepbrothers, so that makes life easy. We are really good friends now and she seems happy.'

'Oh well that is good, especially for Evie,' Jess said, far too exuberantly, hoping that Dan would never ever find out what she knew, as it would most certainly destroy him on two counts: the first that Evie was not his and the second that she had betrayed him so greatly, in her knowledge of that fact. 'Right, let me open a bottle of red. It can breathe while we get those girls to bed,' Jess suggested, untangling herself from Dan's legs.

Dan followed Jess into the kitchen. He put his arms loosely around her neck. The old electric current flowed between them and Jess smiled at him openly.

'In answer to your question of earlier: Yes, I do love you, Daniel Harris.'

Dan hugged her tight, kissed her forehead, and gently sighed. Just loving him wasn't enough. He wanted Jessy Morley to be so in love with him that she would never ever let him go.

Chapter Thirty two

Emma waited until Monday night to phone Jess. 'So come on spill the beans, how was the weekend? Fireworks or damp squibs?'

'Well he slept on the sofa so there were certainly no fireworks.'

'Oh,' Emma said, slightly shocked.

'No it's all good. He thought it best for Evie not seeing us together in the same bed the next morning.'

'Well, well, at least ten years has made him a bit more respectful.'

'Yeah, that's what I thought,' Jess replied. Every time she spoke to Emma she still found it really hard that she couldn't tell her about Evie's parenting, but realised again that it was for the best. The fewer people who knew, even if she trusted them explicitly, then the less of a chance there was of Dan ever finding out.

'What's Evie like now?' Emma said.

'Well she's turned from a screaming brat into a charming young lady. She is really well-mannered and seems kind and balanced. It was a pleasure to spend time with her.'

'Well, that's lovely. And how was Freya with her?'

'Couldn't have been better, despite the age gap they still played together very well. We are all going down to Cornwall for the first two weeks of the summer holidays.'

'Ooh, hark at you. You sound like a family already.'

'Oh Em, I do love him very much but I'm so frightened of getting hurt again.'

'Well just enjoy the moment for now, Jess. It's not like he's proposed or anything is it?'

Chapter Thirty three

Freya was beside herself with excitement. 'Mummy, how many sleeps 'til we go to Cornwall with Evie and Dan?'

'No more, darling, as soon as you finish school today we are going to be on our way.'

'Yippeeeeeee.'

Jess laughed. 'I love you a million zillion two trillion dollars.'

Freya squealed. 'And I love you more than cola bottles.'

Dan pulled up outside Jess's house. Evie waved frantically at her through the window. 'Jesus, we're only going for two weeks,' Jess exclaimed as he opened the boot.

'Well I thought we could maybe go camping, I've packed a tent!'

'Camping!' Jess exclaimed.

'It's OK, Jess, you won't have to use a chemical toilet or anything nasty like that.'

Jess laughed. 'I can't wait to get down there.'

'Nor can I. Now get in the car and let's go get that baby girl of yours from school.'

It was getting dark as they arrived at the cottage. Dan unpacked the car as Jess opened all the windows to let out the stuffiness. The girls ran upstairs squealing to choose their bedroom.

'OK, Mrs. Robinson?' Dan enquired as he dumped the last of the cases in the hallway. 'More than OK thank you, Mr. Harris. For the first time in months I actually feel like I'm home.'

The girls awoke early. Dan and Jess still sleepy from last night's passionate lovemaking, groaned.

'Evie will see us in bed together,' Jess stated.

'Its fine,' Dan replied. 'I explained that we would probably be sharing a bed here, as we were very good friends.'

'Keep quiet and hopefully they will play amongst themselves until we get up.' Just as Jess said this, the bedroom door was flung wide open.

'Mummy, Dad,' the girls said in unison. 'Can we go to the beach now?'

Jess and Dan smiled at each other. 'OK, now you two go and get dressed. We will have some breakfast then make a plan for the day,' Jess replied sensibly.

'I want to go on a boat,' Freya shouted as they approached the bustling harbour.

'Evie?' Dan questioned.

'Yeah, what fun!' Evie exclaimed.

'Well we have the option of a glass-bottomed boat, which doesn't leave for another hour, or there is a fishing boat, which means we would be out for half a day, which leaves soon,' Jess stated.

'I want to go now,' Freya cried.

Jess smiled. 'Up to you, Dan, it is such a beautiful day, I'm happy to come along and get a suntan if you want to fish with the girls.'

'Come on then the lot of you,' Dan said as they all clambered aboard.

Jess sat on the bench seat at the back of the boat and tipped her head back towards the sun. She fleetingly thought of Sam and how he would have loved this. She did try and remain positive in her memory of him, but, every time a good thought hit her mind, it was immediately replaced by a dark one. She imagined him with all those other women, which made her feel felt physically sick. She also thought of his ready dismissal of Evie, even before she was born, and this too upset her greatly. Freya had been surprisingly resilient and rarely got upset. Just asking Jess occasionally what she thought her daddy was doing with the angels. 'Just playing around I expect,' Jess would reply, tongue in cheek.

A flock of gulls flew overhead as they left Looe Harbour. It was if they were crying out for the boat to hurry back soon with its tasty bounty. The boat made its way out to sea. 'This is such fun,' Evie cried as she ran up to Jess.

'Hey, be careful running,' Jess said. 'I bet you used to love living on the boat with your dad didn't you?'

'I don't remember much about it really, we moved off of it when I was four. How did you know about our boat anyway?' Evie quizzed.

'I used to be friends with your daddy a long time ago.'

'What, boyfriend and girlfriend type of friends?'

Jess wished she hadn't started this conversation. Evie continued her interrogation.

'So why did you not stay friends with Dad then?'

'I guess sometimes people just drift apart, but it's great we are friends again don't you think?'

Evie put her hand on Jess's arm. 'I'd like it if you stayed friends with my dad for a long, long time.'

Jess welled up. 'I think we can manage that,' she replied..

Archie, who was skippering the boat, scurried around making sure the children put on life jackets. 'Up to you if you want one, my lovely,' he said to Jess in his thick Cornish accent. 'Wouldn't want to ruin your suntan now would we? He was tubby with a white whiskery beard and a ruddy complexion. 'It's so still out there today, you should be fine. If you have any questions just ask for me grandson Adam up there. He pointed to a dark haired lad at the front of the boat. He must be about twenty-four, Jess thought. She looked at him and he seemed so young. She actually found it hard to believe that when she had been forty, she had been dating a man as young as him. Mind you, Dan had always looked that bit older and she had always acted much younger.

Jess looked across at Dan. He was a good looking man. She studied him in his trunks. She had always adored his back and manly chest, even his slight beer belly was an added cuddly attraction. She squirmed on her seat as she thought about last night. It had been gorgeous. Gone was the hard furious sex they used to have when they were younger, replaced by pure meaningful lovemaking. She was comforted to know that she was the only woman he wanted and, unlike Sam, she knew that he would always be honest with her. That was a major quality of Dan: his honesty. Even ten years ago, despite breaking her heart in two, he had at least been honest in his reasons for leaving her. She felt quite sick that now it was her who had to keep the biggest secret from him.

Jess shouted down the boat to Evie and Freya who were midway through helping Dan put bait on his hook. 'When you've finished that come down here and I'll put some sun cream on you both.'

'OK,' they shouted in unison. The girls dutifully went to Jess who administered their sun cream.

Dan cast his line over the side of the boat. He was in a row with three older looking guys, who all seemed to be taking the whole experience very seriously. On the other side of the boat a couple of young lads were messing around. Dan, with line now hanging over the edge of the boat, sat down and turned his head to the sun. He was already on tenterhooks about his proposal. Special plans had been laid to make sure that everything was perfect. The antique ring that Jess had marveled at, in the window of a jeweler in Prague, was hidden in his case. He'd even pre-arranged for Phoebe and Glen to come down and take the girls away for the night so that they could be alone. In five days he thought, I am going to be engaged to the most beautiful woman in the world.

They'd been fishing for an hour when the sun went in and it suddenly started to get a little windy. Big black clouds appeared on the horizon. 'Boo, we could do without rain,' Jess stated to Archie as he walked to the back of the boat.

'Aye, we could that,' Archie replied then went to the front to chat with Adam. He then put his hands on his hips and shouted, 'Ladies and gentleman, looks like a storm maybe brewing over yonder. We didn't expect this at all. I'm afraid we are going to have to head back early, we don't want you all getting too wet now do we?' Just as he finished his sentence a large flash of lightning filled the now blackening sky, followed by a giant clap of thunder.

'Please can you all put on your life jackets,' Adam instructed. 'We have sou'westers and wellies too if anyone wants them.'

Large drops of rain began to slowly fall, making a clanking sound on the deck as they did so. Freya and Evie huddled next to Jess, and Dan came over to sit with them. There was nowhere to escape from the rain and the boat began to rock from side to side as the wind started to build.

'I'm frightened,' Freya said.

'It's fine darling, it's just a little storm. It will be over before we know it,' Jess said. As she said this Jess looked at Dan with concern, as a streak of lightning fell out of the sky, proceeded by an even louder clap of thunder than the previous one. Evie screamed.

'It's OK, Evie,' Dan reassured her. 'Jess is right. It'll be over in no time.'

The rain began lashing down and the wind became stronger. The boat was now listing quite heavily from side to side and Jess began to feel sick. She knew she had to remain strong for the children, but then couldn't hold it in any longer and threw up over the side.

'Mummy!' Freya wailed.

Dan held her to him while trying to stroke Jess's back.

'My darling girls, hold on to me.'

'Are you OK, angel?' he asked Jess as she stood back upright.

'No,' she replied and leant back over the boat again. She was green.

They struggled to keep their footing. The younger lads who had been messing around were now silent. Two of the three older guys also had their heads over the side of the boat being sick.

'Sit down everyone and hold on,' Archie instructed. 'We're in the eye of it now, my lovelies, just hang in there.'

The wind was getting stronger by the minute. The rain was pelting down so hard it stung everyone's faces. Thunder and lightning were now persistent. All of a sudden a huge wave lifted the boat and almost tipped it on its side.

'Evie,' Jess screamed. The force of the wave, made her lose grip of her and the young girl was thrown right to the other side of the boat, bashing herself hard as she landed against the side.

'Help me,' Evie screamed to Dan, she was now sobbing her eyes out.

Everybody held on to each other as tightly as they could, spray was covering them every time the boat bashed down again. Dan, in rushing up to help Evie, who was now hanging on to a rope at the side of the boat, was knocked over himself by the force of yet another wave. He crawled to her and just as he reached her feet, was thrown back over the other side again. Jess, aghast at what was happening, knew that she should just hold on to Freya with all her might. Archie couldn't leave the helm so Adam jumped up to help get Evie on her feet. Just as he did so another huge wave covered the boat and filled it with at least a foot of water.

'Evie,' Dan screamed. 'Oh my God, Evie, she's gone over. I can't swim. Quick somebody do something.'

Jess was already in the water. She choked as the raging swirl hit the back of her throat, and was terrified as she was lifted by the torrid waves. She talked herself into not panicking. She could see Evie, all she had to do was swim to her.

'Help me, help me,' Evie screamed.

'I'm here, darling, I'm here,' Jess croaked.

Every time Jess took two strokes the strong waves pushed her one back, exhausted she eventually reached Evie who clung to her for dear life. Adam had now joined them in the water with two life rings. Archie and one of the older guys helped drag them all up the side of the boat. A now ashen-faced Dan clung on to the sobbing Freya with all his might.

'Hold her please,' Dan instructed one of the young lads to look after Freya. He ran over to Evie and Jess.

Jess, now sitting on the deck, was promptly sick into a fish bucket. Evie was crying and her cheek was bleeding from her initial fall against the boat. The wind suddenly dropped but the pelting rain was still persistent. Adam made a makeshift bed out of tarpaulin in the little bit of cover there was at the helm and helped Evie and Jess shakily up, so that they could lie down out of the lashing rain. Dan rushed to their side.

'Oh my god, are you both alright?' He was shaking.

'Dad, it's OK I'm fine,' Evie bravely replied.

Freya clung to her mother's legs. Dan reached for Jess's hand and held it tenderly. She was weak from her swim and was shivering from the cold. Her wet hair streaked her face and she started to cry from the shock. He leant down to kiss her and felt a sudden surge of love for her stronger than he had ever felt before. Without hesitation he looked right into her eyes and asked. 'Jessica

Ann Morley, will you marry me?'

Jess could barely speak, but through her tears she managed to smile weakly and reply. 'Yes, Daniel Harris, I will marry you.' She then added, 'As long as you learn to bloody swim.'

Chapter Thirty four

The coastguard had received a distress signal from the fishing boat and an ambulance was already at the harbour. The storm had now subsided and a crowd had gathered awaiting the vessel. Dan, holding Freya's hand tightly, helped Evie off the boat, while Adam guided Jess up the harbour wall steps. The paramedics then led her to the back of the ambulance.

'Jess, you better get checked out,' Dan said caringly, then to Evie. 'And you, little lady, better get your face cleaned up.'

Jess had swallowed a lot of water and was still feeling sick. She lay in the back of the ambulance as they checked her blood pressure and asked her a series of questions.

They cleaned up Evie's face and put a butterfly plaster on her cheek, luckily she did not need stitches. Once the paramedics were happy that they were OK they drove all four of them back up to the cottage.

'Jess are you sure you are OK to come back to the cottage?' Dan asked.

'Of course I am,' she replied weakly. 'Just want to get in my own bed.'

It was early evening when they actually got back to the cottage. Despite it being mid-summer Dan turned on the heating, made them all hot drinks and ran a hot bath. Jess insisted that Evie and Freya got in first. Evie winced as the hot water stung the cuts and bruises on her legs, Freya delighted in playing nurses tending to her with a flannel. The children then moved to the comfort of the sofa while Dan ran another bath for Jess, who had just gone to lay straight on their bed.

He pushed open the bedroom door slowly and lay down next to her. He cuddled her gently and pushed her soaking wet hair back off of her face.

'How's my heroine doing then?'

'Not too good actually, Dan, I feel a bit shaky.'

'Probably shock darling,' he replied. 'I can never ever repay you for what you did, Jess, you saved my daughter's life.'

'Anyone would have done it,' she said modestly. 'Now don't worry about me, how are those girls of ours?'

'OK actually. Freya is relaying it all as a big adventure now. Evie is a bit sore but she's in good spirits.'

'Now come on you, let's get you in the bath to warm you up.' Dan helped Jess off the bed. Just has she had lain back in the warm soothing bubbles and closed her eyes, Dan bounded back into the bathroom. He got down on one knee and propped himself on the edge of the bath.

'Just to make sure.' He laughed. 'Jessica Morley, will you do me the honor of being my wife?' He produced a ring from behind his back. Jess looked at him with a deadpan face.

'Jess?' A look of panic went across Dan's face. Then, just like Julia Roberts in *Pretty Woman*, ducked her head back right under the water then emerged with a huge grin on her face.

'Of course I will, Daniel Harris!'

They both laughed and Dan kissed her gently on her forehead.

'Oh my God, Dan, the ring, it's the one from Prague, I can't believe you did that! It is beautiful.'

'Well you know, only the best for the future Mrs. Harris,' he said modestly.

Just then Jess heard her mobile ringing in the bedroom. 'Can you get that please, baby?'

Ten minutes later Dan came running into the bathroom,

pulled down the toilet seat and sat on it. 'It was Hope. I told her what had happened. She had some news for you, was going to wait and tell you herself, but thought you might need cheering up. She and Jack-the-Lad are tying the knot too.'

Jess managed a smile. 'Good old Hope she never disappoints me. Husband number four. She vowed she'd never do it again! Have they set a date yet?'

'Next month!' Dan replied.

'No! How funny. That is just so Hope though, I bet she wants to snare him before he gets a chance to run away.'

'Jess?' Dan said softly.

'Yeeeesss,' Jess said wondering what was coming now.

'I did plan a proper romantic proposal and everything. I wanted it to be really special.'

'Just asking me was special enough, Daniel Harris.' Jess replied matter of factly. 'Now, dear husband to be, do you want my bath water or not?'

'And who said romance was dead eh?' Dan smiled and replied. Jess threw a sponge at his head and they both laughed heartily.

Chapter Thirty five

'Hiya mate,' Matt greeted Dan at the door. He had baby sick on his shoulder and looked very tired.

'And how are you today, madam?' he asked Evie.

'Fine ta, Uncle Matt, where are the twins?

'Upstairs with Auntie Sara, go on up.'

Evie ran upstairs.

'Can of Stella?'

'Cheers, mate.'

'Long time no see,' Matt stated.

'Yeah, sorry, mate. We've been away with Jess and the girls to her cottage in Cornwall.'

'Very nice.'

Dan looked a little embarrassed. 'I've got something to ask you actually.'

'Fire away, Danny boy.'

'Well I'm getting married to the lovely Jessica Morley, and I would really love it if you could be my best man.'

'Hey you're a bloody dark horse, Harris. Congratulations though, mate. And of course I'd be honored to be your best man.'

'Great, thanks, mate.'

'I can't wait for my speech already.' He smirked and continued. 'Must get my geriatric jokes up to scratch.'

Dan laughed. 'I know, I know, who'd have thought it eh?'

'You were adamant she wasn't the one for you and I tended to agree all those years ago. Funny how time changes everything.'

Dan nodded. 'I really love her, mate, always did I

think. Just couldn't see it at the time.'

'I'm genuinely really pleased for you. Sara will be delighted as well. She was just saying she needed a good night out. We are both run ragged looking after the twins. Never realised quite just how hard work it would be.'

'Anyway, have you set a date yet?' Matt asked.

'No not yet, I only asked her a few days ago, we need to sit down and talk about it.'

'And how has Evie taken the news?'

'She absolutely adores Jess, and gets on so well with her little one, Freya, so it's all worked out perfectly.'

'Chuffed for you, mate. And dare I ask about Charlie, is she OK about the news?'

'I'm leaving that one to Jess.' Dan laughed. 'But I'm sure she'll be cool about it.'

'Hiya, Dan,' Sarah shouted down the stairs. 'I'll be down in a minute. Matt, stop gassing and get that chicken in the oven now, or we'll all be having roast dinner at midnight.'

'OK, my love,' Matt replied and laughed to Dan. 'Oh the sweet joy of matrimony!'

Chapter Thirty six

'Darling girl!' Hope greeted Jess at her front door in miniscule shorts and a boob tube. She ushered her straight through to the garden.

'No Freya today then?'

'No, she's spending the weekend with Charlie.'

'Wine?' Hope offered.

'It would be rude not to.' Jess winked as they settled at the garden table. 'Congratulations on your upcoming nuptials, Ms Adams. I'm not even going to ask if you're sure after such a short time. Bloody impressive rock though.'

Hope waved her hand in the air so that her huge diamond engagement ring sparkled in the sunshine. 'Darling, you know I don't work in time, but in carats!' Hope took a slug of wine and continued. 'Seriously though, he is such a sweetheart, Jess. I can actually see me staying with this one. Surely, there are only so many men a girl can sleep with and I'm running out of options.'

Jess laughed. 'Umm, I've heard that three times from you before, but you go, girl.'

'Pretty in pink I've decided,' Hope continued. 'Seen a gorgeous little designer number in the boutique in Swift Street. I'm so excited, Jess.'

'And where and when exactly are you consummating this one?'

'Well obviously it has to be a registry office. Have pulled some strings and found a smart one in Mayfair who can take us. I've booked it for September 13th. We want to have the reception at The Soho Hotel, was hoping you may be able to pull some strings in getting me a good deal. I'm only inviting fifty people, so hope they'll have the space.'

'You're cutting it fine, Hope Adams, and not sure if it's the same management at the hotel, but let me make a call for you. You should be OK though, as it's a Sunday and a small affair.'

'Talking of affairs, have you told Charlie yet about you and Dan seeing each other?'

'Well first, dear friend, I've actually got some big news for you too.'

'Really?'

'Dan proposed to me in Cornwall?'

'No!' Hope exclaimed. 'And what did you say?'

'I said yes.'

'Well you don't sound too happy about it?'

'I am, I am,' Jess said.

'So was it a romantic proposal? He's usually spot-on in that department.'

'Well yes and no.'

Jess relayed the storm story and Hope listened in horror. 'Jesus, I'd have asked you to marry me too after all that,' Hope exclaimed. Jess laughed.

'Congratulations to you though, Jess. I'm so happy you're happy again. I love the ring too!'

'I'm sure people will think it's just too soon after Sam dying but to be honest I don't care. My lack of respect for him since finding out about the affairs has really helped for me to get over grieving for him anymore.'

'So tell me, what did Charlie say?'

'I fronted it this morning when she came to pick up Freya. I told her the whole story from ten years ago actually.'

'Wow, and how did she react to you sleeping with him the day of the funeral?' Hope asked.

Jess grimaced. 'Well, OK I wasn't that honest. I said we were together ten years ago and we didn't realise we still had feelings for each other until after she and Dan had split up.'

'I think that's fine, Jess. Sometimes it is more hurtful to tell the complete truth and she knows how it is now at least.'

Thoughts of Dan and Evie ran immediately through Jess's head. She brushed them aside and continued. 'She is an amazing girl. She's coming to the wedding, so she must have been being genuine about being happy for us.'

'So have you set a date yet?'

'Not yet, there's no hurry.'

'Jess, are you sure you're OK?'

'Oh, Hope, I do love him and Freya adores him and Evie, but if I'm honest I am worried myself about the age gap now. I mean when I'm sixty, he will still only be forty-four. Looking back I was so young and vibrant at that age. I'm worried he may decide to swap me for a younger model.'

'Jess, don't be so ridiculous. You are still young and vibrant now, in fact you will be until you are one hundred and five! He loves *you*, Jessica Morley. The wonderful, kind, generous, sexy, loving person that you are.'

'Bless you, Hope, you're so sweet. I really hope so,' Jess replied, not utterly convinced.

'And anyway by the time you're sixty, I'm sure they'll be able to lift boobs and botox fannies on finance!'

Jess nearly choked on her wine. 'Hope Adams, you are unbelievable!'

'But oh-so gorgeous.' Hope smirked. 'Right now let's finish this bottle and get another one open, we have reason to celebrate!'

Chapter Thirty seven

'Get your sexy arse over here, Jessica Morley.' Dan grabbed her around the waist and threw her on to the huge bed in their suite at The Soho Hotel.

'I have something here for you.' He smirked.

'Oh my god, Dan, I am so not taking an ecstasy tablet again.'

Dan laughed out loud and remembered back to their erotic night in this same hotel all those years ago. 'More like an ecstasy lollipop actually.' He took her hand and placed it on the obvious swell in his boxer shorts.

'No Dan. Come on. We've got to get ready for the wedding. We'll be late and Hope will kill me.'

'Jess, we've got loads of time.'

'Later, Dan, later.'

A frustrated Dan sighed and walked into the bathroom to take a shower.

Hope looked amazing in her glamorous pink gown and long pink gloves. Jack-the-Lad was beaming throughout the short ceremony and gave his new wife such a long, lingering kiss at the end of it, that some of the elderly relatives had to look away with embarrassment.

Hope had arranged for a London bus to take the guests to the reception, and was horrified when she noticed that her husband had put a sun visor strip on the front of the bus with their pet names for each other: Honey Pie and Stallion.

The smart waiters, all dressed in black gaily served pink champagne and canapés as the first guests filtered into the trendy Swirl Room. Swing music filtered out over the speakers.

'You look amazing,' Jess exclaimed to her beaming friend.

'You surely would expect nothing less!' Hope exclaimed.

Jess hiccupped. She had already had two glasses on an empty stomach and was already feeling quite drunk.

'Your turn soon,' Hope added and flitted off to mingle with the rest of her guests.

Dan walked up behind Jess and kissed her on the lips. 'Has anyone ever told you how beautiful you are, Jessy Morley?'

'I've lost count.' They both laughed out loud.

'I mean it, Jess, you are the most beautiful woman in this room.' Jess smiled as Dan continued. 'We really must set a date soon. I cannot wait for you to be, Mrs. Harris.'

'Let's get today out of the way first then we can talk about it,' Jess replied and helped herself to another glass of champagne.

The evening progressed smoothly. Hope had decided that she didn't want a formal affair, just copious amounts of champagne, an elaborate buffet, and her favourite swing tracks playing all evening. Just as Jess was reaching for her fourth glass of champagne, Phoebe approached. Jess hiccupped again and lost her footing.

'Whoa there, sis, too many sherbets already?' Phoebe rested her hand on her shoulder to level her.

'Whoops,' Jessica slurred. 'I'm celebrating my friends' nuptials, don't you know.'

'You quite obviously are,' Phoebe exclaimed. 'Now let's talk about you, dear sis. I simply cannot wait for your big day. Have you set a date yet?'

Jess raised her eyebrows. 'If anyone bloody asks me that again.'

Phoebe was taken aback by her sibling's curt reply. 'Hey, Jess, what sort of reply is that? Anyone would think you are not looking forward to it.'

Jess didn't reply. Phoebe, detecting something was wrong, ushered Jess to seating in a dark corner of the room.

'Are you OK?'

'I'm drunk,' Jess stated.

'I mean, is everything OK with you and Dan?'

'Yes.'

'Jess?'

'Oh, Phoebes, I'm really not sure if I'm making the right decision.'

As Phoebe was about to reply, Dan came bounding over to them. 'Hello, wife and sister-in-law to be.' Dan smirked and Phoebe smiled broadly back at him.

Jess was struggling. Struggling with the fact that she knew that Evie wasn't Dan's. She had begun to feel that every time he talked about how much he loved his beautiful daughter, that in fact she was betraying him. She also knew that she couldn't discuss her concerns and angst with anyone else. It was breaking her heart and unconsciously she was beginning to push Dan away

'Dan, can't you see we're talking?' Jess said grumpily.

'What on earth's the matter with you?' Dan enquired realizing that Jess was acting completely out of character. Phoebe mouthed that she was drunk.

'Give us a minute, Dan.'

Dan walked away disgruntled.

'Jess, you were so mean to Dan then. He's so lovely to you,' Phoebe stated. 'Now come on, tell me why the second thoughts?'

'I just have some doubts, that's all.' She put her head in her hands. 'Mac the Knife' belted out of the speakers. Jess so wanted to tell Phoebe the truth about Evie, but even in her drunken state knew that she couldn't.

'I love him, Phoebe, but not with the intensity I think I should. I can't see us growing old together.'

'Oh, Jess. He is a good man. I know I said that about Sam and was proved oh-so wrong, but I do honestly think that Dan is completely head over heels in love with you and would never betray you.'

'I don't want to just settle, Phoebe. I don't want to always be looking over my shoulder feeling insecure that he's going to leave me for a younger model.'

Phoebe, in realising that Jess, in her current state of mind, would not be able to rationalise her feelings, clasped her hand and helped her up. 'Come on let's get some food in you and we'll talk again tomorrow when you're sober.'

Jess picked at the buffet then, realising she had been curt with Dan, looked for him to make her apologies. It wasn't his fault she bore this secret. He was nowhere to be seen. She negotiated her way to the toilet and checked herself in the mirror. She was mortified to see how red her eyes were and how her lipstick had smudged on to the side of her face.

'God I shouldn't have drunk so much,' she said out loud and reapplied her make-up. Just as she was rounding the corner to go back into the party she caught sight of Dan in the corridor, talking animatedly to a really pretty girl. Dance music filtered out from the main bar of the hotel. The girl must have been in her late twenties, with straight long blonde hair and a trendy designer blue mini dress. Jess backed herself behind a pillar and continued to watch. They ended their chat with Dan kissing her on both cheeks.

Jess began to shake. She tried to get a grip of herself but the alcohol didn't allow her to see any sense. She had never ever really been a jealous person but since Sam's revelations she felt she could trust nobody. She marched back into the reception room which was alive with chatter and music. She spotted Dan chatting to Hope and swung him around roughly to face her.

'Who the fuck was that?'

'Jess, what? Who are you on about?'

'I saw you kissing that blonde bimbo!'

Before Dan could return her onslaught, Jess turned on her heels and fled out of the room. Dan ran after her to their suite and swung the door open with force.

'Jess, what on earth is the matter with you?' he demanded.

'Who was she? I want to know now,' Jess cried.

Dan wasn't quite sure how to deal with Jess like this. She had always been so cool and had never ever shown any sign of jealousy before. Part of him was flattered, as it made him realise how much she must care, but the other half of him didn't like to see this ugly side.

'Jess, come here.' Dan softened. He went to take her in his arms.

'Get off me,' she screamed.

'Calm down, angel. That was just Louise. She is a work colleague, nothing more, nothing less. She happened to be having a drink in the bar here, so I had a chat with her, then kissed her on both cheeks goodbye, like you know I do with everyone.'

'And do you fancy her?' Jess continued her drunken rant.

'Of course I don't, Jess. I love you. I love you with my whole being. I would never ever do anything to hurt you.' He continued with exasperation in his voice. 'I'm actually upset that you think I even would.'

'Oh you can say that now, Dan, but what about when I get older and you don't fancy me anymore? Face it, Dan, when I'm sixty, you'll still only be forty-four.'

'And what has that got to do with anything, Jess. I love *you*.' He put his hand to his forehead in exasperation and continued. 'Jess, listen to me. We are meant to be together. Our outer bodies are just a shell for the person within, and the person within you, Jess, is the most beautiful being I've ever met in my whole life.'

Jess failed to take this in and continued. 'What if I don't want sex as much as you? What if you meet someone younger and prettier than me who does?'

Dan put his fingers to Jess's lips. 'Shush now, Jess.'

'Don't you bloody shush me. I'm just being realistic, Dan. I've just been shit on from a great height by somebody who used to say I was the most beautiful woman in the world, and we were similar ages. Sixteen years, Dan, not four, not six, but sixteeen. It's a huge age gap by anyone's standards.'

It was then that Jess dropped her bombshell. 'Dan, I don't think we should get married.'

Tears filled Dan's eyes. 'Don't say that, Jess, you're drunk, you've overacted. In the morning things will seem different.'

'In the morning Dan, I will still be fifty and you will still be thirty-four,' came out of Jess's mouth, when what she really wanted to say was, 'In the morning, Dan, I will still know that Evie is not your daughter, and I don't think I can bear to keep something so huge from the man I really do love.

Chapter Thirty eight

'Jess, Jess, wake up.' Dan shook Jess's arm gently. 'I have to go. It's Evie, she's been taken ill.'

Jess groaned. 'What time is it?' she said dozily, not registering what Dan had just said. In her half asleep, drunken state, she hadn't even heard the hotel phone ring.

'It's 4 a.m. Look I'm gonna have to take your car.' Jess half opened her eyes.

'Jess, did you hear me!' Dan said loudly, turning the light on and rushing to pull his clothes on.

'Turn it off!' Jess murmured moodily. Dan lost his patience and shouted. 'Jess, my daughter is in hospital, I'm taking your car. I have to go now.'

Jess came to her senses. 'Evie, oh my God, what's wrong with her? Which hospital? Do you want me to come with you?'

Dan rushed towards the door, pulling a shoe on as he did so. 'She just woke up with terrible stomach pains and has been violently sick. She's at Wexham Park in Slough. Turn your mobile on. I'll call you as soon as I've got some news.'

Within minutes of the bedroom door shutting behind an anxious Dan, Jess was up, washed and packed. She was ashamed of herself for not supporting Dan in his hour of need. She asked the concierge to get her a cab. Her hangover was so bad, that she embarrassingly had to ask the driver to pull in to Heston Services so that she could be sick. 'Never again,' she whimpered as she crawled back in to the waiting vehicle.

An hour later she walked up to the hospital reception.

She had downed a litre of water in the taxi and was beginning to feel slightly better. 'Good morning, I wonder if you can help me. I'm here to see how Evie Meadows is. She was brought in a few hours ago.'

'Are you a relative?' The bespectacled, grey-haired lady behind the counter enquired.

'Er, yes,' Jess replied hesitantly, and put her hand to her forehead. She was very pale. 'Are you OK?' the receptionist enquired. 'Yes, yes, sorry,' Jess added. 'I just need to go the, the ladies, I'll be right back.'

Jess headed for the toilet, her head was spinning. Yes, she was a relative. In fact on paper she was Evie's stepmother and probably even had more of a claim to the beautiful Evie Alexandra Meadows than her beloved Daniel Harris. She felt sick again. All of this was too much to bear. If she really wanted to, then she could legally be entitled to look after the second child that she had always wished for. What a mess!

'She's in theatre.'

'Theatre?' Jess exclaimed.

'It's OK dear, nothing serious. She's having her appendix out. There is a relative's waiting room, first floor. You'll see the signs. Her parents are up there already.' She pointed to some stairs.

'Thanks, thanks very much,' Jess uttered.

Jess hovered outside the waiting room. She could see Dan and Alex sitting next to each other through the glass. She suddenly felt really awkward. It seemed wrong somehow for her to see them together. There were a few seats in the corridor. She sat on one to gain her composure, before she faced them both.

She fleetingly thought back to the night of the Christmas party all of those years ago when Dan had spent the night with her. The fun, the passion. Everything was simple then. She had loved him, loved him with an intensity with which she doubted she'd ever love anyone else again. And here she was sitting here now, almost eleven years on, with the same man in the room next to her, but a million miles away from those heady first days of their relationship.

And here also was Alex Hargreaves, nee Meadows: the woman who had not only slept with Jess's husband and lover, but had also brought on the death of Sam, plus nearly killed her and her precious Freya. Everything about the situation suddenly seemed very dark, and it was at this precise moment Jess knew her final decision had been made. She had to move on. There were too many secrets, too many betrayals, too much heartache. With a little girl's lifelong happiness at stake, Jess had to remove herself from this whole situation. A situation that seemed almost dirty. A situation that she didn't want to be part of anymore. Yes, she loved Dan but not with the blind intensity that she had felt before.

She was older and wiser now. Life was hard enough as it was, without having to live with betrayal. By holding on to this secret she couldn't give one hundred per cent to Dan, and it would destroy her. By giving it away, she would destroy him and maybe Evie. It was time for Jessica Morley and Freya Beresford to start a new life and find the happiness they truly deserved, without any secrets and without Daniel Harris.

It wasn't the right time to talk to him now. She would speak to him when Evie was on the mend. Just as she stood up to leave, the door of the waiting room opened and Dan appeared.

'Jess? You came. Poor little angel, she was in *so* much pain. She's having her appendix out as we speak.' He had tears in his eyes.

Jess couldn't bear to see Dan looking so sad and held her arms out to him to hug him.

'I love her so much, Jess.' he said.

Jess stroked his hair to comfort him, as if he were a

small boy. 'I know you do Dan,' she soothed, and realised that actually it didn't matter who Evie's real father was. Dan would love this little lady more than anyone in the world. And for him not to know the truth, was the right decision. It would most certainly break his heart in two if he knew.

'I love you too, Jess, you know that don't you?' Dan continued.

'I know, baby, I know,' Jess replied with tears in her eyes.

'I have to go now, Dan.' Jess broke away from their embrace and continued. 'Have you got my car keys please?'

'Sure, sure, here they are, but where are you going? Don't you want to wait and see Evie?'

'Home, Dan, home. Give Evie all of my love and tell her to be brave and get better very soon.'

'But you can tell her that yourself, Jess, can't you? Later or tomorrow?' Dan's voice started to crack. Jess was hurting inside. She turned her back and walked towards the stairs. Dan followed her outside. 'Jess, please don't leave me like this. I love you so much and Evie does too.' Jess was now crying. 'Dan, I have to. Something just doesn't feel right between us now and I'm not prepared to settle. You were the one who said I was an all or nothing kinda girl.' She smiled weakly. 'But, Jess, we can make it work, I know we can. Look at how Freya and Evie get on too. We've got our own little family now.'

Jess swallowed hard.

'You said you loved me,' Dan whispered.

'I do, Dan. You are a very special person and don't you ever forget that, but I've made my mind up and there's no going back.'

'If this is to do with your age, Jess, like you said last night, then please don't do this to me, to us.'

Jess shook her head. 'It's not just that.'

Dan raised his voice. 'It shouldn't be *not just that* at all. I've told you a million times that I love you. God!' He pulled at his hair with both hands. 'If we didn't have bloody passports or birth certificates then there wouldn't even be an issue. What is it with this society and age!' An old man in a dressing gown, who'd sneaked outside to have a cigarette, stared at the commotion.

'Dan, stop! I know you love me, but I've got to go now and find my happiness elsewhere. I'm so, so sorry. Goodbye.'

Chapter Thirty nine

Jess drove straight to Emma's. She was in tears when she reached her. She was pleased to see Freya playing in the garden. Emma had kindly had her for the night, whilst she was at Hope's wedding.

'Jess, what on earth is wrong?'

'I've left him, Em. For good. I had to finish it now.'

'Oh Jess. Come here.' She gave her friend a big hug.

'I had to do it now, before it got too far down the line. I told him that age was an issue, that I wouldn't ever feel secure.' Jess whimpered.

'And how did he take it?'

'Really badly, he is completely in love with me. I feel so terrible doing it but I have to think of myself and Freya on this one.'

'I'm proud of you, Jess, I actually was reading an article in one of the Sunday supplements yesterday that said to let go with love is one of the hardest things to do. But I think you've done the right thing.'

'You do?' Jess wanted reassurance.

'Yes, you are always saying to me, "If in doubt don't do it" and this is definitely the case here. And who knows further down the line what will happen.'

'I'm not to'ing and fro'ing to Dan if that's what you mean, Em. That is the worst thing he did to me, all those years ago. I love him enough to leave him alone and let him get over me. I can't bear the thought of not having him in my life, but I think that is what has to happen to be fair to him.'

'And what about Evie?' Emma enquired gently.

Jess's eyes filled with tears. Now was the time. She

couldn't keep it in any longer.

'Em, I have the biggest secret to tell you. You are the only person who is going to know this, but if I don't get it off my chest I am going to explode.' She took a deep breath. 'You have to promise me, Em, that this one will go to the grave with us both.'

Emma held Jess's hand. She hated to see her friend this troubled. 'Without question, Jess, and you know that.'

'Not even Mark,' Jess added.

'Not even Mark,' Em replied softly. 'You know you can trust me mate.'

'Evie is Sam's.'

'Oh my God, are you sure?'

'Yes, positive. Alex told me the whole story and there is no reason whatsoever for her to lie.'

Emma made tea as Jess relayed her encounter with Alex after the will reading.

'So you see why it has to be a secret? Dan and Evie must never know.'

'I agree totally. Why make two lives unhappy for no reason and now with Sam dead anyway, it's not like Evie can get to know her own father.'

This mention of Sam made Jess suddenly feel really sad. Tears filled her eyes again.

'Look, Jess, you are so doing the right thing being on your own again. You have been through so much in such a short space of time. You do still need time to get over Sam. However much of a bastard he was, you spent a lot of years with him and you did love him.'

Jess nodded. 'And being realistic, age is an issue with Dan. It is a big gap and I know you, you would start feeling insecure whatever he said to reassure you. And you would probably end up pushing him away and being on your own anyway.'

Jess nodded as Emma continued. 'And as for keeping it from Dan about Evie, it would destroy you. Leaving him is the only way forward for you.'

'Thanks, Em, you've helped me make sense of my own head. I can't live a lie with Dan. And if I did tell him the truth it would make him so unhappy and I *do* love him enough to not want that. He was so upset when I left him though.'

'Time is a healer,' Em uttered.

'God I remember that saying.' Jess smiled weakly. 'But, yes it is.' She took a sip of tea and continued. 'On a positive note, Dan is still young enough to meet someone else and start a new family. He will be fine.'

'And you, my lovely ,Jessica Morley, are still young and gorgeous enough to meet somebody wonderful and be very happy for the rest of your life.' Emma rested her hand on Jess's shoulder. 'So have you thought about what you are going to do now?'

'I have actually. I'm going to move to Cornwall for a while. There is a really good school in Looe for Freya and it will give me the chance to write that novel. There's a book in everyone so they say.' She attempted a smile.

'I'm going to miss you big time, Jess, but I think it's a really good idea. A completely new start.'

'That is the only downside not being near my friends,' Jess continued. 'But on the big upside, Seagull Cottage is such a party house, and with so much space, anyone can come and stay anytime. I was thinking of having everyone down for Christmas actually.'

'That sounds like a lovely idea. I'm definitely up for that.'

'So when are you going, Jess?'

'As soon as I've got everything tied up this end, so in a few weeks probably. The school says they can take Freya anytime. I'm actually looking forward to having some me-time. Freya and I will be just fine.'

'I know you will, Jess. You're a brave lady and I love you very much.'

Chapter Forty

Dan had never before felt such sorrow. He had always thought broken hearts were a myth but the pain he was actually feeling inside made him think that one half of his heart had actually fallen into his stomach. He felt that if he cried any more he would surely have no more tears left for anything else that may upset him. He asked Alex to look after Evie and he stayed in bed for two days, just venturing downstairs for Stella to try and numb his hurt.

Somehow he felt safe under the duvet. Like the real world was not happening, he could escape and feel safe. He could see no purpose in being here without Jess. Light turned into dark and dark into light. Never before had he loved anybody with such a passion and he felt she would never love anyone again. He prayed that one day they could be friends as the thought of never seeing Jess again was too much to bear.

Chapter Forty one

Phoebe, Glen and the girls were the first to arrive at Seagull Cottage. Freya ran down the stairs screeching with excitement.

'Mummy says its three more sleeps until Father Christmas comes, is that right, Auntie Phoebe?'

'Yes it is, darling. Now I hope you've been a good girl or he might not come.'

'He will come,' replied Freya adamantly. 'I wrote him a letter and asked him to.'

Jess smiled at her beautiful daughter's exuberance.

'How you doing, big sis?' Phoebe enquired lovingly.

'Really good actually. Freya is enjoying her new school, which is a relief and I've already made a couple of friends through a writing club I've joined.'

When everyone was settled in bed, Jess went downstairs to check she had locked the door. She looked out of the front window and noticed the full moon had created its twinkly pathway right across the sea. She thought of Dan and the night he had surprised her here at the cottage. Tears began to fall silently down her cheeks. She loved him. Loved him like she had never loved any other man in her life. She knew however that she had made the right decision this time. At least now, with him gone from their lives, she and Freya could move on, with no deceit hanging over them. Just pure honesty, trust and love.

Christmas Day arrived. 'Do they know it's Christmas Time' blared out of Jess's speakers.

Jess looked around the room at her friends and family

and felt a surge of love for them all. Freya, Georgina, Annabel, and Emma's three, excitedly opened their presents. Even though there were four teenagers present, they still had the same look of excitement on their faces as the youngsters. Karl tenderly looked at Shelley as she waddled out to the kitchen. Their baby was due any day now and they were both really excited. Hope and Jack-the-Lad sat holding hands on the sofa giving each other butterfly kisses as usual. Even Emma and Mark had managed not to bicker for the past hour. Phoebe and Glen discussed when the turkey should be ready. Jess's Dad and Maria both sipped on their sherries.

'Right has everybody got a drink?' Karl enquired.

'Yes,' they all shouted in unison.

'I'd like to make a toast to our wonderful host, my beautiful sister Jessica.'

'To Jessica!'

'Mummy?' Freya suddenly piped up.

'Yes, darling.'

'I love you more than Father Christmas.'

Everybody laughed out loud.

'And I love you more than mince pies.'

Epilogue

Jess sat back in her chair and re-read the first three chapters of the novel she was writing. She could hear the cry of gulls but could barely see them against the white, winter sky. Waves crashed on to the rugged Cornish coastline below.

'Come on, Mum, we better go, I'm going to be late for school,' Freya urged.

Jess pulled on her hat and scarf and opened the door. White flakes fell onto her face and she laughed out loud.

'Fresh Snow, Freya! Fresh Snow!'

THE END

Printed in Great Britain
by Amazon